The Creat...... ..

Manic

The Manic Chronicles

A.W. Entwisle

For my loving partner Sami, who's listened to me talk about almost every sentence of this book for years. How you've not gone mad I have no idea.

Contents

Prologue

Wind and snow roared through the skies, crashing into the mountain as picks hacked into the frozen rock. A small expedition of climbers was attempting to climb the western side of Everest, something that few have ever attempted, and none have ever survived.

"Jessie! How much further?" yelled Hunter, his shout distant through the pressing wind.

Jessie replied, the icy wind stealing his breath and stiffening his cheeks, "Not much! I can see it just up ahead".

On and on the group climbed. The ice cracked as they slammed pick after pick into the sturdy ice. Reaching the precipice, Jessie, with the last of his waning strength lifted his arm and reached out to grasp hold of the final ridge. Finding his grip, he hefted his elbow onto the edge. He clenched his teeth and pressed hard against the ground feeling the strain through his back and shoulders, as he hoisted himself back onto solid ground. Relief swept over him as his eyes fell upon a huge cavern, large enough to shelter them from the storm. He reached out his hand to a younger woman. "Sara! There's shelter here - we have to get inside!".

Sara pulled herself onto the ledge with Jessies help. She pulled her hood further over her face, shielding herself from the storm. Her brown dreadlocks dangled out of the hood quickly getting covered in a thick layer of ice and snow, as her boots crunched with hurried steps towards the cavern.

One by one Jessie pulled his companions to salvation, each of them rushing into the cave. Finally, Jessie hoisted the last member onto the ridge and made his way with the last

4

of the party into the cavern. They began to remove their hoods, shaking off the snow from their coats as they looked up in amazement. The walls of the cavern were like a dark obsidian, with strange indentations that seemed to sweep across the walls into the darkness. The group removed their outer layers of clothing to help dry their clothes.

Jessie looked around the group, "Right, do we have everyone here?". He began to count.

First there was Hunter, an American that Jessie had met back in college. Hunter had a classic climber build, with floppy brown hair, which showed a similar resemblance to that of a mop. Jessie had known Hunter for years and he'd often taken him on photography expeditions around the world. Hunter always made Jessie laugh with his, 'why is it always me' attitude, recalling stories of him nearly being eaten alive by mosquitoes or having his blood sucked by leeches. Then you had Hunter's sister Helen. Jessie knew her well, only because her and Hunter were almost inseparable. She had quite the competitive streak and was always out to get Hunter, the only reason why she was here was that she had trained for a year to prove that she could be just as good as her brother. Hunter had already removed his outer layer and was rummaging through his bag, he pulled out two chocolate bars and offered one to his sister Helen. She shivered and took the bar forcing herself to speak, "Thank you, you have no idea how much I need this". The two then collapsed against the shining black wall and began to scoff the bars.

The German Bogohardt, or Bo as he preferred to be called, was removing a small pocket stove from his backpack and was beginning to prepare some coffee. Jessie wasn't overly familiar with Bo, as he joined the expedition pretty late and only seemed to because Sara was coming. Something that seemed to not pass anyone's attention was Bo's attention to detail, and that detail was Sara. He would accompany her on every adventure she went on. The guy was clearly in love with her, but clearly, she had no clue. She would hug into his masculine frame, his triangle shoulders embracing her whilst she would say something cliche like "you're like the brother I never had". But he never seemed to care, he would just carry on being like a brother. He was smart, he would play the long game until she knew how great that chiselled chinned German really was. His only undefining feature about him really was how bad his coffee tasted, it sucked...bad.

Sara's curiosity had ventured her straight to the back of the cave.

"Guys this cave goes crazy deep, I can't even see the back of it" she shouted.

"We should remain here for the moment, these guys have the right idea, first, we eat and warm up, then we can explore further". Jessie replied, ensuring the safety of the group.

"Ok fine" she smiled and headed back over to Bo who had prepared the team a fresh cup of coffee. The group gathered in a circle passing around a mess tin full of boiling coffee and filled their cups. Helen held her cup with both hands, feeling the warmth through her fingertips. She took a deep breath, allowing the smell of ground beans to fill her senses as she took a sip.

"Oh god", she spattered, trying not to spray the coffee. Bo threw a deep laugh "Tastes good yes?" he replied, his thick German accent evident. Jessie drank deeply and coughed, "tastes delicious Bo, strong as ever" his sarcasm poorly disguised. Bo looked over, "you English... so ungrateful" he chuckled "how's yours Sara?". Realising she'd been staring down the cavern she turned back to Bo, "oh sorry I haven't tried it yet" she took a sip "hmmm yeah it's definitely um... warming" she said raising her cup in appreciation, "yes, I definitely like the way it makes your... eyes water, not many drinks can do that!" she said, with the colour returning to her pale cheeks. Jessie laughed and turned to Hunter "except your brandy maybe" slapping him on the shoulder.

"Hey! those are tears of joy because my brandy is just something so unbelievably incredible" he replied.

"Ha! You keep telling yourself that Hunter" replied Helen elbowing her brother.

"Hey! I think you'll find making brandy is a very emotionally engaging process. It's made with love, care and just because I shed a tear when I tried my first batch doesn't mean it's a bad drink".

"So, you crying wasn't because you dropped your first and only bottle?" Said Jessie throwing Hunter a sly grin.

"That was just a minor mishap, these things could happen to anyone" replied Hunter. Bo looked over to Hunter, "Yet they only happen to you I hear?". Hunter's head dropped in his hands, "oh god not you too. He's only known me for five minutes and he's already taking the piss, this is all your fault" he said accusingly to Sara and Helen.

"It's got nothing to do with us, it's not our fault you give off that vibe" responded Sara shrugging.

This to and fro continued for another half an hour until Sara stood up and addressed the group.

"Right, we're all warmed up now let's go and explore this cave!".

"I guess it wouldn't hurt exploring for twenty minutes", Said Hunter, looking at Jessie for his approval.

Jessie looked back out of the cave and rubbed at his stubble. The snow and wind had continued to batter the mountainside for the past two hours and didn't seem to be lightening up. If they went back into that now they'd either freeze to death or take a tumble down the mountain. He didn't see any good going back into it now so he replied, "I don't see why not, looks like we might be set in for the night anyway, so I guess we can make camp here and move on in the morning" he said approvingly.

"Yes!" Sara shouted, pumping her fist before flinging her bag onto her shoulder and heading down the tunnel. The rest of the group laughed as they pushed themselves off the wall and collected their gear, before disappearing down into the tunnel.

They'd only been on the move for a couple of minutes before they all had to remove their torches from their packs and place them on their heads. As Sara was hell-bent on leading on this little expedition, Jessie decided to follow up behind the group, taking note of each turn they made and ensuring the team didn't get lost.

The walls of the cave were grey with what seemed to be jet black streaks that marbled through the rocks.

"Have you taken a look at this rock? It almost looks like glass", Hunter said to Helen.

"Yeah, I saw something similar to that earlier in the opening of the cave" she replied.

"It seems to almost be getting darker" added Jessie rubbing his finger against the black glass. Helen placed her fingers against the indentations, "These groves are all over the rock it's almost like claw marks" Said Helen.

"Yeah, claw marks of a freaking giant bird maybe?" Hunter said, his face breaking into a large smile which suddenly shifted as he slipped on a smooth section of ice. Hunter recovered quickly. "Watch your step Hunter, you wouldn't want to trip", Helen said strutting past, flaunting her superior balance. Hunter felt a hand pat on his shoulder, "   Stop messing around Hunter, you listen to your sister". Jessie said sarcastically.

"I hate you guys" said Hunter as he hurried to keep up with Helen.

Bo and Sara were ahead of the group reaching a slight decline. The centre of the rocky walkway was bedded with icy gravel, which Bo found exceedingly difficult to manoeuvre without sliding and colliding with Sara. "That might not be so bad", he thought to himself. Sara, on the other hand, was tiptoeing her way along the sides of the walkway, hitting each icy rock with precision, making great headway. Suddenly, she stopped. Bo raced down to catch up with her. It was there that he noticed there was a huge opening within the cave. A small crack had formed within the mountainside above them which let in the occasional dust of snow which slowly drifted through the opening. A bright light shone down into the centre, hitting a huge collection of stalagmites which illuminated the cave with a brilliant blue glow. Amazed, Bo looked over to Sara. The radiant blue shone through her dreadlocks, highlighting the soft rose-tinted skin of her cheeks, and coaxing the blue of her eyes.

"Beautiful isn't it", Sara said faintly as her eyes filled with childish amazement. Catching Bo off guard he stumbled, "oh yeah, yeah, that really is something isn't it?". He turned back to see the opening once more and exhaled in amazement "Ach du großer Gott".

Hunter and Helen passed into the cavern closely followed by Jessie. The entire group stared on in awe.

"Have you ever seen anything like it?" exclaimed Jessie. The entire group shook their heads almost in unison. Snapping themselves from the trance, Sara jumped down from the ledge into a large ice trench which ran around the giant stalagmite sculpture like a moat. The group disbanded and began to explore the opening within the cave, investigating every nook and cranny for any new wonders that the cave might bring.

Hunter jumped off the ledge into the frozen moat with a satisfying crunch, as frozen bubbles of air crushed beneath his feet. Removing his ice pick from the side of his bag, he stabbed it into the ice giving him enough of a hold to pull himself up onto the stalagmites centre. Climbing up the front of the cave's frozen nucleus, Hunter stood in front of the stalagmite sculpture. Removing his glove, he brushed his fingertips over its smooth rippling surface. The ice was cold to the touch, slightly melting onto his fingers leaving a gooey ice water upon their tips.

Hunters upper lip curled "Urghh?".

Bo and Helen had begun to explore two of the passageways that led from the cave when they heard Hunter shout.

"Guys! Guys come here you have got to see this". Bo and Helen ran from the passages, removing their ice picks and then scrambled over the icy ring to Hunter. His voice calm and quiet he turned to them both. "Rub your hand over the ice, let the warmth of your hand melt it, it's a little gooey, but it becomes clear as glass, and look… there!" Hunter investigated the icy window. In the centre of the stalagmite sculpture was a single large oval rock. The rock beautifully mottled with bright blue streaks, its edges were jagged like scales climbing all over the stone.

Jessie emerged from one of the passages curious from all the commotion. He climbed over to the group, only to stop suddenly as he saw the brilliant blue stone.

In the other side of the cave Sara stood next to a wall of perfect sapphire blue. She placed her hand along the sapphire wall feeling its icy chill. Looking up through her condensing breath, she noticed that it was surrounded by the same black obsidian streaks that covered the cave. Each streak became more apparent near each passageway. As she looked down, she noticed something strange that almost looked like a piece of clothing wedged behind the wall. She began to move closer to get a better look at the object, clearly so alien in a place like this.

Jessie looked again at the strange rock within the stalagmites and then again at the surrounding cave. Jessie thought it was strange that the cave was so perfectly rounded and what was with the icy circle surrounding the sculpture? He looked deep into the stalagmite sculpture and stared at its strange, scaled shape.

"No... it can't be..." he thought.

"Hey Sara come quick; this rock looks like some kind of egg!" shouted Bo from the centre of the cavern.

Sara turned to look back at Bo as a low rumble ricocheted through the cavern, causing stalactites to crack and break free from the ceiling. Ducking and covering their heads the group cowered from the falling daggers. Finding his breath, Jessie got back onto his feet and called out to the group, "Is everyone alright?". The group nodded in unison, as they stood brushing snow from their clothes. Jessie looked over to Sara as she pushed herself up.

"I'm okay!" she replied, brushing shards of ice from her coat. Silence descended in the cavern as Sara looked up to see horror on her teammates faces and blinked.

"What? I'm alright, honestly" she replied.

Not one of the group responded, their gaze distracted by what was above her. She turned to the wall as two fiery blue globes peered down at her accusingly from behind the sapphire glass.

"Run!" shouted Jessie as he jumped from the icy pedestal. But before anyone could react, a monstrous white and blue creature crashed through the sapphire wall, smashing Sara aside with its giant scaly shoulder, shattering blades of ice all over the cavern.

A blade of icy glass soared through the air slicing a deep cut through Jessie's forehead as he was flung to the

11

ground. The ice beast turned to the siblings and reared on its hind legs exposing its scaled underside. It began to pull its head back like a snake coiling to strike, then as if triggered, the creature threw itself to the ground spitting vast amounts of blue flame into the cavern engulfing Hunter and Helen. They screamed in agony as they tried to cover their faces from the creature's icy breath. Jessie looked up in horror at the siblings, only to see their terrified bodies frozen in place. The creature swung its gigantic icy tail and Bo dove down into the icy moat, the tail swiping dangerously close. He scurried over to Sara who collapsed on the ground, a large piece of glass jutted out from her neck. Bo cradled her in his arms, holding her tight against his chest.

Blood bubbled and flowed from her throat and mouth. The ice monster turned its huge bulk around to the two climbers and again reared. As it did, Jessie dove at the creature wielding his ice pick, embedding one deep into the shoulder of the beast and the other ripping into what appeared to be a wing beneath its clawed arm. The creature roared in pain causing the ice above to shake. The creature shook Jessie from its body and smashed him with its muscular tail, flinging him into one of the passages. Huge sections of ice crashed down from the ceiling, trapping Jessie in the tunnel. A spine-chilling crack like thunder echoed through the cave as a large section of ice above broke free and descended into the centre of the cavern shattering the two frozen siblings and the frozen stalagmite sculpture containing the scaly orb. The creature roared in anger and turned back. Bracing its claws, it reared again in frustration and pulled its head back. Sara looked to Bo helpless and scared as she coughed blood trying to speak. He could see the life in her eyes beginning to fade away.

"It's ok, it's ok" he repeated, holding her tight. Bo wept as he rocked her gently in his arms, and as tears formed in his eyes Sara's body became limp and lifeless. His voice

12

broke and tears ran down his cheeks as icy blue flames engulfed the couple causing their skin to freeze into a dark glacial blue.

Silence again fell in the cavern, except for the ragged breaths of the creature and the tiny echo of a frozen tear that broke away from Bo's cheek. The tear echoed for eternity as it bounced from rock to rock, finally resting in the icy moat next to the bleeding scaled rock that once lay soundly in the centre of the cavern.

Chapter One: A Day in the Life of Jasper

Vandelhammer fell from the keeps walls and crashed to the ground, landing on his back. He looked up in horror. From the top of the wall, a huge bony hairless creature with no eyes stepped to the edge. The creature's giant claws clung to the rock as it tilted its enormous head down towards its attacker, saliva dripping from its long teeth. The creature unleashed an ear-piercing screech. Vandelhammer scrambled to his feet, kicking back dust as he raced to create distance between himself and the gangly creature. Running as fast as he could, his stamina decreased. When it reached zero, he stopped to catch his breath. The monster, sensing this opportunity, launched itself from the wall, causing sections of the stone to crumble and shatter beneath its feet. It landed with the grace of a cat and sprinted towards Vandelhammer, its slender legs stretching further with each stride. Vandelhammer composed himself, turned to the creature, raised his shield, and lifted his sword high. Steadying his breathing, he readied himself for the battle ahead. The creature's claws tore into the ground like a plough and its tentacle-like tongue flapped in the wind as it closed in on its prey. A small quiver came from the bushes to its left, rustling the leaves mid-bound, the monster turned its head to follow the sound. It shrieked as an arrow glowing with purple flame shot through its enormous teeth, ripping through the back of its head, splattering vertebrae and flesh in all directions. The monster crashed to the ground and slid to Vandelhammer's feet. Pop-art style letters appeared above the creature's head. "Headshot!!!" echoed a deep omnipotent voice followed by 5000 points above the creature's body.

Jasper slammed his desk with both hands and shouted down his headset, "No! Come on! Lucy, that was my kill!"

"Don't be such a baby. It's not my fault you didn't kill him quick enough", Lucy said.

"You are so smug. I can even hear you smirking. You never could have taken out that ragecrawler without my help". Jasper glowered at the screen.

"Yeah, yeah. You're just a sore loser – you couldn't have taken it out without me either", Lucy said. He could hear her laughing as she said it.

"Anyway, I better get going. I should actually eat some breakfast this morning", Jasper said, putting his character into logout mode. It always took a few seconds for their characters to leave the server.

"All right, catch you later, Vandelhammer".

"You too, Dreamreaver". Jasper watched as Vandelhammer sat down in the wasteland and disintegrated into a cloud of pixels while Dreamreaver raided the corpse of the fallen ragecrawler for loot.

Jasper jumped off his computer chair and stretched his arms, cracking his shoulders and feeling the stretch across his back. He opened his mouth wide, letting out a loud Wookie-like yawn. He shook the tension out of his body and ran downstairs, only to be greeted by his wagging, bumbling mess of a cocker spaniel, Maxie. Maxie's bum wiggled back and forth, and his long tongue splayed out the side of his mouth in greeting.

"Good morning, little buddy!" Jasper said, rubbing Maxie's squishy cheeks with both hands. Maxie flapped his tongue whilst shuffling in place, his eyes wide with excitement at seeing his person.

"Come on, buddy, I've got to get on". At that, Maxie ran out of the hall and darted into the living room. Jasper peered in. His mum and his brother, Johnny, were both sat in front of the TV, watching whatever disaster was happening in the news that day. Jasper yawned. The news was always the same: just absolute misery. Someone murdered here, a terror attack there, or a natural disaster that has devastated somewhere else. Every day his family sat in front of the TV, kick-starting their day with depression, death, and misery. What an excellent way to start the day. At least he was spending time with his friends and doing something fun in the mornings.

He filled the kettle and began to prepare his usual breakfast of honey on toast with a strong filter coffee. Once the kettle had boiled, he filled the cafetiere. The coffee bubbled and frothed as the rich aroma of roasted beans filled the air and Jasper took it all in, letting the warm scent embrace his lungs. Jasper filled his mug, grabbed his toast, and walked out of the kitchen. He was taking a large satisfying crunch out of his toast as he passed the living room but paused when he heard the news anchor on the flatscreen.

"Good morning, England, it's seven fifteen, and what a beautiful morning it is".

"No! Seven fifteen already! I've gotta get out of here!" Jasper cried. He downed his steaming coffee, yelping as it scalded his throat. Wincing from the coffee, he slid his shoes onto his feet, kicking his heels to make sure they were properly on and not folded over at the backs. Swallowing the last of his toast, he shouted, "Bye, Mum!" grabbing his rucksack and a large fluorescent yellow bag full of newspapers, he hopped out the door.

The sky was a beautiful clear blue, with a cold spring air that clung to your cheeks and refreshed your lungs. Shutting the door, Jasper ran round to the side gate. It was always locked but he knew how to open it. Every day he'd slide his hand down the side of the door and using two fingers he'd shimmy the bolt across, before swinging it open to reveal his bike. It was an old rusty mountain bike, complete with dodgy brakes, no suspension whatsoever and an unreliable chain which was always popping off.

Hopping on, Jasper began to pedal as fast as he could to the first house, trying to complete his paper route before college. As he rode the wind pulled at his short reddish-brown hair, lifting it above his forehead. The cold air bit at his cheeks and made his hazel eyes water. Jasper bombed it as fast as he could around each block, dropping his bike almost every twenty meters to run to each set of houses. The town was a small one and many of the houses had relatively well-tended gardens, but like every small town one was always an overgrown mess. Jasper reached the door of old Mr Alberts, who always gave Jasper a hard time. Maybe because he was retired and didn't have anything better to do. The old man opened the door.

"What time do you call this?"

"Sorry... it is still before eight thirty, though", replied Jasper apologetically, as Mr Alberts's ginger cat, Churchill, rubbed his body up against Jasper's leg.

"Yes, but I like to read my paper at quarter past seven whilst having my morning cup of tea and my jam on toast", Albert said, scowling. As if on cue, Churchill bit Jasper, who jerked back. Churchill flicked his tail high displaying his ten pence as he strutted back towards Mr Albert and the house. Averting his eyes Jasper shook his head at the cat's audacity as he lugged his bag back onto his shoulder and jumped on the bike.

"Sorry, I'll try harder tomorrow!" Jasper shouted, already cycling away.

17

"You'd better!" the old man replied, waving the newspaper. He turned and walked back into the house.

His paper round only took him an hour and half, but best of all his chain only came off twice this time. He pulled his bike up to the college. It was nothing out of the ordinary, steps led to a large rectangular building with hundreds of windows and walls which had once been cream-coloured but were now dirty and stained. They probably hadn't been cleaned in about ten years. A few other buildings were scattered around, in a similar state to the main building: not too old but clearly not well maintained. Jasper's family couldn't afford anything like a private education anymore. Not since his father left when he was a kid.

As Jasper locked his bike he saw Billie with his usual oversized superhero T-shirt. Today it was Iron Man swamping his tiny frame. Opposite Billie was Lucy, her dark-brown hair just covering her shoulders.

"A polar bear would easily win! It's got thick skin and fur; the skinny ragecrawler would have a much harder time landing a killing blow", argued Lucy.

"No way! The ragecrawler isn't even real. For all we know it could be so much stronger than a polar bear – and it's lightning fast!" Billie said, adjusting his glasses.

"I doubt it, not with those skinny arms". Lucy said folding her arms.

Jasper butted in. "Come on, you can't even be arguing about this. Of course, the ragecrawler would win – it breaks stone just by gripping it with its claws. A polar bear wouldn't stand a chance!".

Lucy turned to look at Jasper, shock in her green eyes. "Well … the ragecrawler is desert dwelling, so if it was to fight a polar bear it would surely lose in the snow". She pouted.

"That I agree with. In each of their ideal climates the winner would probably be the niche species; however, on a level playing field it would have to be the ragecrawler", Billie said, hoisting his bag onto his shoulders.

"That's if the ragecrawler didn't get pounced on by an elf in tights, right before the polar bear was about to get it". Jasper cocked an eyebrow at Lucy.

"Oh she got you again! That's brilliant! Every time, man. She's really kicking your arse", Billie said, grinning a little too widely.

"Jasper is just way too slow, obviously", Lucy said, as the trio began to make their way into the campus.

"I'll get it next time for sure, and you won't have a chance of getting that last shot in", Jasper said.

"Whatever, *Vandelhammer*" she said drenching the word with derision "I'd like to see you try".

"Ouch! She's taken to mocking your name. Dude, I'm not sure if I'd take that", Billie said opening the door that led them through the entrance of the college.

"It's okay. I'm not the one who has to steal other people's kills, just to get ahead", Jasper said.

"You guys are just the worst. Right, I've got to get to my electronics lecture. I'll catch you two losers later", Billie said, as he patted his two friends on the shoulders and disappeared off into the crowd of students.

"We'd better get a move on as well, otherwise Mr J will lose it again", Lucy said.

"You've got that right. He always comes down on us like a tonne of bricks". Jasper and Lucy scampered off to their biology lesson.

***

19

The classroom was dark, with a projector lighting the front of the class. Around the room were various specimens in jars. Posters covered the walls showing all sorts of animal anatomy and physiology. In one corner of the room there was a selection of vivarium's housing reptiles and invertebrates.

Mr Jackson strode around the room, talking to the class. Stopping next to a large vivarium, he leaned in. The light from the tank illuminated his face and glistened off the grey hairs that patched the side of his head.

"The chameleon isn't the only creature in the animal kingdom that can change colour, we also have many others that can do the same. Can anyone think of any examples?" Silence fell around the classroom. Mr J cast his eyes around the room full of blank faces staring back at him. Removing his glasses, he rubbed the bridge of his nose, replaced his glasses, and spoke again.

"I know it's scary to speak up, but it does help the class flow faster if you answer".

A scrawny teenager at the back of the class, with long dark hair that poked out of the sides of his grey cap, raised his hand before answering. "How about the cuttlefish?"

"Very good! A cuttlefish is the perfect example as it can perfectly change colour to suit its surroundings. Different from a chameleon, which mainly changes colour to fit its mood as a warning to predators".

Jasper was busy sketching drawings of goblins and trolls when he felt someone looking over him.

"Hey, nice drawings", Lucy said.

Jasper reddened and quickly closed the book, then turned to Lucy. "It's nothing", he whispered.

Mr J stopped abruptly at the front of the class and turned. "Jasper! Now, tell me – what was it that allowed the cuttlefish to change colour again?" Mr J theatrically scratched at his head. "I know I just said it, but it seems to have just slipped my mind. Can you please jog my memory?" He knew full well that Jasper wasn't listening.

Jasper swallowed. "It's the, uh, the pigment cells in their skin which allow them to change the hue of their hypodermis?" he said with an awkward smile.

Mr J raised his eyebrows. "Very close, Master Collins, very close. It's the chromatophore cells which work like a pigment organ to change the colour of the hypodermis".

The bell rang, and all the teens began to pack their things and make their way out of the classroom.

"Now, everyone, don't forget we have a quiz next week on predator–prey relationships. This all helps towards you're A levels so make sure you revise!" Mr J looked back at Jasper. "Jasper, would you stay behind a moment? I want to have a word".

"Ouch! Good luck Jasper", Lucy whispered.

"I'll meet you outside, Luce. I shouldn't be long".

Lucy nodded then grabbed her things and made her way out of the room.

Jasper walked over to the desk at the front where Mr J was collecting up some paperwork. Mr J's hair was short, a little posh but also a little scruffy. Jasper noticed a large scar just below Mr J's hairline on one side of his forehead.

"So, Master Collins, have you completed that last assignment for me?".

"Oh yeah, sorry, I've got it right here". Jasper reached into his bag and his sketchbook fell open on the desk revealing his drawings of creatures, one of which resembled a bipedal dog.

"So, this is what you're doing when you're meant to be listening to my class. What is this meant to be?" he said, gesturing to the strange canine.

Jasper handed over the late assignment his face rapidly going a shade of red. "It's not really anything. I just drew it. I'm always coming up with different creatures", he said, shrugging.

"So, you've never seen anything like this before?" Mr J asked, looking at Jasper with narrowed eyes.

Puzzled, Jasper replied, "No, why?"

"It's just an incredibly detailed drawing; I'm impressed. You know, if you spent less time drawing in my class and more time listening you might actually learn something".

"Sorry, Mr J. I just get distracted and once my concentration has gone, that's it, I'm done for".

"Well, that is something you will have to work on. Let's try and stay focused on the class next time, shall we? And we should also be sure to get our assignments done on time", Mr J said, handing the book back to Jasper.

"Yes, definitely, I'll be sure to get the next one in on time. Thanks, Mr J". Jasper lifted his bag over one shoulder and walked out of the class.

"Oh, and Master Collins?" Jasper turned to look at Mr J. "Don't forget to revise for the quiz next week. You're doing well, but if you ace this test, I might be able to put you forward for a scholarship".

Chapter Two: One Rotten Apple

After the final bell, waves of students poured out from the doors of the college. Many heading to their homes to procrastinate from doing their homework. Jasper emerged from the front doors, shouldered his rucksack, and ran down the steps towards Billie and Lucy. They had waited for him because it was Thursday, that meant only one thing, Demon Sword. Every Thursday they played it without fail. Jasper always played as his warrior Vandelhammer because he was always at the front with his shield soaking all the hits. Lucy enjoyed her rogue class and always played as her character Dreamreaver. It was the sneak attacks from the shadows that really got her attention. Billie liked his engineer classes. He was a tinkerer in games, just like he was in life.

"Sorry guys. Wasn't planning on getting stuck after class".

"Man, how did you get busted again?" Billie asked, as the trio began to wander home.

"You know me, Billie, lose my focus then time just runs away from me".

"As usual!" Lucy chipped in.

"I swear other people in his class talk as well, but I'm the only person that ever seems to get caught". Jasper slung his bag over his shoulder with a scowl.

"Aren't you forgetting something?" Lucy asked.

Jasper stared at her. "What?"

"Your bike, you pleb".

"Oh, yeah!" Jasper looked back towards the college.

He thought about the unreliable rusty chain. He shrugged then made a shooing motion in the direction of his bike and turned back towards his friends. "It'll be all right, no one's going to steel that rust bucket. I fancy walking with you guys for a bit anyway. How was electronics, Billie? Did you manage to piss off Lee again?"

"It was over-explained and underwhelming, as usual. Lee was on form doing his best ape impression for the entire lecture. If I didn't know any better, I'd say he'd make a great addition to London Zoo. Maybe the apes there could show him how to use some tools. Oh, and when those lecturers teach me something I haven't already learnt online, I'll personally fly you both to Mars", Billie said, nonchalantly adjusting his glasses.

Both Lucy and Jasper broke into hysterical laughter.

"Oh yeah, are you going to invent the first genetically enhanced flying pig as well?" Jasper asked, sharing a glance with Lucy.

"The teachers at this college couldn't tell the difference between an atom and an anvil. It would be more likely that they couldn't put down a book on anti-gravity than they could teach me anything the internet can't".

"Maybe they could teach you modesty?" Lucy blurted out, she and Jasper roared with laughter.

"Unlikely! Anyway, did you two hear about those animal attacks on the news this morning?" Billie asked, clearly willing to change the subject.

Calming his laughter, Jasper replied, "No, what happened?"

Billie shrugged. "Well, they keep finding dead sheep on the moors, mauled and in a total mess".

"It's probably just some failing farmer trying to get money from the council, or even just a loose dog", Lucy said as they rounded a corner and headed down a cul-de-sac of new builds.

Jasper's mind began to wander as he thought of all the creatures that could be the real culprit: dragons, a ragecrawler or even trolls. *That would be so freaking awesome.* His mind conjured up towering beasts with giant tusks wandering the moors, chasing terrified sheep up and down the hills. He imagined a sabre-toothed tiger chasing the sheep through open fields and a confused farmer watching the whole commotion while scratching his head. He smiled.

"Whatever it is, I wouldn't want to bump into it!" Billy said.

"Yeah, but it could be something awesome. We should go check it out!" Jasper said, his excitement taking over.

Billie turned to Jasper. "You're having a giraffe, Jasp. There's no way on this earth you'd get me there! I think someone has been playing too many games – and that's coming from me! They're getting to your head. Or maybe biology is just sending you loopy".

"*Someone* sounds like they're a little scared", Lucy said.

"Wouldn't you be scared? Imagine it's a wolf or a panther that's escaped a zoo or something! They say that it's happened before, and they've never been caught. Reckon you could fight off a panther?" Billie asked, as they came to the end of the winding cul-de-sac.

"Yeah, right!" Jasper rolled his eyes. "The beast of Bodmin or Exmoor or whatever". He and Lucy erupted into laughter once more.

"Hey, I'm not saying it's that, all I'm saying is that I wouldn't want to bump into it on a dark night!"

"Fair enough, Billie, we'll let you off. I wouldn't want to fight off a sheep-eating tabby cat either", Lucy said, shifting a sly grin to Billy. "But anyway, I'd better get going. I'll catch the two of you later".

"I'd better dash as well. I've got a date with a battleground that I'm already late for. No Demon Sword for me tonight". Billie said.

"No worries Billie, I'll catch you later. Luce, maybe you'll get a chance to take out another ragecrawler", Jasper jeered.

"Yeah, because you'll never get a chance to get one without my help". Lucy pushed Jasper playfully, then ran off down the road.

"I'll take one on with you later. It'll have to be after my arena battles. See you, Jasp!" Lucy shouted, as she and Billie both disappeared down a tiny footpath between two houses.

Jasper laughed and began to fantasise about different ways that he might be able to beat the ragecrawler without the help of the other two.

Jasper had been walking for some time when he realised that dark clouds were rolling in overhead.

"Damn it! I'm going to get soaked", he muttered, and chastised himself for not going back for his bike.

Hoicking up his rucksack and pulling the straps tight, Jasper began to jog down a main road. Turning down an alleyway he spotted his short cut, slowed to a walk before taking three large strides and launching himself over a fence. He twisted his body and landed in a crouch. He leapt into a run and vaulted three more fences before interrupting a family barbecue. Three kids sat around their garden table happily eating burgers when Jasper gate-crashed their lives. A small ginger boy holding his burger in both hands dropped his jaw at the sight of Jasper landing in their paddling pool.

Jasper looked down at his soaked shoes and cursed.

"Oi! What on earth do you think you're doing kid?!" shouted a beer-bellied man that emerged from behind a cloud of barbeque smoke wielding a large, pronged fork.

He gave the man an awkward smile. "Sorry! I'll find my own way out".

Jasper stumbled as he waded out of the paddling pool, flinging fountains of water with each movement. The ginger boy stared as Jasper ran to the other side of the garden and vaulted their garden fence. Gawping, a dollop of tomato sauce dripped out of his bun as he stared on in shock.

"Oh, Tommy!" the man sighed, as the small ginger boy realised in horror that he'd dropped tomato sauce all over his shorts.

Jasper finally stopped to catch his breath in a near-by alley next to some bins and put his hands behind his head, relieved that he'd narrowly avoided being barbequed. He was pacing back and forth, when a garbled rustling sound came from the bins next to him. His body froze, he could feel his heart beating in his chest as he slowly turned towards the source of the noise.

One of the bins tumbled over and he leaped back as the bin lid sprawled open and out rolled a small green furry creature. The filthy creature scrambled around the rubbish, clearly searching for something. Wrappers and bits of dirt clung to its green fur as it lifted its prize into the air. In its claw it held its trophy... a brilliant, stunning, fantabulous, and rotten... apple. The creature garbled something heroically unintelligible before shoving its entire claw into its mouth, swallowing the apple whole and covering its claw with a thick coating of saliva.

"Ugh!" Jasper winced as he witnessed the creature devour its prize. The creature froze, its large ears twitched and shifted like two large satellite dishes. The creature's fur stood on end and its back arched like an agitated cat. Its small, hunched form turned slowly, locking its glowing golden eyes onto Jasper. For a moment they both froze staring at each other.

The creature gave a garbled yell and with short leaps charged towards Jasper in a blur of movement. Still stunned by the encounter, Jasper didn't move fast enough, and the creature pounced onto his leg and sank its teeth into his shin. He yelled in pain. Finally, Jasper forced himself to move, he kicked out his leg, trying to get the strange creature off. The creature finally let go and hopped a few meters away before turning and staring back at him. Its movements were similar to those of a ferret or a small bouncing rodent but its body looked more like a tiny bear.

"What on earth are you?" Jasper said, rubbing at his leg. The creature glanced at the bins, back at Jasper, then cocked its head curiously at the bag on Jasper's back. Jasper caught its eyes as the creature looked back to him and then again to his bag.

"Oh no, no, no, no!" Jasper screamed as the creature braced its claws into the ground and launched himself at Jasper.

***

Tommy's dad had finally wiped the ketchup off his son's shorts and sat down to enjoy the rest of the family barbecue. Tommy finished his burger and beamed up at his dad with ketchup-covered cheeks. Tommy's dad smiled back to his boy and picked up his burger.

Just as the man was about to take a bite, someone crashed through the fence, smashing it to bits. The same boy that had jumped the fence before had now fallen through it and was spinning around trying to grab his bag. Jasper frantically clawed at his back, and shredded paper was flung out of his bag in all directions, as though the bag was possessed by an angry photocopier. Tommy's ketchup-covered jaw dropped again, but this time at the strange, garbled sounds that were coming from the boy. Finally, Jasper clawed off his bag and launched it into the paddling pool. Jasper was hunched over, breathing heavily, when a little green creature emerged from the pool. Its fur was dripping and had clumped together over its eyes. The creature climbed over the side and dragged Jasper's sopping bag out of the pool. Shaking the water from its fur like a dog, the creature blinked at Jasper then scarpered, bouncing back through the hole in the fence with Jasper's bag.

"Hey! That's mine!" Jasper shouted, as he chased after the creature.

Tommy stared mouth wide at the carnage left in the garden. He blinked stupidly, then looked up to his dad. The beer-bellied man gawped in horror at his ruined garden when unknowingly a large dollop of ketchup dropped onto his shorts.

***

Jasper sprinted around the side of a fence and out onto the main road, then slowed to a stop. Out of breath, he looked around, searching frantically for the creature. It was nowhere to be seen.

"Man! What the hell was that?" Drenched and defeated, he began the laborious walk home.

Opening the front door, Jasper was assailed by Maxie. Maxie's tongue hung out of his mouth, and his bum wagged from side to side trying to keep up with the excitement from his tail.

"Hey, little buddy", Jasper said, kneeling to stroke Maxie, who rolled over to expose his furry belly.

After giving Maxie a quick belly rub, Jasper stood and ran up the stairs. He shut his door, stepped over the pile of clothes on the floor and collapsed on his bed. He could still see the creature that had terrorised him. It's curious and angry golden eyes were now burned into his memory.

He mulled over the day's events for a while before pushing himself up, moving over to his desk and grabbing a pencil and one of his sketchbooks. He sat down and began to flick through pages and pages of imaginary creatures: serpent men he'd named Naga, giant ice dragons and flying tigers.

He finally got to a blank page and began to draw. The graphite scored the paper as he glided the strokes of the creature's strange green fur across the page. He recalled that the size of the strange creature's ears were oddly similar to those of a German shepherd.

Maybe it was some kind of dog? He quickly disregarded that idea. No dog he knew bounced like that and they definitely didn't walk on two legs. He drew the body, recalling its stubby proportions.

Jasper placed one elbow on the desk and began to tap the pencil against his lips. He couldn't help but wonder why the creature was so ... *green*. It looked almost like an angry, mossy koala bear that had spent a bit too much time with raccoons and had drunk way too many energy drinks. Jasper continued to draw for another fifteen minutes before he was happy that he'd sketched a rough idea of what the creature looked like. Staring at the garbling green gremlin on his page, he realised that there was absolutely no way anyone was going to believe this. But he knew he'd have to find a way to get people to believe.

Chapter Three: Sparks

Billie was hunched over his desk, soldering a section of circuit board. Bolted to his desk was a cacophony of different scrap metal, pipes and wiring that all combined to make what looked like an artist's impression of a human arm. Surrounding the arm was a collection of old rusting tools. He wore bronze goggles that extended from his face. He looked like he was about to pilot a steampunk blimp. Billie was arguably even more obsessed with engineering and electronics than he was with gaming. It didn't mean that his college work suffered; college didn't challenge him so, other than his electronics class where he paid some sort of attention, he couldn't really be bothered with the rest. He was better than college. Pressing the solder into the iron, he carefully attached it to a fuse. A small stream of smoke rose from the iron and curled around his goggles, and he grinned at the circuit board.

"I've done it! I've only gone and bloody done it!" He threw his arms into the air – still holding the solder in one hand and the iron in the other – as he spun in his chair. Not too bad for a seventeen-year-old.

Setting down his tools, he pulled on a single glove, which had sensors and wires trailing up the fingers and along the palm. He peered at the robotic arm through his goggles as he lifted his gloved hand, pressing his thumb and middle finger together with an audible snap. The robotic arm sprang to life and began to mimic every movement from Billie's hand. He curled and uncurled his fingers, marvelling as the robotic hand did the same. Sitting opposite the arm, he reached out and touched its shoulder. The robotic arm reached out to place its rusted metallic palm on Billie's shoulder. Billie looked down at the hand on his shoulder with a grin.

"Billie! Billie! You're not going to believe what happened!" shouted Jasper, as he swung open the garage door. Billie jumped and his arms flailed, causing the robotic hand to flail in turn. It slapped Billie around the back of his head, knocking him to the floor.

"What on earth are you doing?" Jasper asked, looking down at Billie in a pile on the floor. Billie pushed himself up, rubbing the back of his head and scowling at Jasper with giant, magnified eyes.

"I finally managed to get my robotic arm functioning". He looked over to the limp arm, sparking and smoking. Billie sighed. "Well, I did get it working".

"Really? Doesn't look like it's functioning ..." Jasper said, looking somewhat sceptically at the smoking limb. "Anyway, you're not going to believe what happened!"

"Oh, I don't know … maybe you went to college, Mr J kicked your arse for not doing your assignment, you realised that the world is pointless and ran over here to tell me that you've decided to end it all?" Billie said, with a little more venom than he intended. Jasper gave Billie a strange look.

"Wow, that was harsh! Sorry for interrupting you – I did just see something amazing though".

"Sorry, Jasp, I'm just under a lot of stress right now. My mums lost her job and she's taking it out on me; she won't leave me alone. She's being way too attentive, so I've retreated in here. And you did essentially just backhand me as well, so you know, that's a thing".

"Yeah, I bet you're going to blame it smoking on me too, eh?" Jasper said, shifting his weight to one leg and crossing his arms.

Billie rubbed his forehead. "Go on, what's this amazing thing that happened to you?" With a grin, Jasper unshouldered his bag, and threw it onto the table. Billie saw Jaspers bright blue bag with a stegosaurus stitched to it and looked at Jasper with a smirk.

"It's my little brothers". Jasper then unzipped the baby blue bag and reached in. "So, I was walking home down this little shortcut – and that's where I was attacked!"

"What? You were attacked? By who?"

"It wasn't so much of a who as a what". Jasper removed a sketchbook from his bag. "I was walking along, minding my own business, when this creature rolls out of a bin and attacks me! It stole my bag too, and I'm fairly certain it destroyed everything in it. Or maybe it ate it. I dunno. I saw it eating a mouldy apple core, so I wouldn't be surprised. Anyway, I tried to get my bag back, but the thing was way too quick". Jasper began to flick through the pages of the sketchbook. "So, I came home and drew exactly what I saw, then grabbed Johnny's bag and shot straight over here". Finding the right page, he turned the book to Billie. Billie lifted his goggles and placed them on his head. He looked at the drawing, frowned and looked back at Jasper.

"You're telling me that you were attacked by a fluffy green rabbit?"

"It was not a rabbit! It had big teeth. Not massively sharp but they could definitely do some damage".

"So, it was a toothy rabbit?" Billie raised an eyebrow at Jasper.

"It wasn't a damn rabbit!"

"Okay, okay, it's not a rabbit. What was it then?"

Jasper took the book back and gazed at his drawing of the creature. "I've got no idea, but whatever it is, it's fast and it's got my bag. Let's give Lucy a call and see if she's got any ideas".

"Sure, but I'm fairly certain she's going to be knees' deep in ragecrawlers right now, making sure you don't beat her", Billie said, with a sideways glance.

"Ugh, you're right. Maybe it's best if we just talk to her tomorrow about it", Jasper said, clearly too distracted to take Billie's bait.

"Probably the best idea", agreed Billie.

"Right, I'd better shoot off. I'll see you in the morning". Jasper slung his bag over his shoulder and ran out of the garage.

"Bye!" Billie frowned as he half-heartedly waved after Jasper. "I have no idea what on earth he was on about", Billie muttered, looking back at his mechanical arm. "Let's get back to you, shall we?" Replacing his goggles, he picked up a screwdriver to remove one of the burnt panels of the arm.

A shrill shout came from outside the garage. "Billie! Dinner's ready!"

Billie jumped and flung the screwdriver across the room. It clattered off some shelves before hitting the ground. Billie dropped his head to his hands.

***

Jasper opened his front door, stroked Maxie's head, and made a dash for the stairs. Halfway up, his mum called from the kitchen.

"Jasper! Dinner will be ready in five minutes!"

"Okay! thanks!" Jasper said.

Walking into his room, Jasper threw his bag onto his bed, then slumped onto his computer chair, which creaked as he leant back. He rubbed his face with his hands before throwing them down and staring blankly at a wall. That thing was unlike anything he'd ever seen. If Billie won't believe him about this, no one would. Hell, if he'd told himself what happened he'd think he was mental too. Everyone will think he'd gone completely mad. Maybe it wasn't some weird creature – maybe he was just imagining it to be something more incredible than it actually was. It's probably some weird dog or something. Something small like a Jack Russell. He thought back to the colour of the creature. A green Jack Russell, that had just been spray painted by some mean owners, who had even gone through the trouble of training their dog to stand on two legs and give him yellow contact lenses. But that doesn't explain the way the thing moved, or its massive mouth. That's even less likely than mythical creatures being ... real.

Jasper's imagination began to run away with him again. Or what if it was a failed science experiment that managed to get away. Jasper smiled: that was probably the most plausible of all the options so far, yet still a little far-fetched. He shoved his hands in his pockets and swivelled on his chair from side to side. His hand touched his phone in his pocket and an idea came to Jasper. He brought out his phone and turned it over to look at the camera. "There's only one way I can get them to believe me".

***

Jasper ran as fast as his legs could carry him, heart racing and eyes wide with panic as he ran down an empty street illuminated by streetlamps. Each time he passed a streetlamp it flickered and cut out, leaving darkness in his wake. Sweat dripped down his forehead. He glanced back into the darkness and a loud growling sound rumbled through the streets, filling his stomach with dread. He ran around a corner and hid behind a wall to catch his breath. The abrasive bricks clung to the fabric of his clothes and scraping his back as he pressed his body tight against the wall. Jasper's chest heaved. His feet tingled with the urge to run, but he was determined to see what was chasing him. He pressed his hands against the wall and peered around the corner at the empty street. He couldn't see anything except the tungsten glow coming from the remaining streetlamps down the street. With a sigh of relief, he leaned back against the wall. Jasper's eyes widened as a warm sticky fluid landed with a thud on his shoulder and began trickling down. His body clenched and his breath caught in his throat. Raising his head, he saw two giant milky-white eyes staring menacingly through the darkness. The creature's mouth contorted into an abnormally wide smile with long, sharp teeth. It looked at Jasper with all the curiosity of a praying mantis about to catch its prey. Jasper was just about to scream when the creature lunged at him with a deafening screech.

Jasper woke with a jolt. His alarm clock had sprung to life, and Wham was telling him it was time to get his lazy arse out of bed. Hitting snooze, Jasper rolled over and looked at the drawing which he'd left open on his bedside table. He thought about his dream and the events of the day before. There was literally nothing on earth like that thing. He felt the soft warmth of his pillow and he began to drift back into sleep.

His alarm began to sing to him again and he groaned. He flung out his arm and hit the alarm with a thump. "I'm up, I'm up", he said, rubbing his eyes.

He swung his legs off the bed and padded downstairs, past his family in the living room who were, as always, watching the news with square eyes. Today an angry farmer was being interviewed about the mysterious killings of his sheep on the moors. "Standard doom and gloom", he said to himself, rubbing his eyes and heading into the kitchen.

Having brewed his coffee, Jasper poured it into his mug and walked out of the kitchen. He turned the corner and lingered in the doorway of the living room to watch the end of the news story on the farmer. The comparatively short, brunette, female news reporter stood next to the stubbly greying farmer and turned to address the camera.

"Attacks like this have been happening throughout the moors for the past week. The big question is, is it some monster? Or is it just another loose dog?"

"I ruddy be gone told you already, it ain't no dog!" butted in the farmer.

The reporter glared at the farmer then smiled. "Or maybe it's just another nutty farmer. Back to you, Jim". The farmer's face turned sour, and he seemed about to shout at the reporter when the screen abruptly cut to a studio.

"Thank you, Clare", said Jim, a news anchor with slick black hair and a freshly shaven, chiselled chin. "Who knows, maybe we'll be seeing gremlins running all over the moors next?" Jim and his co-anchor, a slender blonde woman, both laughed.

The co-anchor turned back to the camera. "Enough with tall tales! Up next, how many germs do hand dryers really spread?". Jasper gave an exasperated groan and gulped down his coffee. He plodded back upstairs and forced himself to eat some toast, that way he'd have more energy for his paper round.

Walking papers from house to house, Jasper was beginning to regret not bringing his bike with him the night before. It occurred to him that he was coming close to the place where he first saw the creature. Rounding the corner, he saw the bins the creature had tumbled out of. They were all upright and completely tidy – not a single scrap of rubbish in sight. Jasper blinked. "That's strange, I didn't imagine it, did I?"

He kept on walking, but after about ten metres he halted in his tracks. In front of Jasper, splintered pieces of treated wood were strewn all over the path and there was a gaping hole in the neighbouring fence. He looked down to see some of his drawings scattered around the path. He grabbed the pages, frantically shoving each one in his bag.

"Oi! Sandra! It's that bloody kid again!" shouted the man he'd run into yesterday, staring at him from the end of the garden ahead. He had no barbecue fork now and was only wearing pants and a half-open dressing gown. Jasper chucked the bag on his back and sprinted away. Turning back, he saw the man standing in the middle of the hole in the fence shouting something which can only be described as unflattering in Jasper's direction.

Chapter Four: Detention

"You know what? I think he's always late because he just needs a little 'alone time' in the morning, if you know what I mean" Lucy said, as she swung her legs back and forth whilst sat on the bike racks with a Cheshire grin.

"Ha! Yeah, maybe he just needs to 'Relax' a little in the morning" Billie said laughing. At that moment they saw Jasper running as fast as he could, completely drenched with sweat.

"Guys, guys", he said heaving.

"Wow, Jasp, don't you want to take fifteen minutes to yourself to... relax, a bit", Lucy said as she threw a look to Billie.

"Like he needs fifteen", Billie sniggered.

"What? No, guys seriously! Billie, remember I told you about that creature last night? The one that attacked me".

"Creature, what creature?" replied Lucy.

"Oh yeah Jasper said he got attacked by a creature yesterday, but I still think it was a rabbit", said Billie.

"It wasn't a rabbit! Anyway, I was thinking this morning that maybe I was just imagining it, maybe it didn't actually happen".

"Or maybe it was a rabbit?" interrupted Billie. Just as he was about to say something else Jasper shouted.

"Shut up Billie! I was doubting it myself, so after my paper round, I walked past the garden that me and the creature crashed into. The place was completely trashed! Even the guy was there, and he definitely remembered".

"What makes you think that?" asked Billie.

"Well, the biggest clue was him shouting" then Jasper imitated the beer bellied man "Hey it's that dumb kid! Get back here you little..." Jasper paused "I think he also insulted my mum a bit too".

"Well, he got the dumb kid bit right", laughed Lucy.

"Guys come on this is serious, I was attacked!" pleaded Jasper. Billie and Lucy began to walk up the steps to the college entrance laughing. Jasper gritted his teeth and ran after them.

Later that day Jasper was sitting in a very ordinary maths class with twenty other teenagers, not listening to the droning meanderings of Mr Newton who was trying to teach math. By the many drawings in Jasper's book, it was not going well. Jasper sat in his chair chewing the end of his pencil. It splintered with an audible crunch, which caught the attention of a girl with long dark hair and dark wiry glasses that sat next to him. She looked at the deranged beaver chomping its pencil, her freckled nose wrinkled with disgust, and she turned back to the teacher. Jasper stared at the clock unblinking. How could time be going so slowly? It was like the damn clock was broken. As the clock ticked, he made another audible crunch.

"Mr Collins, do you intend on using that pencil? Or will you continue to use it as a chew toy? In which case you can go outside like the other dogs", Said Mr Newton, who had somehow managed to teleport from one side of the room to the other.

"Sorry Sir", said Jasper, lowering his head to his book. *How did he manage to do that?* Looking at the pages in front of him he saw that there was the start of an equation that seemed to end in a detailed illustration of the furry creature. Mr Newtons leathery jowls drooped as he looked down at Jasper's work and swiped his book. Pushing his glasses to his face, his mouth opened a little, exposing brown teeth and accentuating his gaunt features as he glared at the drawings.

"Ahhh" he drawled "Mr Collins, it appears that you're drawing dogs as well as acting like one". This caused a small rumble of laughter to echo in the classroom. The classes approval just bolstered Mr Newton and he went on. "Maybe you'd also like to sit and, 'stay' in after school detention too", he smirked. That caused a chorus of "oooooooos", to flood the classroom. "Yes, thirty minutes of detention at the end of the day should do the trick. Maybe it'll teach you to focus more on class. Don't be late Mr Collins, I wouldn't want to castrate you". Jaspers face paled and Mr Newton through his book back to the table. Jasper's head fell to his hands. Through his parted fingers he looked up at the clock. *What?! not even a minute has passed.* Exasperated he dropped his head to the table. Moments later Jasper felt something bounce off his head. Sitting up he saw a scrunched-up ball of paper, looking around he spotted the culprit. Lucy made a gesture for him to open it. Like peeling an orange, Jasper unfolded the ball.

Ouch that was harsh! Funny as hell though! How do you manage to get yourself into these situations? Billie and I are going to take on the next boss tonight.

Join us!!!

PS, don't get castrated.

Jasper read 'join us' exactly how Lucy would have said it. Just like a hungry zombie.

The rest of the school day carried on for Jasper without a hitch, until he found himself stuck just as that old leathery handbag wished, in after school detention. Jasper was sat in a standard classroom scribbling down his math work in complete boredom. The classroom had twelve seats and educational posters all over the walls, some with mathematical equations, some with planets and some with human anatomy. There were a few other students in the classroom and one very bored teacher, Mr Malack. Mr Malack was the kind of teacher that really didn't want to teach at all. He probably wanted to be a guitarist or something else equally cool, but realising he needed to make money he resorted to teaching. Jasper recognised one of the girls in the room. Her name was Molly. Jasper always thought that she looked like a gorgeous rocker, with her hazel eyes and messy mousy brown hair that hung over her Guns and Roses t-shirt. Unwittingly Jasper realised that he was staring, his biggest clue was the young rock chick flipping him the bird. A little embarrassed he turned back to his work and fumbled with his half-chewed pencil.

If Billie could do it, so could he. Moments later he found himself staring out the window. Next to a large willow tree was a squirrel that bounced along the ground, its big fluffy duster like tail bobbing behind him. *No! Focus!* He shouted internally. Jolting back to his work he stared at the equation again, $X5 / X2 = X5\text{-}2 = X3$. He paused in complete and utter confusion

"Well, what the hell is X?" he muttered in frustration. Catching the eye of the young rocker, who glanced at him through her mousy hair. Frustrated, he put his fist on the side of his chin and stared out the window.

Jasper dropped his pencil as he saw what was outside. The strange green creature that attacked him was hunched over next to the Willow tree, its arms shot out left and right as bits of fur flew all over the grass. It turned and the squirrels tail drooped from one side of its mouth. Hunched over, the creature slurped the tail into its mouth like spaghetti, then made a small belch and bounced off through the college courtyard. Perplexed, Jasper blinked.

"You have got to be kidding me!"

Mr Malak looked up from his magazine and frowned. "Are you alright Jasper?". Jasper looked around the class. Everyone was staring at him, he looked at Mr Malack, then back out the window.

"Errr, yeah" Jasper scratched the back of his head "all good thanks, can I please just leg it to the toilet?".

Mr Malack sighed, "go on then, but don't be long".

"Sure! No worries", Jasper replied as he was already grabbing his book and his bright blue dinosaur bag.

"Urm, Jasper what do you think you're doing?" shouted Mr Malack half-heartedly, as the young man ran out the room with all his things.

Running through the empty corridors, Jasper grabbed onto the side of lockers so he wouldn't lose momentum as he ran. Sprinting through the main doors of the college he scanned around before making a snap decision and ran down the steps to grab his bike. He prayed that just this once the chain would hold. Unlocking his bike, he cycled towards the courtyard where he'd seen the creature. Jaspers skidded to a stop as he saw the lone willow with no sign of the creature. The clouds began to disperse, and the sun broke free. Squinting in the sun Jasper raised his hand over his eyes so he could see. Suddenly he spotted the creature bouncing across the road on the far side of the courtyard. Smiling Jasper pressed his foot to the peddle and shot after the creature.

Jasper rounded a corner on his bike and stopped suddenly when he saw the strange creature gnawing on the tire of a parked car. Each time the creature clenched its jaws, it creaked like an old boot. Its eyes shot to Jasper and they both froze. Jasper knew that no one would believe him unless he had proof. As slow as he possibly could he reached into his pocket to grab his phone. The creature's eyes flicked to the phone, then back to Jasper. Jasper had never been a hunter, but he knew the concept from his late grandfather.

"You must know the land, what's in your pack and no sudden movements damnit or you'll startle your quarry".

As slowly as humanly possible he raised the phone. The creature blinked, then clenched his jaw tight, the tire squealed then popped, the burst of air flapped the creature's ears and caused it to squint as it stared menacingly at Jasper. Jasper lifted his phone as slowly as he could, the creature's eyes glanced back to the phone and the creature suddenly bolted, scarpering away. "Get back here!" Jasper shouted and continued in pursuit. The creature turned sharply down an alley followed closely by Jasper. The bike swayed back and forth as Jasper peddled like a steam train after the creature, who stopped suddenly next to a pile of bins. Jasper skidded to a stop, his back tire sliding out to the side so as not to hit the creature. Breathing heavily, he looked down at the creature. It looked at him curiously, then out of nowhere it kicked up a can into its clawed hand and threw it at Jasper hitting him cleanly on the forehead. Jasper flinched at the sudden attack "ouch!" Jasper shouted as he raised his arms in defence and rubbed at his forehead. The creature then tilted his head observing this strange tall creature covered in rags. It then dove into the bins and began pelting Jasper with a volley of old yogurt pots, cans, and banana peels. Jasper fell from his bike and scarpered behind some bins on the other side of the alley in an attempt to avoid the onslaught. The creature then tilted its head back with a maniacal laugh, as it threw dirty nappies at Jasper who winced at the smell. Finding his steal Jasper picked up a nappy and launched it at the creature hitting him square in his laughing mouth. It stopped laughing abruptly and began spitting on the floor, clawing at its tongue. Jasper threw his hand over his mouth to stifle a laugh, which he didn't hide well at all. The creature then turned back to Jasper and growled like an angry terrier. Jasper stopped laughing at the sight of the new danger and picked up a bin lid, put it to his side like a shield and shouted to the creature. "Come at me crap bag!". The creature, dropped to all fours pushed his body back, his hair standing on end and launched himself at Jasper who brought up his tin shield at a slight angle, and slammed it into the creature bouncing it into the air and out of the alley. It rolled to a stop at the side of the road and instantly got to its feet and roared a garbled yell. Jasper could almost see the KO above the creature's head as the yell was abruptly cut short. The creature suddenly went under the tires of a small blue Nissan Micra with a red magnetic L on the back. The Micra bounced over the creature then came to a stop. Jasper threw down his shield in horror and ran over to the creature. The car paused for a moment, then as the young driver saw Jasper run after what must have been his pet, the passenger next shouted "forget that, just drive". The Nissans engine rumbled and the exhaust popped as the learner slammed on his accelerator. Jasper gave the Micra a last imploring glance as it began to slowly trudge away as fast as it could.

The creature led on the road, still as death. Jasper knelt next to the creature, remembering what he had been taught about first aid back when he was in the Scouts. He placed his ear next to the creature's mouth and looked down its chest. He saw the creature's thick green fur rise and fall with each shallow breath. Jasper felt its warm breath against his ear, then it made a small groan like an old man attempting to get out of a chair. Jasper jumped and saw that the creature was still passed out. A crowd was beginning to gather, moving towards him. Seeing the approaching horde Jasper considered. There was absolutely no way people were going to be okay with this little guy, they'd probably go mental. They'd grab their torches and pitchforks, failing that he would become an internet sensation for killing the thing. He wasn't about to let any of that happen. He quickly took up the little guy in his arms, cradling the creature and ran over to his bike. With one hand Jasper opened his bag, sliding the creature feet first into it and zipped it up leaving a little gap at the top. Jasper gently slid his arms into the straps of his bag putting it on his front so he could keep an eye on the creature. Reaching down Jasper lifted his bike, climbed on, and began to peddle home, the bag on his front and the little German shepherd ears of the creature just poking out of the zip.

Chapter Five: Bogart

The day rolled on and the sky was beginning to grow dark. The heavens had opened drenching the roads in a slick layer of water. Jasper peddled as fast as he could home, water sprayed up his back from his rear tire. The creature was tucked away in his brother's baby blue bag on Jaspers front, keeping the creature safe from the elements. This also allowed Jasper to keep a close eye on the creature. Just in case it decided to go all Tasmanian Devil on him again. Panting, he looked down at the creature on his front.

"You are keeping me fit little guy, I've never cycled so much in my life". The creature groaned. Jasper's breath caught in his throat and his feet pressed firmly into the peddles. Thankfully, the creature was still asleep or knocked out and he loosened his grip on the handlebars. Jasper could just imagine the creature waking up and launching himself at Jasper throwing him from the bike. They'd probably end up rolling along the floor for a few meters then just start brawling again, or he'd end up having to fight the little guy for his brothers bag this time. *Not a massive loss*. The creature stirred again spurring Jasper to cycle faster. The journey took him a little longer than he'd like. There was no way he was going down that short cut again.

Panting, Jasper pulled his bike up to the house and took it around the side gate. Locking the bike, he saw the creature stir, it blinked and began to wriggle in his bag. Throwing his hands over the bag he zipped it up completely, trapping the creature. He ran out of the side of the house, closed the gate, and opened the front door.

"Hi Mum!" he shouted, shutting the door.

"Hi Jaspy. Dinner will be ready in 20 minutes" replied his mum.

"Thanks! and don't call me Jaspy" he replied, running upstairs. Maxie darted around the corner to greet Jasper but was too late, he'd already run upstairs. Jasper stopped suddenly, as his little brother Johnny stood outside his room. Johnny was holding a triceratops and stegosaurus, his two favourite toys. Johnny was just like any other 'normal' four-year-old, obsessed with dinosaurs. He knew all their names and would probably give a struggling palaeontologist a run for his money. The to be fossil hunter looked at Jasper tilting his head and raised an eyebrow.

"Why does my bag sound angry?" said Johnny. Thinking on his feet Jasper replied,

"That's because it's hungry". Jasper then pulled in his elbows and made two claws with his hands. "Like a T-rex!" He chased Johnny into his room roaring and tickling Johnny until he submitted on his barely visible bedroom floor surrounded by plastic and fluffy dinosaurs.

"No, no stop, stop!" Jonny cried with laughter. Johnny threw his toys as he tried to cover every vulnerable area from the tickling tyrannosaurus. Jasper smiled and shut Johnny's door, but not before poking his head around the door "I told you that the T-rex was hungry". Johnny smiled, sat up and then carried on playing with his toys.

Jasper hurried into his room and pressed his back against the door slowly clicking it shut. Closing his eyes, he released a sigh of relief. He carried his squirming bag over to his bed. Tentatively lowered the bag on to the bed. Jasper brushed his hand through his hair as he gazed at the bag that lay motionless on the bed. What was he even thinking bringing him here? The creature would trash everything. He wasn't expecting him to actually wake up, he just wanted to keep him safe from a close-minded horde. Jaspers eyes lit up as an idea came to him. Leaving the bag squirming on the bed he ran downstairs, throu-h the hall, into the kitchen and past his mum, who was finishing up cooking what smelt like a delicious roast.

"Jasper David Collins! What's this I hear about you skipping after school detention?" Said Jaspers mum.

Jasper flinched. He didn't have time to deal with this right now! He reeled internally. *Just be honest, honesty and truth can never send you wrong. If you always tell the truth no one can accuse you of lying. That is, unless your truth is so outlandish that everyone thinks that you're lying anyway.* "I never skipped detention. I was there". He protested "I just had to leave early that's all. There was an emergency". His mum pierced her lips as she turned to him, her frown tightening.

"An emergency? What kind of emergency?"

"I saw an accident". Jasper paused. *Why are my palms sweaty?* He wiped them on his trousers. "It was outside the window, so I had to go help". Her eyebrow raised then she turned to back to the food.

"That's funny, because your teacher said that you were going to the toilet but never came back", She said stirring the roasties with the calm of a detective. *Stupid Malack why couldn't he stick to playing guitar. Well, that's one lie caught out. Time to tell the truth.* He looked at his mum, then looked down to his feet.

"That's the problem, that was the emergency. The emergency was me, I had an emergency". He paused realising he'd already gone and done it. His entire body deflated as he said "it was a, a, toilet emergency". *What am I doing, I'm in a bed of lies!* He screamed internally. Her face turned to concern.

"Oh god what happened?", she said, setting down her wooden spoon. *Okay you're in the hole now, so sell it like a goblin selling a kidney.* He had to raise his voice over the sound of sizzling chicken.

"I had drunk a lot of water and I didn't want anyone to know, but... I wet myself". He signalled to his drenched trousers. "Wet myself bad, just started as a trickle then as soon as I got out of that room. Whoosh it was a torrent. Honestly it was a miracle no one saw me. I think I would have been ridiculed for life if they had. Honestly if you must feel bad for anyone it would be the poor janitor that finds the trail. Right! Well, I'd better go get changed anyway, can't be standing around in wet trousers" She raised an unconvinced eyebrow.

"Come on then take them off".

"What? Here? Mum, no" he protested.

"Off now! No son of mine is going around in trousers drenched in a 'torrent of urine'". At that moment one of the pots bubbled over, which drew the attention of his mother who promptly took the pan off the hob. Seizing his opportunity, he ran out of the room, "I'll get changed and pop them in the wash."

"Thank you and you can also be grounded for a week as it's clearly rain! Oh, make that two weeks for lying to your mother!" she yelled from the kitchen. Jasper gritted his teeth; he just couldn't catch a break.

Jasper tentatively creaked open his bedroom door and peered over to his bed, the bag was still motionless. Glad that the creature hadn't escaped, or destroyed his room, he brought in a dog crate, a water bowl, and some dog biscuits. Then as quiet as a ninja he locked his door and placed the large dog crate in the side of the room. Taking some blankets from his wardrobe and thick pillow from his bed he made a small bed inside the crate. He then placed the dog food next to the crate and turned back to his bed "right little guy, let's get you sorted". The bag made a growling noise and Jasper felt a rush of adrenaline as his body tensed. Forcing himself he walked over to the bag *Here we go*. He picked up the bag like a loaded bomb that could explode at any moment, suddenly the bag began to wriggle and snap. Suddenly Jasper felt an intense pressure on his hand as the creature bit him through the fabric. The creature's teeth pressed hard against his wrist. He felt a pop and crack as his hand dislocated from his forearm. His face creased and he clenched his jaw tight in pain. Hurrying, Jasper gently as possible (all things considered), unzipped the bag, through it into the dog crate and shut the door. The creature sprawled out like a bowling ball, rolling onto the blankets. Springing up on two feet, the creature had a brief intense look at his surroundings sniffing loudly in each direction as if he were taking in the entire room. The creatures focus shifted to Jasper. Jasper could see dried blood staining the green fur on the creature's shoulder. The creature's eyes narrowed. It rolled its eyes and gave a disregarding snarl and began to thoroughly lick the wound on his shoulder. Each lick smothered the fur in saliva leaving it wet and clumped together. "Well, that could have gone much, much worse" said Jasper as he wiped a nervous sweat from his forehead and popped his hand back into place.

Relieved Jasper sat at his computer, rubbing his wrist he watched the creature before turning on his computer. The fan quietly hummed as it powered up. The computer had a classic lock screen where it showed beautiful photography of fantastic places on earth, most were likely taken by some National Geographic adventurer. This shot had a campfire in the centre of a tribe, sitting under the stairs. Members looked at each other with joy as some played instruments like wooden shakers and drums, whilst others danced the night away in the light of fire. Jasper was about to put in his password when the photo gave him pause. He looked to the tribe then looked back to the creature "where are the rest of you guys? Surely you have a family? I guess I'll have to work out what you are before I can do anything". Said Jasper as if he were talking to a lost puppy. He typed in his password, Adventurer23 and his home screen popped up. It was a beast not too dissimilar to a tyrannosaur, however this one was armoured to the teeth. A creature that you would not want to meet on a dark night, or any day for that matter. "Okay little guy, time to work out what you are". said Jasper. He first typed 'green creature' and the first thing to pop up was a stop motion animation from the 1980s of a clay character named Morph. In the video Morph had found a little green ball, which was 'obviously' alive. Jasper watched the video with a raised eyebrow as the creature made an awful squealing noise with each movement. Jasper winced as the creature tried to talk to Morph with this same insufferable squeal. "Yeah, not that". Jasper clicked off the video. He then tried typing 'green dog' with equal failure, this just brought up pictures of photoshopped dogs and irresponsible owners who had cruelly dyed their dogs' coats green. With little success his search was cut short when his mum shouted from downstairs.

"Jaspy, Johnny, dinners ready!".
A small snarl came from the cage at Jasper's mum's voice. "Hey, it's alright little buddy, I'll see if I can grab you something nice" The creature looked at Jasper with a sense of loathing then groaned and curled into a ball, resting his head on his claws. "Okay, okay, I'll get something really tasty", the creature shifted his eyes to the dog food then to Jasper, "Something tastier than that". The creature grumbled, rubbed his face into his fur and closed his eyes. Jasper couldn't help but smile at the creature's seemingly disinterested reaction.

Jasper pulled in his chair to the wooden dining table in a beige rectangle room. The smell of roast chicken filled his nostrils. "Mum this looks great" he said instantly picking up a chicken leg to devour it. Before he could his mum came in carrying the gravy and said sternly
"Jasper! Wait for Johnny"

"Arrghhh ok fine" he replied putting the chunk of chicken flesh back onto the plate.

"Johnny! Come downstairs, dinners ready!" shouted Jackie. Jasper had an odd sinking feeling in his stomach and all of his instincts screamed at him from Johnny's absence. His eyes widened and his chair clattered to the floor as he darted away from the table, almost knocking over his mum and the jug of gravy.

"What is wrong with these kids?" Said Jackie.

Thundering up the stairs Jasper caught Johnny just about to go into Jasper's room. "Johnny what are you doing?! I told you, you can't go into my room".

"But I can't find my stegosaurus?" said Johnny pouting.

"Look, dinners ready we'll find your steggo later, okay?". Johnny looked down to his feet.

"Okay" he said before he shuffled past Jasper and down the stairs.

Jasper and Johnny stuffed their faces with all the goodies their mums roast had to offer. Crispy roast potatoes, roasted chicken, stuffing and Yorkshire puds. There was also brussels sprouts, but some kind of strange force field must have surrounded those, because no fork even came close to them. Jackie watched Jasper and Johnny for a moment before breaking the silence.

"So, how's Lucy and Billie?"

"Yeah fine" Jasper said with a mouthful of chicken. "Billies gone mad with his engineering. Made a robotic arm in his garage. Never seen it working but he seems to think it's worked," said Jasper.

"Cool!" threw in Johnny, gravy dribbling down his chin.

"Yeah, really cool isn't it! He's going to make a massive robot one day. One so big it could fight off your T-rex".

"No, it couldn't!" Johnny giggled.

"That's incredible and what about Lucy? What's she up to?" she asked, cutting into a crispy roastie.

"I dunno really, she's into her gaming a lot, she's even entering into a load of championships". Johnny interrupted the conversation and began to explain the eating habits of a pterosaur. Picking up a bit of cabbage with his hand and dripping gravy all over his top, Johnny tilted his head back and began to scoff loudly, with a sound like a choking seagull. With this perfect and slightly peculiar distraction, Jasper took some food from his plate and put it in a small bowl he'd hidden under the table. Johnny stopped his scoffing and gave a cheeky grin to his mum with a giggle. Jasper looked at Johnny, slightly confused as he could still hear a quiet slurping, munching sound. Lifting the tablecloth, he saw Maxie, the spaniel licking the bowl completely clean. The sneaky pup looked up at Jasper, greedy eyes asking for more.

Well, wasn't that a brilliant idea! Jasper thought scolding himself for being so foolish.

"Jasper. Jasper, Jasper!" Said his mum looking at him curiously.

"Huh? What? Yeah, yeah definitely" Jasper said lifting a glass of water to his lips, not knowing what he'd just agreed too.

"Brilliant I'm so glad you two are dating now, Lucy's a lovely girl. We'll have to invite her around for dinner on the weekend". Jasper inhaled the water, coughing and splattering all over the table. Johnny flailed as he was drenched in the spray.

"What? No, no we're not dating, she's just a friend". he said trying to regain some sort of natural rhythm to his breathing.

"Really? Oh, that is a shame", said Jackie. "Well, you'll have to invite her over anyway, she really is a lovely young woman".

"No way mum, we're just friends, I don't want to put her through that embarrassment". Jaspers eyes shot to Johnny. He was staring at Jasper wearing a stupid chubby gravy covered grin.

"You love her", Johnny said raising his eyebrows like a creepy old man.

"Right!" Jasper said, standing and removing himself from the dinner table. "If anyone wants me, I'll be in my room doing homework". Smiling Jackie shouted back.

"What about desert?". Quick as lightning Jasper replied.

"I'm not hungry!"

Without even a glance back to them he slammed the door. He then heard a roar of laughter come from the dining room. Jasper huffed and gritted his teeth in annoyance when an idea washed over him, and he darted to the kitchen.

Jasper pressed his back lightly against the bedroom door, he used his elbow to push the door handle open. Pushing his back against the door and an inevitable pile of clothes, he maneuvered a tray of assorted nibbles into the room. The creature unmoving sniffed the air and opened one eye to look at the source of the smell. Sniffing again the creature's eyes widened as it caught all sorts of scents. Immediately it jumped up on two feet with its paws against the bars sniffing up at Jasper. Bending to one knee, Jasper placed the tray in front of the cage. The creature reached out, squeezing his good shoulder through the bars as much as he could and grabbed a cold sausage. Yanking it through the bars the creature sat holding the sausage with two paws before devouring it in two large bites. It then looked up at Jasper chewing loudly like a happy toddler. Jasper couldn't help but smile as the creature chomped in front of him and he offered it another sausage, which it demolished just as fast. Tilting his head Jasper looked curiously at the creature munching away. "I'm going to have to think of a name for you little guy, I can't keep calling you 'the creature' or 'the thing'", he said that last part with a slight mocking tone.

The creature finished the sausage then got to all fours and stared over to the tray. Jasper looked at the food on the tray weighing up what to give him next, he offered the creature chocolate which he sniffed at, then turned up his nose and batted it away in disgust. "Hah okay, you don't like chocolate. I wonder if you can't eat it? Like dogs". Jasper then offered the creature some crisps which he had poured into a bowl. The creature pulled the bowl closer to the cage and began stuffing fists full of crisps into its open maw. "Slow down buddy, you'll get indigestion" the creature stopped, looked at Jasper then exhaled sharply, huffing at him like a disgruntled horse. The creature then turned back to the bowl and continued stuffing his face. "Alright maybe you won't get indigestion". Jasper paused for a moment "It was almost like you understood me then" he said looking at the creature. The creature continued to scoff the crisps. "Or not?" Jasper said, raising one eyebrow. Jasper sat cross legged in front of the creature and looked at it closely. "Scoff, yeah that's what I'll call you, Scoff". Scoff then pushed the bowl away and led back, his little belly protruding from his body. He then stretched out, licked his chops, and sprawled himself over the bed Jasper had made for him. "Scoff, yeah I like that, it definitely suits you" said Jasper looking at the creature stretching out before curling up into a fury ball. His eyes then shifted to a strange chewed up clump of plastic in his bed, which strangely resembled a stegosaurus. "Ah balls!" Jasper said. The creature opened its eyes and glanced over as Jasper's head fell to his hands. "Johnnies steggo"

A few hours had past, and it was rapidly becoming the middle of the night. Jasper's hair had become a little wilder and his eyes were having the pull of an all-nighter. He sat staring at the computer screen perplexed. Putting his face to his hands he drew down his cheeks exposing the red veins underneath his eyes. "What are you Scoff?" he muttered to himself before releasing his face. He had hundreds of tabs open on his screen, all of varying creatures all slightly resembling Scoff but not one even really coming close. "It's almost like you're a cross breed of dog. A German shepherd, crossed with a staffy then crossed again with a koala or something. "Right let's try a different approach" Jasper said as he typed frantically into the keyboard. He began to search for genetically mutated animals, thinking that maybe he was an experiment that had gone horribly wrong. "Dolly the sheep? No. Super pigs? Doubt it. Ha, glow in the dark fish! Definitely, not. Genetically enhanced cats that are allergy free?" He turned his head to look at Scoff sleeping soundly. Scoff had now sprawled himself out, starfished in the middle of his bed snoring loudly. "Nope really don't think you're any kind of cat" Jasper said looking back at the computer. Scratching his head, he decided to take a completely different approach. "Alright let's try creatures of myths and legends". Instantly he was bombarded by myths of Dragons, Panthers that roamed the moors and even ghosts. *That's kind of cool, I wonder what other mythical creatures might have lived around here.* Jasper thought but he knew already that he was procrastinating. But his curiosity was sparked now, and nothing could stop him when he really focused. Sipping a coffee, he read into all sorts of other mythical creatures that 'used to live in these parts'. There was a huge array of different creatures, pixies, goblins, ogres, something called the Fiskerton phantom and there was even a creature called a Knucker. "The Knucker, in old English folklore means water monster, and it was a type of water dragon. Awesome!" Jasper said nodding to himself.

Jasper continued to read for hours about countless mythical creatures, until his coffee went dry and his eyes turned mothy. Leaning back in his chair he turned to Scoff "Sorry buddy, I don't think I'm going to be able to work out what you are tonight" He said as he began to prepare to turn off his computer. Dozens of monsters and beasts flashed across the screen as he began to close tabs, monotonously clicking until something caught his tired eyes. Something called a Bogart, his face brightened as he moved closer to the monitor. "The Boggart has a few different descriptions as no one could quite crack what they actually look like. Some say that they were as tall as a human and strong as six horses and some say that they were as big as a small calf, had shaggy hair with saucer like eyes". He turned to little Scoff sleeping in the dog crate and tilted his head "well your hairs kind of wiry, but I guess it could be thought of as shaggy and you're about half the size of a small calf". Scoff opened his large golden eyes and looked at Jasper begrudgingly. For a short moment they both stared at each other. Then Scoff huffed and snuggled his face back into the pillow. "And your eyes are definitely like saucers" Jasper said thinking allowed. He then looked back to the description on his monitor "Uncontrollable and destructive. Well, it took getting hit by a car to knock that out of you, for a little while anyway". Jasper then lifted the chewed steggo in his hand, mulling over the descriptions. "Hmm a Bogart, Scoff the Bogart. I like that".

Chapter Six: The Lure

Jasper woke up to the sound of his upbeat alarm 'Wake me up before you go-go' by Wham. The happy upbeat tune droning in his ears, he groaned in irritation as if a ragecrawler was screaming in his ear. "Urrggghhh" he murmured as he fumbled around, then slammed his hand onto the phone silencing the world ending annoyance. Opening his tired eyes, he looked at his phone "it's 6:45 am already urghhhh. I've only had two hours sleep", he said removing his quilt and swinging his legs out of bed. He rubbed his eyes looked up at Scoff who was sprawled out in the cage. "Well looks like you had a good night at least" he yawned and walked out of the room and into the bathroom.

The shower was hot, filling the small white room with steam. Jasper hung his head under the running water, feeling it warm his muscles. He relaxed and began to stretch, loosening his body. As he climbed out of the shower, he pondered the night before. There were so many arrows pointing to Scoff really being a creature of myth and legend. Stepping out of the shower he rubbed the towel across his arms, feeling the rough cotton pull at his skin. He looked into the mirror seeing himself, *nope can't be. He just can't be from myths, must be some kind of mutant, experiment or something. But I checked everything I could find last night and there was nothing about mutant bipedal dogs with golden eyes.*

He walked out of the bathroom and yelped as he stepped on Johnny's triceratops. *Ouch! awww man I'll have to break the news to Johnny about steggos close encounter. Close encounter... maybe he's an alien?* Jasper walked into his room to see Scoff sniffing at the food tray left by the cage. "Well, I doubt you're an alien, I can't see you flying any alien spaceships anytime soon, or ever for that matter.

For now, you'll be my dog, or bogart until I can find out where you're actually from. But for now, I'd better get you some more food". Then Jasper disappeared downstairs, leaving Scoff scrabbling at the side of the cage trying to get to the empty tray.

A short while later Jasper returned and on one arm, he carried a bowl of Sugar Puffs and a plate of toast. In his other hand he held a freshly brewed black coffee. Scoff began to perk up jumping all over the cage smelling the food, "alright buddy, so we didn't have much and I kinda like my honey, so it's either Sugar Puffs or honey on toast". he then placed the two foods in front of him to see what he'd go for first. Slightly timid at first, Scoff smelt both the cereal and toast before reaching his good arm through the cage towards the cereal bowl trying his best to grab it. "Cereal it is" said Jasper picking up the bowl and moving to the front of the cage. "Okay buddy, I'm going to open the cage now and give you this" said Jasper gesturing to the Honey puffs. Scoff then pressed his two clawed arms against the front of the cage wiggling his bum in excitement staring at the bowl. "You can't stay in here forever, so here goes nothing" he said sliding open the deadbolt.

Scoff burst out of the cage throwing Jasper off his feet and he went flying into the side of his bed. Winded Jasper looked up at Scoff, with his face submerged in the cereal bowl immobilized. "Errr Scoff? Are you ok?" Jasper said wheezing at the fury stone gargoyle with its head in a cereal bowl. At the sound of Jasper's voice, Scoffs ears twitched turning towards him like two fury satellite dishes. Scoffs jaw then began moving and he began making a slurping crunching noise as he demolished the entire bowl's contents. Jasper pushed himself up and back onto his bed. Scoff's head popped up from the empty cereal bowl and turned to Jasper. Scoff starred for a moment before cocking his head. Milk and cereal clung to Scoffs fur turning it into green matted knots.

Jasper bit into a slice of toast. He noticed instantly that Scoffs eyes followed wherever the toast went. Jasper decided to test this theory and waved his arm in a circle over his body, Scoffs eyes were locked onto the toast and his entire head followed in any direction that the honey covered delight travelled. Laughing Jasper took another bite.

"Ha you are a funny little guy aren't you?" he said with a mouth full of toast.

Scoff then took a little shuffle forward towards Jasper. Jasper's jaw paused mid chew as he noticed Scoff's eyes shifting back and forth from Jasper's eyes and the toast in his hand. Jasper had a sudden sinking feeling when he saw Scoff's bum wiggle again, this time just like a cat preparing to pounce. He dove backward trying to protect his toast, as Scoff jumped at him garbling. The two then began to scrap on the bed, Jasper trying his best to keep Scoff away from the toast. Jasper held the toast in the air, trying to keep Scoff down with his other hand. Scoff was clawing up Jaspers top, dragging the neckline halfway down Jaspers chest. Jasper then took the toast and shoved the whole thing in his mouth, stuffing his cheeks as much as possible. Scoff saw this treachery and froze halfway up Jaspers body. Scoff looked in horror at Jaspers honey covered mouth. There was a moment of silence before Scoff and Jasper both in unison looked over to the desk, where on the plate lay the second and last piece of toast.

Both Scoff and Jasper rolled around in a pile of claws and feet. "You had a bad arm! You were hit by a car! How do you have so much energy?" Jasper reeled, frantically battling with the determined fluff ball. Finally, they both grabbed the toast and shot backwards. They were both holding half a piece of toast in their hand, they looked at each other, then at the others piece of toast. Jasper laughed "half each, I can deal with that" he said taking a bite of the toast. Scoff looked at his half of toast and examined it. He then turned to Jasper and threw the toast aside and dove at Jasper and his prize.

"What! You had half!" Cried Jasper.

The scrap continued. Jasper was trying in vain to shove the food into his mouth with both hands. Scoff was holding both hands as tight as possible with both feet pressed against Jasper's chest. The toast was just millimetres away from Jasper's mouth and he could almost taste the honey when they locked eyes. *Did Scoff just smile?* Confused Jaspers eyebrow rose, and Scoff let go of both arms slamming the toast into Jasper's face. Scoff landed on the ground with the grace of a cat, then fell back in maniacal laughter. "You pug ugly snot rocket! You didn't even want the toast!" Said Jasper coughing and splattering the toast from the back of his throat.

Straightening out his clothes and wiping his face Jasper composed himself. Whilst also trying to ignore the laughing coming from the little creature that was now walking away from him shaking his head and slapping his leg. *He's slapping his leg!* Scoff walked back to the cage leaving the door open, then fell back into the soft pillow linking his claws behind his head. *That little terror. What even just happened?* Jasper thought rubbing his jaw. Looking at the time, he realised he was late for his paper round "damnit, not again!" he cried, grabbing his things, and dashing to the door. He looked at Scoff for a moment contemplating taking him to school. Scoff still was wearing a Cheshire grin. He even had the audacity to pick up a piece of cereal that was on his bed and throw it in his mouth as if it were a grape and he some roman emperor. Jasper could swear he was even chewing like he was triumphant. Checking there was enough water and food in the room he looked back at Scoff "Yeah, you can stay here" Jasper said, this time locking the door.

Jasper cycled from door to door doing his round and though he was physically there, his mind really wasn't. Too many things were flying around his head about the creature in his room. The creature was possibly called a bogart, Jasper realised then that he was still no closer to knowing what the creature was. *If bogarts are real, what other mythical creatures are real? Are ogres real? Dragons? Bigfoot?* Jasper shivered at the thought of ragecrawler's and other beasties from people's imagination roaming around the planet. Opening a small wooden gate surrounded by lush evergreens, he made his way to the front door of a small cottage. As he went to post the paper, something caught his eye. On the front cover he saw a headline "FARMER HARASSED AND THE DISAPPEARING SHEEP" he then unfolded the paper and looked at the photo, there was an older man, maybe in his late 50s, wearing tweed standing in a lush green field surrounded by mist. *I think I heard about this the other day when Mum and Johnny were watching the news*, Jasper thought as he read on.

Farmer Barric was out checking on his herd when he heard an awful garbling, roaring noise and he said that he had to investigate. "Initially I thought one of the ewes had got caught in a fence you see. Because that does happen from time to time. But when I went to see where the sheep were, I couldn't believe me eyes. I wasn't just missing one ewe, no mam, I be missing a third of my flock. You often lose one or two to bad weather, disease or animals but not a third of my flock! Unheard of that is!" Obviously, the farmer was in distress over the loss of so much of his flock, not only are his sheep like family to the farmer but they are also his source of income. Now the big question on everyone's minds is what happened to these sheep and will we ever know?

He looked at the photo of the farmer and the land, noticing the misty hills behind him. Thinking back on the night before, he recalled where it was speculated that the Bogart would have lived. It was said that they often were found in small towns and villages, harassing families, even eating children and family pets. It then went on to say that it's thought that they could live on moors and Marshland, keeping out of humanity's way until they're feeling particularly mischievous. For a moment he thought of Scoff eating Johnny, but quickly disregarded the idea before thinking about it again... And then disregarding it again. *Okay this is getting serious now, either I need to stop those Bogart's from killing sheep. If it's them that are even doing it, or I need to release Scoff back into his natural habitat. If that's where bogarts are from.* He paused. "Oh god, I have no idea what I'm doing. I need to talk to Billie and Lucy".

Later that morning Jasper locked up his bike and looked around for Lucy and Billie. "I guess I'm a little early", he thought, looking at his watch. With time to kill he hopped onto a wall next to the bike racks and began to search more about bogarts on his phone. He discovered something else rather disturbing.

Not only are boggarts thought to be very dangerous, but they're also thought to turn your milk sour and also be incredibly bad luck

Jasper frowned; *I really don't think that he's caused me any bad luck. In the past few days, I've only been attacked, shouted at by an old fat man, grounded, had after school detention and almost got hit by a car... Maybe I have been*

64

having bad luck? At that moment two feet appeared in his eye line, he looked up slowly to see a girl wearing a red and black checked skirt and a black iron maiden t-shirt. Draped over her slender shoulders was the messy mousy brown hair of the rocker from detention.

"Hey, Jasper, isn't it?" She said chewing gum.

Jasper nodded dumbly "urh yeah, Jasper, but my friends call me Jasp".

"Well, Jasp. That was pretty cool what you did last night, flunking off detention like that. Very cool" she said, swinging her body from side to side.

"Ha yeah, no one's going to hold me in detention!" he said trying to act cool and hide his embarrassment.

"Well, me and a few of the crew are going to go up to the old, abandoned sewers wanna come? It's sick skating around there, if you're down for it?" she said before playing with her gum, wrapping it around her finger as she looked up at him.

"Ace, yeah, sick. Cool I'll be there" said Jasper the words falling out of his mouth as he fumbled with his hands on the railing.

"Ace?" She said in a mocking tone, "we'll see you there, shall we say around five-ish?" she said with a grin chewing her gum, her beautiful white teeth catching Jasper's eye.

"Yeah, cool see you at five-ish" said Jasper nodding his head with all the cool of an ogre doing long division.

"Ace" she said walking away, she turned her head around to him, her mousy hair flicking over her shoulder. "The name's Molly by the way, but you know, my friends call me Molz" winking at him and flashing that white smile again as she continued to walk away.

What the hell just happened? thought Jasper catching himself.

"What the hell was that?!" Shouted Billie and Lucy in unison. Jasper jumped and turned to see both Billie and Lucy.

"It's, er, not what it looks like, I just urgh, well, um" His face turned red. "Honestly, I don't really know what just happened" Jasper said, rubbing the back of his head still confused. Billie looked at Jasper with a predatory grin, nodding.

"You sly dog! I thought I'd be making you a robot girlfriend before you actually got one of your own. Man, you proved me wrong, you my friend are a god!" Billie said, turning Jaspers face a bright red colour. Lucy stood stone faced with her arms crossed.

"Yeah, congratulations, stud!". Billie completely lost it at that.

"Oh my god you're a stud! What happened? Tell us everything!" Billie said dragging Jasper off the wall and leading up the steps of the college. Lucy stood behind them, anger boiling in utter disbelief at what she was seeing and stormed after them.

Billie was dragging Jasper through the corridor, passing classrooms, lockers, and hundreds of students, some of which were already eyeing Jasper.

"What's going on? How do people know already?" asked Jasper.

"How indeed" said Lucy angrily behind him. Billie looked up to him.

"Are you kidding me, who cares? Anyway, you have to tell me, when did you two first talk? Have you kissed? What are you going to do tonight? Are you going to bring a skateboard too? Can you even skate? I don't think I've seen you skate. How long were you two talking? Ahhhh I'm so excited! Can I come?" Said Billie.

"Yeah, how long were you two talking? We were meant to do that boss raid last night remember?" Said Lucy folding her arms.

"Oh my god the raid! I'm so sorry guys, honestly, I didn't mean to miss it. This huge thing happened to me after I left detention" said Jasper coming to a halt.

"Leave it Jasper" Lucy said storming off, leaving Jasper staring at her walking away into a blur of teenagers.

"Oooo Lucy said Jasper rather than Jasp, that must have stung" said Billie nudging his side.

"Yeah, it did" said Jasper, his pained expression evident.

The bell rang and students began disappearing into different classes.

"Well at least you have a hot date with 'Mollz'. The chick of rock!" said Billie triumphantly raising his fist in the air whilst walking away from Jasper towards the workshops. He pointed at Jasper "I'll catch you after college though yeah?" called out Billie causing a few of the other students to look at him.

"Nerd" one of the teens said, shouldering Billie aside knocking him into a locker. Jasper glared at Lee, the large curly haired teen that shouldered Billie, he then stared back at Jasper shouldering him aside, causing him to stumble. "What are you looking at, freak?" scowled the bull storming through the corridor. Stumbling Jasper looked back at Billie.

"Yeah, I'll catch you later", he said. Waving Billie disappeared into the crowd. Jasper looked over his shoulder and saw Lee storming down the corridor *what an arse hole, I'm too tired to deal with that today. I'm staying way away from him.*

Jasper was sat in his biology class listening to Mr J. The class was filled with the familiar scents of various reptiles

67

in the room. Leopard geckos hid in their little caves, a panther chameleon peered curiously at the students, its eyes following each of them independently, whilst they jotted down endless notes, and you had the African green leaf mantises which glared motionless at the students as they worked. Crickets chirped loudly as Mr J was going through the importance of adaptation within nature. Jasper was looking down at some sketches he'd made of various creatures in his notebook thinking to himself.

Man, why can't I concentrate today. Maybe it's the serious lack of sleep, a mythical creature in my room, some random girl asking me out. Or maybe it's the sound of those god forsaken crickets! he shouted internally. Jasper then forced his attention towards Mr J.

"So, within each environment, when there is too much competition for a resource, to put it bluntly wildlife will either adapt or die. Some may become scavengers, or use deception, others will just become dominant over others, using their strength to overpower them and in some cases, animals may move on to a new environment all to gain vital resources, such as food or territory. Essentially what I'm saying is animals will find their niche. So, knowing this, what do you think would happen if we took an animal from, let's say America and put them into another environment or even country, like the Galapagos in Ecuador?" Mr J asked the class. A girl at the front of the class wearing glasses spoke up. Jasper recognised her from the Maths class, then he remembered she was the one he'd chewed his pencil in front of and he turned back to Mr J hiding his face.

"It would either die or it would have to adapt to suit its environment, like the mosquito did" said the girl at the front of the class. Jasper thought her name could have been Hannah, but he wasn't sure.

"Exactly!" Said Mr J pointing at her, the enthusiasm evident in his tone. "This has happened all over the world, where countless invasive species have been introduced to an environment, they've had little to no competition another example could be the Burmese pythons in Florida, grey squirrels in the UK and 'even' those pesky mosquitoes in the Galapagos islands. If those creatures go unchecked in those environments, where they have not evolved to be, they will either die or they'll adapt and take over". Mr J was clearly very good at his job because instead of rambling on he stopped and let the students mull over what he's just said. Jasper found himself thinking back to Scoff and where he might have come from, wondering if maybe he had accidentally found his way into an unknown environment, or maybe he was pushed out? A thought dawned on him. *Now I've got to get him back to the moors, where he belongs. All I need to do is just find a way to get there"*.

"Now the big question is, how do we stop these things from happening in the future? What else is out there? And what creature might take over next?" as if on cue the bell rang and all the students packed up their books and began to file out of the room. That was all the students except for Jasper who couldn't get Mr Js last comment out of his head. Jasper walked to the front of the class using his most nonchalant walk to where Mr J was collecting up some assignments. "Ah Jasper" he said turning around "what can I do for you?".

"Well, it's a bit of a weird one really".

"Oh no! don't tell me another student has got you to tell me they've got a crush on me, have they? I can't be having that again, I'd lose my job, and I like teaching here" said Mr J looking quite dishevelled.

"What? No. Wait, does that happen often?" Said Jasper completely forgetting about what he was going to say.

"Oh, you weren't? Thank God! I had it in my last class, but luckily, I put that end to that straight away. Anyway, what can I do to help?".

Casually Jasper walked over to the Chameleon and watched its eye staring at him "So, let's say you found an animal that was currently in an environment it wasn't meant to be in? What would you do? Obviously, this has happened all over the world, and it's killed loads of animals already, how would you deal with the situation?" Said Jasper desperately trying to not give anything away.

"Well that all depends really, if for instance it was a pest like mosquitoes, you'd probably just have to exterminate them". Instantly this made Jasper physically recoil at the thought of having to exterminate Scoff. The whole thing unravelled in front of his eyes, him having to shoot Scoff, the creature that had been such a nightmare to him, but he was beginning to kind of like that little terror. "But then if it was a creature that might have got out of a private collection, zoo or something similar, you'd probably try to capture or sedate it to take it back to its rightful home, if you could, and obviously if it's safe to do so". Jasper relaxed a little. *At least I wouldn't have to sedate him, he seems to have calmed down a lot... kind off* Jasper thought. "Why are you asking anyway? Have you found something?" Asked Mr J crossing his arms.

Jasper turned abruptly "No, no of course not. I was simply curious that's all. You know with everything that's going into the news now, it just makes you think". Said Jasper trying to bait Mr J to see if he knew anything. "Ha! Yes, definitely makes you think! I wouldn't worry about that in the news. It was probably someone's dog that got loose and killed a couple of sheep, and the others ran off that's all. I wouldn't worry about it", Said Mr J laughing.

"Alright thanks for your help Mr J".

"You are very welcome Jasper, anytime you have any questions feel free to ask". He said brushing his fringe to one side. Jasper spotted that just below Mr Js hairline was a scar that he'd never noticed before. Shouldering his rucksack Jasper smiled "Thank you, I will definitely". Just before Jasper was about to walk out of the room, he turned back to Mr J, who was now just finishing a cold cup of coffee from his desk.

"I hope you don't mind me asking Mr J but out of curiosity how'd you get that scar?" Jasper said pointing on his own head where the scar would be.

Mr J swallowed, "oh this?" He said pointing to the scar. "I got it in a climbing accident year ago, still gives me nightmares!".

"Awesome! Very cool" said Jasper nodding and walking out of the biology lab.

Mr J looked at Jasper walking from the lab and drained the last of his coffee before muttering to himself. "That kid is definitely up to something".

Chapter Seven: The Chewed Steggo

Luckily the rest of the school day went as any other. Jasper went to classes, got bored, he learnt a couple of bits, you know the normal school thing. But today there were way too many things on his mind for just his two hours of sleep, so he decided to leave any big adventures or decisions until tomorrow, when he was a little bit more rested and could think straight. Thankfully he hadn't had any backlash from leaving detention early, but he still wasn't planning on repeating that again, just in case. There were still two other things he knew he had to deal with today, first was Molly and whatever she had planned for tonight. Then he still had the Bogart stuck in his room. This one Jasper was starting to get an idea of how to deal with and was a lot easier to deal with than Molly, so he was going straight home before things got any further out of hand.

Jasper ran down the steps of the college to Billie and Lucy who were already waiting for him.

"Whoop, there he is!" Billie howled.

"Billie shoosh", said Jasper. Billie's face dropped as he instantly deflated. "Right, before either of you two talks, I have something insane to tell and show you".

"Better not be what you're planning to show Mollz". said Lucy raising an eyebrow, it almost goes without saying that Billie sniggered.

"Guys please, this is serious. Come with me you guys aren't going to believe this!" as he unlocked his bike. "Let's go!" he said impatiently as he placed his feet on the pedals and pelted down the road. Lucy looked to Billie and shrugged.

"He's probably going to get himself into trouble again if we don't follow him", said Lucy hopping onto her bike.

"Nice, I look forward to seeing this!" said Billie riding after her.

Peddling frantically Jasper took the shortcut home.

"Normally I'd take the longer route, but I have got to show you guys something else, that's before I show you the really big thing". He said shouting back to Lucy and Billie.

"I really hope he's not talking about what you were thinking Luce, I don't want to see that", Billie said in a very loud whisper.

"Jesus guys get your dirty minds out of the gutter for one second". They rounded the corner to the alley where Jasper and Scoff had taken a tumble through the fence. The three skidded to a halt in the alleyway in front of a gaping hole in a fence. Shards of wood scattered the floor and the garden, draped across the hole in the fence was some police tape that drummed in the wind. A cold breeze whipped past the three, standing their hair on end.

"Jasp, did you do this?" Asked Lucy, dropping her bike and peering around the fence closely followed by Billie.

"Well, it wasn't just me. It was me and the bogart" said Jasper, he could already feel the weight of everything he'd been holding secret lifting from his shoulders.

"A bo-what?" said Billie, the two turning to him.

"Okay so I think the creature I found was called a Bogart. I know it sounds mad, but I was running through the gardens taking a bit of a shortcut and I literally just stumbled into it rummaging in those bins". said Jasper pointing to the bins. "It attacked me as soon as it saw me, that's how we ended up crashing into this fence… and that one" he said pointing to the other fence a little awkwardly. We'd better go before we get caught; I need to show you something at mine. Billie and Lucy exchanged concerned looks before they all mounted their bikes and cycled in the direction of Jaspers.

"I saw him again outside the window in after school detention" Jasper panted.

"That's why you ducked out of detention!" said Lucy, finally understanding his strange behaviour.

"Yeah, I had to. You two were never going to believe the creature was real, so I had to take a picture. You would have just laughed and said it was my overactive imagination or something. So, I went after him". He said looking around to the other two trying to keep up with him, "we ended up having another little scrap in an alley just past the college, before he got hit by a car. Luckily, he was ok, it was only a Micra". The two cycling behind Jasper both nodded in understanding, as if the Micra explained it all. "But he was knocked out, so I took him home to make sure he was okay. Luckily other than a bit of a bad shoulder the little guy seemed fine. He spent the night in my room, whilst I did some research into what species he was. I can't be sure because all the descriptions were pretty vague, but I'm fairly certain he's something called a bogart". Lucy and Billie looked at each other suspiciously as they pulled up to Jasper's house. Throwing down their bikes Jasper turned to them. "Right, before we go in, I need both of you to be very quiet when you meet him. Don't make any sudden movements, don't look threatening and I wouldn't hold anything he might want. No food and nothing shiny". Jasper looked at Billie's glasses but dismissed the thought. He then ran to the front door and went in followed by Lucy and Billie.

"Yeah Billie, don't look so threatening" which was followed by a scowl from Billie. Both of which Jasper promptly ignored.

Jasper ra up the stairs and stopped in utter shock. His bedroom door was ajar.

"But I locked it! How could it be open?" Jasper panicked. He swung open the door saw that his room was completely trashed (even more so than usual). Clothes were strewn all over the room, dog food scattered the floor, and the bedroom window was wide open. "No, no, no! How could this have happened? I locked the door, why is it open? I'd shut the window too!" He checked the door which was completely scratch free. "I don't understand" he then looked over to Johnny's room where Johnny was playing with his Dinosaurs. "Johnny what happened? Why is my room open?" Jasper demanded storming into Johnny's room. He looked down to see Johnny playing with his chewed up steggo. "Johnny, how did you get this?" Jasper said, raising his voice and snatching the toy from his hands. Johnny looked up at Jasper with glistening eyes and burst into tears. "Come on you have got to be kidding me!" he gave Johnny back the toy and returned to his room. "Well Johnny's still here and is alive, so that means that Scoff must have got out before mum let Johnny in, so he could find his toy". Billie and Lucy looked at each other confused. He looked at the window and spotted scratch marks by the latch. "Yeah, definitely must have got out the window first. Guys, we've gotta get out of here before mum goes mental! She would have seen this room and thought I was keeping a dog here or something".

"And she wouldn't be too far off, this place is a mess", said Lucy. They all began creeping downstairs when they heard a shout from the kitchen.

"Jasper David Collins is that you?!"

"Oh yeah I forgot to say I'm grounded too". Billie and Lucy looked at each other as if to say, could this get any worse? Suddenly Jasper heard movement from the kitchen and shouted at them.

"Run!"

All three of them charged out of the house and got onto their bikes and rode off as fast as their legs could carry them.

The three teens cycled to a long, abandoned road, surrounded by overhanging trees and bramble bushes that intruded on all sides making the road their own. "Jasp what the hell is going on?" asked Billie, collapsing onto the concrete, breathing frantically.

"Yeah, I'd really like to know that too" said Lucy with both of her hands resting on her knees as she caught her breath.

"Okay, so I got grounded for skipping detention and the bogart got out the window of my room, so he's back out terrorising the town somewhere" said Jasper throwing his arms in the air before rubbing his forehead. Billie pushed himself up.

"Okay so he got out and is back in the town terrorising, what's the problem with that?".

"Billie, you don't understand. You guys have heard about the sheep that have been going missing all over the moors".

"Yeah, it's all over the news. What about it?" Said Lucy.

"Well, I'm pretty sure that that's more of the bogarts. All this only started happening around the time when I bumped into this guy. It can't be a coincidence. It has got to be to do with him. I read that bogarts are from the moors, so it must be his family. They must be going nuts without him or something. So, we have to find Scoff and bring him back".

"Scoff?" asked Billie, raising an eyebrow.

"Oh yeah, I named him Scoff" Jasper said with a Cheshire grin.

"You named it! I can't believe you named it!" Said Billie slapping his hand to his forehead.

The three sat in a triangle on the concrete of the abandoned path. Jasper sat cross legged peering at both Lucy and Billie with hopeful glances as they mulled through everything he'd just told them. Praying that they didn't think he was going completely mad. Lucy was deep in thought, her dark brown hair now tied up in a ponytail. Billie sat with his knees up and with his hands on his face drawing down his cheeks exposing the red underbelly of his eyes, as he looked into space in confused bewilderment. Lucy spoke up first.

"Let's say hypothetically, that we believe you and you have found a violent angry creature that could potentially eat children, family pets and has attacked you on multiple occasions. Why should we help you find it?" she said looking over to Jasper. Jasper placed his hand on his knee and in turn looked at them both in the eye.

"Don't you always tell me that you wish life could be more like a video game?" Jasper looked to Billie "That life could have more wonders, like dragons, ogres and hell beasts? This is your chance to find and save a creature from myth and legend. A creature that almost no one has ever even seen before. You're not going to leave behind such an incredible adventure, are you?" Said Jasper.

Billie removed his hands from his face. "Well, I'm not sure if I actually want to meet hell beasts" he grumbled.

"Scoff would eat pets and he would probably eat kids too. I saw him eat a squirrel once. It wasn't pretty, slurped up the tail like it was spaghetti". Lucy and Billie sat back in silence. Jasper looked at them both. *Are they not going to say anything?* The moment felt as if it dragged on for an eternity. Jaspers palms began to sweet and could feel the pull of anxiety to his heart, beating it faster. Lucy and Billie shared a knowing glance.

"Alright, I'm in" said Lucy with a nod.

"What!? You're in? I thought you were thinking he was nuts too. Even if it is true, this thing is dangerous, and it kills sheep and eats kids. Leave this to the police, hell, leave it to the military!".

"Billie, they'd never believe us. We are the only ones that can do it", said Jasper.

"You're not being a coward are you, Billie?" said Lucy.

"No, I just don't want any of us to be eaten alive by a fury green gremlin, if that's alright!?".

"No one's going to die Billie, we'll keep each other safe. Stick together, okay?" Billie was quiet for a moment then looked to Lucy and Jasper.

"Sticking together?" said Billie.

"Yep, the whole way", said Jasper. Billie's mouth broke into a large smile, "Alright I'm in".

"Yes! Never doubted you for a second!" said Jasper.

"I did", Said Lucy as a smile crept onto her face. Billie shot Lucy a glare.

"So great adventurous one. What happens now?" Jasper took a moment to think, he really hadn't thought it through properly, but that had never stopped him before.

"First, we have to find Scoff. Every time I've found him, he's either been trying to find food, rummaging through bins, or trying to eat something he shouldn't".

Lucy nodded "Right, so we need to go straight back and search by all the bins? Sounds easy enough".

"What about Molly? You're meant to be meeting her now", Said Billie.

"That's alright we're close to the abandoned sewers anyway, so we can swing by there first and just say that we can't stick around".

"Then we go straight to find the bogart?" asked Lucy.

"Then we go straight to find Scoff" Corrected Jasper.

"Alight let's do this" said Billie, he then threw his fist up in the air "For adventure!" Shouted Billie. Both Jasper and Lucy shied away, grabbing their bikes.

"Whatever nerd" said Jasper Laughing,

"Ha! Yeah, come on Billie, don't make it weird".

"You guys are the worst!" Said Billie picking up his bike and the three cycled off towards the abandoned sewers to meet Molly and her crew.

Chapter Eight: The Abandoned Sewers

Molly and her crew were relaxing just outside the abandoned sewers. A giant pipe surrounded by moss and trees jutted out the wooded hillside like a tunnel. The enormous pipe was broken and cracked, exposing rusted iron bars, making it the perfect half pipe for skating except for a small trickle of water that eternally poured from it into its own little stream. There was also a 'slight' risk of impaling yourself on the iron bars at the top of each side of the half pipe, if one was crazy enough to go that far on it.

Jasper, Lucy, and Billie came to the tip of a wooded hill just before they got to the sewer. Down the wooded hill was a break in the trees. Jasper could see Molly and the Crew down by the pipe, but had difficulty making anyone out, other than one of the crew he assumed was Jordie, as Jordie was the only one of them that could actually skate. He was on his board whipping back and forth on the half pipe, lifting the nose of the board with one foot at each peak performing a perfect nose blunt then diving back into the dip, before repeating it over and over again.

"Remember guys we'll just be here for a minute, then we have to go", said Jasper.
"I just can't wait to see you blow it with Molly before you even start" said Billy loving this moment just a little too much.
"Come on guys, let's just get this over with" said Lucy already cycling down the sloping track, through the woods closely followed by Jasper and Billie.

The three skidded to a stop at the bottom of the hill in front of the half pipe. Jordie came to the top of the ramp and balanced two wheels on the edge, with one foot on the wheels and the other at the top stabilizing the board, he gave a half salute to Lucy.

"Hey Luce! What you doin here?" he shouted from the top of the pipe. Instantly the crew's attention was drawn to the newcomers. There were only four members of the 'Crew' and they were all here, Molly and her friends Lillz, Jordie and Lee.

"Hey Jordie! Just chilling, you know how it is" said Lucy as her cheeks flushed a light shade of red. Billie nudged Jasper.

"She's almost as bad at this as you".

"What do you mean?" asked Jasper. Billie nodded towards Lucy walking over to the ramp to talk to Jordie, who smoothly stepped off the board and slid down the ramp to Lucy.

"Ohhhh! Really? Him?" replied Jasper his face somewhat resembling a bewildered beagle.

"Jasp you came!" said Molly walking over to him and wrapping her arms around him. He stumbled back before he wrapped his arms around her. He closed his eyes briefly taking in the moment, her perfume drawing him in closer. He released the hug. She only half released it wrapping one arm around his waist and guiding him to Lee and Lillz. Molly looked up to him then gestured over to the two sitting on a rug next to a speaker. The tiny speaker was doing its best to fill the clearing with drum and bass.

"You know Lee, and this is Lillz". Jasper raised his hand giving an awkward little wave.

"Hey" he said, not quite sure of himself. Lee looked at him then back to Molz.

"Molz what's going on? What's this guy doing here? and why is the nerd from electronics staring at us over there?" Jasper noticed he said that last part a little more angrily. A realisation hit Jasper like a wet sponge. *I wish I'd known he would have been here earlier else I never would have suggested Billy come along. They get on worse than a bull, and a carefully placed teapot.*

"Ummm, I don't actually know why he's here, or why he's staring at us. Jasp?" asked Molly.

"Oh yeah! Billie, come over here". Billie slowly walked over, ready to bolt at any moment.

"Awww he's like a little deer", said Lillz.

"This is my friend Billie", said Jasper, attempting to exude confidence.

"Hey guys", said Billie, avoiding eye contact with Lee. Lees eyebrows furrowed.

"No", said Lee, pushing himself up.

"What do you mean no?" Said Billie.

"What I mean is, no you can't be here" said Lee who barged past Jasper to tower over Billie, who tried in vain to stand his ground.

"Lee what's wrong with Billie? He's a good guy" said Jasper trying to reason with the brute. Jasper already knew the likelihood of this working was a slim zero, but he had to try. He'd have a better chance of walking a bull through a china shop and the china being left chip free... that little teapot was screwed.

"He's not a good guy!" shouted Lee. "This 'good guy' rips the piss out of me in every class, in front of everyone, just because it takes me a little longer to get things than everyone else. So no, 'Billie' is not a good guy. 'Billie' can get the hell away from me otherwise I'll make sure he can't tell the difference between a wrench and a stick". Said Lee breathing down his nose at Billie. Billie cringed but a moment later something switched in him, and he began to bare his teeth.

"It's not my fault, you're so stupid you can't even pick up a resistor without going..." Jasper knew exactly what was coming next and tried to stop him.

"Billie!" shouted Jasper.

"Derrrr what's this thing do, smacking it against your head", said Billie. Jasper thought that the dumb voice was a real elegant touch on Billie's part.

Not so elegantly, Lee launched his meaty fist into Billies Jaw throwing him tumbling to the ground.

"Wow! Dude what are you doing?" called Jordie from the pipe. Lucy turned around to see Billie on the floor crawling away from Lee.

"You think you're a smart guy huh! You look pretty dumb from up here to me!" roared Lee furious. Jasper unstuck himself from Molly and launched himself at Lee, and they both went tumbling to the ground.

"What the hell is wrong with you lot!" shouted Lucy running over to try and break it up. Lee launched another punch which hit Jasper square in the gut, winding him.

At that moment an enormous roar erupted from within the sewer pipe, causing the whole group to stop suddenly.

"What? The hell was that?" asked Lillz, her voice trembling.

"Get off me" said Jasper pushing Lee away. Lee rolled onto his feet and began to creep closer and closer to the pipe.

"Come on! You want to go? Come on!" he roared into the pipe.

Billie was right this guy really is stupid, what is he even trying to prove?

Again, an enormous roar came echoing from the tunnel, Jasper felt the echo vibrate through his entire body, instantly making his stomach churn. The trickle of water that flowed from the pipe began to swell as if the pipe had just been unblocked. Molly and Lillz started to back away as fear and adrenaline began to overwhelm them. It all became too much for the 'Crew' and they broke from the group, running in terror. All except Lee who was still standing right in the middle of the tunnel.

"Everyone, get out of here!" shouted Jordie as he tripped over Billie. Before scrambling on his hands and feet up the hill and away from the sewer. Lucy ran over to Billie to get him back to his feet.

"Billie we've got to go, you, okay?" Billie ripped his head away from the pipe and looked at Lucy "Yeah, I'm okay" he said trying to convince himself more than anyone. "Jasper! Is that Scoff?" Lucy shouted.

Jasper looked to the pipe and saw a large bloody, slime covered claw slam out of the shadows and hit the wall next to Lee. The giant creature peered its gigantic bear head out of the shadows and peered its one good eye towards Lee, who was now shaking all over. The creature looked like it could have been a bear once, but now it was missing half its face and was covered in blood, sores, and slime. Jasper noticed that the monster was staring around with one good eye, the other looked scared, cloudy, and weeping. The creature's assessed its prey then its good eye fell upon Lee. It let out a low throaty snarl.

"Lee, RUN!!!" shouted Jasper backing away.

Upon seeing the creature Lee's once confident, large stature changed, his shoulders became small, and his knees quaked as he looked up to the snarling creature. Finally, Lee gathered his nerves and turned to run. But it was too late. The creature roared and with one swipe of its enormous claw and smashed Lee to the ground. Its claws tore into his back as it scraped his body against the bottom of the pipe, dragging him closer to the creature. It grabbed lee in its jaws, and he screamed in pain before it shook his body like a rag doll and threw him aside slamming him against the pipe wall silencing him for good. Lees lifeless body fell to heap on the ground. The creature's enormous head turned from Lee's limp body to Jasper.

"That's not Scoff!" Jasper screamed and all three ran for their bikes. The creature bounded after Jasper, leaving a trail of blood and slime in its wake. Lucy and Billie made it to the bikes and Lucy screamed to Jasper

"Quick, it's gaining on you!" Lucy and Billie peddled frantically away from the creature.

Jasper risked a glance back and he saw that the creature had gained on him faster than he thought. He made a beeline for the trees knowing he'd never make it to his bike in time, reaching the treeline Jasper picked up branch, swinging it blindly around. The wood shattered as it pounded the beasts head knocking it aside. The beast shook its large head like a bloodhound, flinging a spattering of blood and slime all over the trees. Darting to the beast's blind side Jasper looked at the remains of his weapon, a handful of useless rotten wood. He threw the rotten wood to a bush on the other side of the beast, and it launched itself at the sound. Jasper turned and ran for his bike jumping over roots and into the opening where his bike lay. The beast heard his footsteps, turned and with a blood curdling roar bounded after him again. Jasper turned to see the beast gaining on him with tremendous speed. The beast was so close, he could see the pain and hatred in the creature's eyes. Jasper tripped over a root sending him tumbling to the ground, grazing his arms. Frantically he rolled to his back and saw the beast lift its claw for the killing blow. A green flash dove into the creature's head and knocked the beast to the side. Not wasting any time, Jasper jumped to his feet. The beast was clawing at its face trying to remove the green creature. The little creature jumped off the beast with a flip landing on two feet. Jasper looked at the green creature to see the beast's good eye dangling out its mouth. Scoff slurped the beast's eye into his mouth and swallowed it whole, before giving Jasper a large Cheshire grin. Unbelievably relieved and revolted, Jasper smiled back to

Scoff. The beast roared in pain regaining their attention as it spat phlegm, blood and slime all over Jasper and Scoff. Behind them they heard the screams of Lucy and Billie as they cycled down the hill, both of their legs pumping the peddles. They held large branches under one arm like lances. They screamed a battle cry so loud their veins popped out the side of their heads. Outnumbered, injured and with only one cloudy barely usable eye, the beast reared giving one last roar in defiance, before turning and bolting back for the tunnel. Its paws pounded and splashed through the water as it disappeared back into the shadows of whence it came. Jasper bloodied and bruised stared at the tunnel. *What the hell was that?*

Saddling up to Jasper and coming to a halt Lucy planted her lance into the ground like a knight. Billie swerved Scoff who easily hopped out the way as Billie's makeshift lance buried itself into the ground and launched him into the air causing him to faceplant into the ground.
"Good thing you didn't have to use that, ay Billie?" said Lucy.
Billie groaned, "shut" - Billie spat out a mouth full of soil - "up!".
Scoff shook off clumps of blood and slime from his fur, when all of a sudden, he was lifted into the air and embraced in an enormous bear hug,
"I can't believe you saved me, you little scruff ball. You could have died!" Scoff yelped at the strength of Jaspers hug and tried in vain to push himself out. Jasper put him back down on the ground and ruffled his hair. "Ha, now I know you like me" Jasper said with a smile. "Lucy, Billie, I'd like to introduce you to our new bogart friend, Scoff". Lucy and the bogart looked at each other curiously. Scoff cocked his head and a large lump appeared from the side of his mouth as his tongue picked out a small chunk of eyeball which he'd clearly missed when swallowing the

rest of it. Scoff then poked out his tongue to look at the chunk of eyeball before looking back to Lucy. They stared at each other for a moment before his tongue retracted into his mouth and he swallowed the chunk of eye. Billie looked up from the dirt to Scoff and adjusted his glasses.

"Fascinating", said Billie, blood still stained his teeth and face from where Lee had socked him. Scoff then looked over to Billie and instantly dove at the floored teenager. "No! What are you doing? Stop!" Billie was rolled around on the ground trying in vain to hold Scoff back as the little creature stretched his arm as far as he could to try and grab the glasses. Lucy and Jasper both laughed as the two brawled on the ground.

"Oh my god, Lee!" shouted Lucy as she sprinted to his limp Body. She placed her fingers on his throat trying to feel for a pulse. "Jasper, he's still alive! His pulse is weak, but it's still there. Call an ambulance now!".

"On it!" said Jasper, pulling out his phone. There was a tooth sized hole in his stomach, she immediately removed her top, leaving her in just a tank top and she pressed firmly on the wound. A groan came from Lee and she shuddered.

"It's alright Lee, you're going to be okay. You're losing a lot of blood, so I'm just going to apply pressure to the wound, okay?" she said knowing full well she wouldn't get an answer. They heard a distant pain-stricken roar eco from the depths of the tunnel, causing them all to tense. Billie walked over to the two of them adjusted his glasses and peered down the tunnel.

"What the hell was that thing?" Billie said. Jasper looked to Lucy and Lee then back down into the darkness of the sewers.

"I have absolutely no idea".

Chapter Nine: Off in an Ambulance

It had only been thirty minutes, but clouds had already rolled in and night was beginning to creep into the clearing. The whole sewer entrance was now lit up with reds and blues as police, ambulances and even animal control were securing the area. The police had already taped off the pipe and had cornered off the area. Word had got around already about the animal attack. Jasper knew that it was probably spread by Molly and the others. People from all over town had come to see what had happened and were attempting to crowd around the pipe and question the teens but were all being held back. Jasper noticed that in the crowd there were even a few grizzled farmers trying to hide their rifle bags, clearly hoping to shoot the beast but did not want to get caught in the process.

The three teens were huddled together wrapped in large foil blankets, drinking tea out the back of an ambulance. Jasper closed his eyes and inhaled, letting the warm vapour fill his lungs. He looked up to a tree at the edge of the clearing and could see Scoff perched on a branch impatiently watching them.

"I'd feel much better if he got out of here already" said Jasper, taking a sip of his tea. Lucy shouldered him a little.

"He doesn't want to leave you, he wants you to be safe, just like you want him to be safe". said Lucy.

"I suppose so, but I still don't like it. Look at them, all it would take is for one to look his way and all hell would break loose" said Jasper looking at the animal control personnel searching the trees around the pipe entrance.

"He's quick and quiet, he snuck up on that bear thing without alerting anyone, I'm sure he can avoid animal control".

"That was pretty amazing wasn't it, the way he snuck up on that bear. He just completely appeared out of nowhere. I thought I was a goner". Jasper looked down to his drink, he swirled the tea thoughtfully. "I still don't like it though".

Jasper turned to Billie, who was hunched over staring into his drink in silence. "Hey Billie, how are you doing?" Asked Jasper. Billie sighed and shrugged.
"This was all my fault" he looked up to Jasper, his eyes glistening. "Not the bear thing but Lee, Lee could die because of me. If I hadn't picked on him so much, maybe he would have run like the others instead of trying to prove something to us. He was right. I really am the bully and now he could die because I couldn't keep my stupid mouth shut". Jasper sighed.
"Billie. It's not your fault. You could be nicer to Lee when he's awake, but this is definitely not your fault. No one could have known that would happen. He's such a knucklehead he probably would have jumped in front of a truck if it made him look more manly". Billie smiled and wiped a knuckle across his eye.
"Ha yeah and he probably would have done it in front of a parked one too". He choked a laugh "he's smart like that".

"So, what are we going to do now?" asked Lucy.
"What do you mean?" said Jasper.
"Well, we just saw a pretty unnatural creature and let's be honest Scoff isn't exactly normal either. So, what are we going to do now?" Jasper surveyed the commotion around them as police began shouting at onlookers to "Get back!".
"We need to protect Scoff, that's the most important thing. We need to get him home wherever that is. I heard that bogarts come from the moors and that's where all the

89

sheep have been disappearing. I think it's probably the bogarts, it only started happening when scoff appeared".

A short stout policewoman with a dark brown ponytail and a scruffy haired man in a tweed suit made their way over to the teens. The woman looked to her notepad then to the teens.

"So, Jasper, Lucy and Billie. Looks like you three have had quite the evening. It's not often we get a bear attack around here" said the policewoman with a thick west country accent. At the mention of the 'bear' the three teens looked at each other all unsure if they should say more. "Mr Jackson here was kind enough to have given me the details of your parents and they're on their way now. Needless to say, they're all very worried. You're all incredibly lucky to be alive, how did you say you got away from it again?" Asked the officer as she raised an eyebrow and peered up from her notebook to the teens. Billie looked over to Lee who was strapped onto a gurney that was being lifted into an ambulance by a group of paramedics.

"It was Lee, he distracted the bear so we would have enough time to get away. But it, it got him, then ran for the sewers.

The officer gave a sympathetic smile.

"Well, you have a very brave friend, the paramedics say he's very badly hurt, but fingers crossed he'll make it. Your parents will be here soon, in the meantime relax and if you want another drink, please feel free to ask". The officer put a hand on Mr Jackson's shoulder, and he gave a knowing smile then the officer walked away shouting orders to the other police.

Jasper then looked up to see Mr J with his arms folded looking down at the three of them. He was just standing there, looking at each and every one of them, staring as if

90

he was trying to stare into each of their minds. He looked to Jasper, then removed his glasses and began cleaning them.

"So, you say a bear attacked you three?" Mr J put his glasses back on, pulled a nearby gurney to the group and sat on it then placed his hands on his knees and leant forward "Go on tell me what happened". They all looked at each other with concerned expressions. Jasper's throat clenched as his mind raced thinking of anything to say, but he was saved as Lucy spoke.

"Well, we came down here to see Molly, Lee and their friends, we were talking and that's when the bear attacked, from that pipe over there" Lucy said nodding over to the pipe. Mr J looked at the pipe then turned back to the group.

"So, was it the bear that hit Billie's chin?" Billie gave an alarmed look and rubbed at a bruise that was already forming on his chin from Lee's fist.

"Not quite" Said Billie "that was when I came off the bike".

"So, you came off your bike too?" said Mr J putting one elbow on his knee and rubbing his chin.

"Yeah, we all did, but I just took the fall pretty hard".

"Ok so you three fell off your bikes and then lee scared off the bear. And how did he do that again?"

"Well, he roared at it" said Billie with all the confidence of a child lying about eating chocolate cake that still smothered their face.

"He roared?" questioned Mr J. Jasper could see Billie squirming in his foil blanket.

"Well, it was more of a yell" Said Jasper, Mr J then turned his attention to him.

"He yelled at the bear, it hit him, then ran away? Okay and the bear what did it look like?" Asked Mr J unmoving.

"Well, it was a bear, big fury, scary, just like any other".

"Just like any other? So, there was nothing different about this bear than from that of, let's say, a Zoo?" asked Mr J. Jaspers eyes narrowed at Mr J and he raised an eyebrow.

"Why? What might have been different about this bear to other bears?" Asked Jasper.

"Nothing in particular. I'm just curious. It's just very strange a bear attack happening around here" said Mr J frowning. There was an awkward silence between Jasper and Mr J. Lucy and Billie watched the two of them as if they were watching a game of verbal ping pong, then peered around Jasper to look at each other. "Hmm, well if any of you do recall anything strange about the creature. You will tell me about it won't you?" Said Mr J.

"Yes of course we will", said Jasper and the group nodded with agreement of "oh yes, of course, yep definitely". Mr J looked at them sceptically before standing up he straightened his Jacket and walked away from the trio shooting them suspicious glances as he left.

Lucy's arm flung at Jasper. "What the hell was that?" she said hitting his arm.

"Ouch!" he yelped, rubbing a large black bruise which had just been violated. "We couldn't have just said about the bear being mutated and zombie looking, could we? He never would have believed us, and he could have ended up finding out about Scoff and we need to keep him safe".

"Keep him safe? How are we going to keep him safe if that bear manages to do to other people what it did to lee?"

"I don't know Lucy; I'm just trying to keep Scoff safe".

92

"I agree with Lucy, we should tell him. We don't have to tell anyone else and Mr J's a good guy". Said Billie.

"I know he is, I'm just worried about the little fluff ball" said Jasper looking a little ashamed.

"I know you're worried, but we can't let that bear attack anyone else. Who knows, he might be able to help us with Scoff too?" said Lucy.

"Alright but we can't do it here, there's no way I'm telling the police about this, if it gets out that there's a mutant bear on the loose, there'd be panic". said Jasper as he pushed himself off the ambulance and walked over to Mr J.

All around him people were shouting and dashing about, searching the entire clearing and a group of police were now forming together and making their way into the pipe. Jasper looked in horror as the five police made their way into the tunnel. Jasper flew into a panic and darted over to Mr J who was observing the commotion.

"Mr J, they can't go in there!"

"What do you mean they can't go in there? What's wrong?" Jasper lost all notion of waiting to tell Mr J and blurted out.

"The bear! It well, wasn't just a bear. It was mutated somehow; I don't know how it happened but the creature" he paused and saw that he was drawing attention to himself and he pulled Mr J aside.

"Jasper, what's going on" said Mr J, becoming concerned.

"Okay look, this bear, it wasn't a normal bear at all, it was crazed, covered in gore, slime, blisters, and one of its eyes was cloudy and scarred. Luckily we managed to tear out the good one but it's still dangerous". Mr J's eyes widened, and he put his hands on Jaspers arms homing him still.

"You're being serious Jasper? You're not lying to me?" he said. Jasper, frightened by this sudden change in Mr J, replied a little shakily.

"No, no I'm not lying it was mutated whatever it was" said Jasper becoming suddenly unsure of himself. Mr J sighed and looked over to the other teenagers.

"Right once this is over, we all need to have a talk, you me and those two". He nodded over to Billie and Lucy "Tomorrow after school, you three now have detention".

"Okay?" said Jasper, a little confused. Mr J then stood up and began yelling frantically.

"Look in the woods over there! It's getting away!" shouted Mr J as he ran off into the woods. Suddenly there was pandemonium, all the police and animal control began springing into action picking up their batons, pistols and torches to chase after the bear into the woods. The police who had ventured into the tunnel ran out and joined the chase. Even the farmers who had been trying to be inconspicuous pulled out their various firearms and ran in the direction of the crowd.

Jasper looked around in shock at the swarm of people disappearing into the woods and walked back to the other teenagers.

"What on earth did you say to him?" Said Lucy.

"The truth. He seemed to be shocked when I told him. Then he told everyone that the bear was in the woods, and they ran after it. I got the idea that he definitely knows what that thing is and only got everyone to run in the other direction to keep them safe".

"Oh, he's good". said Lucy.

"He said that we all have after school detention tomorrow because he wants to talk to us about what happened".

"Well, I haven't got anything better planned, what about you Billie?" Said Lucy.

"Yeah, I'll be there". Said Billie not looking at either of them. At that moment, the engine of the ambulance carrying Lee rumbled into life. The three teens stared wondering if this was the last time that they would ever see Lee. The ambulances lights flashed, and its siren screamed as it accelerated and drove up and out of the clearing.

"Jasper!" Jackie shouted, as she ran over to him and embraced him in her arms. "What on earth are you doing here? Are you hurt?"

"Mum, I'm fine, don't worry about me". Jasper said as if she were simply rubbing a mark off his cheek with her thumb.

"Your room looked like a wild animal was let loose in there and then I hear this happened, how am I not going to be worried?" Jackie turned to Billie and Lucy. "Where are your parents?"

"They're on their way, Mrs Collins", said Billie.

"How are you two holding up? I can't believe you were attacked by a bear, it's awful!". Said Jackie. Billie yelped as she embraced them all in an overly loving hug.

"Yeah, we're fine, just a little shaken up. Nothing bad though" said lucy.

"Thank God none of you are hurt. Well, that is, except for that Lee boy, I spoke to a police officer, and she said that he saved you all. Very brave". Billie looked to his feet.

"Yeah, he was brave".

"Jasper let's go home, Johnny's waiting in the car. I didn't want him to see, well, this". She paused looking around at the ambulances and police cars surrounding the sewer pipe. "Come on, let's go", she said. Jasper walked to the car with his mum and looked over to the branch where Scoff was now nowhere to be seen.

"I hope you're alright little buddy".

Night drew in and rain began to batter the car. Jasper and his mum sat in silence for half of the journey, just listening to the rhythmic squeaking of the windscreen wipers and the constant drumming of rain on the roof. Johnny was fast asleep and led across the back seat with seat belts wrapped around his body. Jackie watched the road but continued to glance over to Jasper who stared out the window, then to Johnny in the rear-view mirror to check if he was still asleep. Jackie sighed catching Jasper's attention.

"Jasper, you really scared me this evening, I had no idea where you were or what had happened. Then I hear you've been attacked by a bear. I can't lose you like I did your father".

"You won't lose me, I'm ok".

"No, Jasper you could have died, and you would have left me with no explanation! What happened to your room and why were you there? Your Dad left just like that, no note, room in a state, I imagined the worst. I can't go through that again". she said, blinking back the tears and checking the rear-view mirror.

"Mum, I'm not going to disappear". Said Jasper unconsciously ringing his hands.

"Well, you're not going to die either! And be quiet, I don't want to wake your brother!"

"What happened to dad?" asked Jasper. His mum sighed and wiped a tear from her face.

"I don't know, he was always so caring of all of us. The best of Dads to you and your brother, then one day he came home white as a sheet, he was acting strange, distant, it was as if his mind wasn't even there. Then when I got back from work the next day, our bedroom was trashed. His clothes were gone and so was he". She pulled up to the front of the house and the car lurched as she put on the hand break. "Your father was stationed in the Himalayas with the army, when he got back, he'd changed, he said that he saw something, something that he couldn't explain. Then he disappeared. He said before he left that it was a simple recon mission and that I shouldn't worry. From the way he looked at me when he got back, he must have seen something horrendous there, I can't even imagine what it was and I'm not sure if I want to. He had been on tours before but never came back in that state, even after being shot, never. Even then he kept a semblance of his personality. I can't lose you too Jasper, you're too precious to me". Jasper looked to his Mum.

"Mum you're not going to lose me, I'm not going to war or disappearing to another country. I'll try and be safe and I'll never leave you like Dad did. For all his bravery he was a coward to leave us like he did" said Jasper reaching over and embracing his mother. He felt her tears wet against his cheek "Mum I'll do everything in my power to stay safe, but you have to trust me okay".

"Okay" she cried.

"Mum? Are you ok?" Asked Johnny rubbing his tired eyes.

"Yeah bud, you know mum. She just really hates the rain" said Jasper releasing the hug and smiling at Jackie. His mum laughed and wiped her face.

"Yeah, awful stuff, come on then little John let's get out of here". The three hopped out of the car and Jasper ran straight into the house, whilst his mum wrapped her jacket around Johnny and they both ran inside.

Johnny was in bed already dreaming about riding a stegosaurus through a giant canyon watching the Pteranodons flying overhead, all the while Jasper and his mother were sitting in the living room sipping hot chocolates. The living room was average. The same magnolia walls and as with most modern houses the TV was the centrepiece of the room. Jasper slurped his hot chocolate, trying to get all the lumps from the top.

"I just can't believe you got attacked by a bear" Jackie paused, still processing what Jasper had told her. "And in the sewer. I mean, what on earth was it even doing there?"

"I've no idea, maybe it escaped from a zoo or something?"

"Possibly, I can't think of any other way it could have got out".

Jasper sipped his drink again.

"Mum do you really not know why dad left?"

"Other than that, he saw something in the Himalayas that scared the hell out of him. No. Whatever he saw changed him".

"But what do you think it was that he saw?"

"Who can know? People see so much in the army. Maybe he saw someone murdered, or worse. Who knows? Whatever it was, it must have been bad to shake your father up like that".

"So, you don't think it was, well um. You know. Another woman?" Said Jasper hiding his face behind his drink.

"Heavens no. Ha, your father couldn't hide anything like that from me. You clearly do not remember how much of a terrible liar he was. Utterly useless. That man couldn't lie to save his life, you remember he had to go through the torture training so many times at work because he was so useless at lying. He'd just start making up a lie which would turn into the truth or be so outrageously incorrect they knew he was lying instantly". Jasper laughed at that.

"Ha yeah I remember he said that the mince pies I left Santa at Christmas were delicious".

"Ha and he couldn't get carrot out his teeth".

The two of them shared a laugh at the memory and stared at their cups.

"Do you think he'll come back?" Said Jasper

"Your father? No, I don't think so. He's been gone too long now. Plus, I think he knows I'd murder him if he came back". She gave Jasper a struggling smile.

"Yeah, I didn't think so either", Said Jasper. He looked at the dark leftovers of his hot chocolate in the bottom of his mug. A thoughtful silence fell over the two of them. "Mum, do you believe in monsters?" Jackie Laughed.

"In monsters? If you mean people that are violent, disgusting and horrendous yes, if you are talking about bigfoot or the boogey man then no".

Jasper smiled, "Yeah I didn't think you would".

"What makes you say that?"

"I don't know. Just tonight was a little crazy I suppose, you know, with the bear and everything".

Jackie smiled and moved over to Jasper and placed her arm around him lovingly. "You know there's many creatures in this world that are big and scary. Like bears, lions and even elephants, they can be pretty scary too, but it's so rare that you'd ever get attacked by any of them. You were just extremely unlucky today. Nothing like this will happen again I'm sure of it". Jackie assured Jasper.

Jasper looked again into his drink, thinking back on the bear attack and about Scoff. "Yeah, I suppose you're right, I'd better get to bed. It's been a long day".

Jackie smiled and kissed him on the forehead. "Whatever happens we'll be there for each other, okay?"

Jasper smiled "Yeah, we will".

We almost died. If it wasn't for Scoff and the other two, I'd be dead right now. Jasper thought as he sat on his bed surrounded by clothes, torn books, and rubbish, even the tissues from his bin were all over the room. *I almost died tonight and there was nothing I could have done about it. I wasn't quick, strong, or smart enough to beat that bear on my own*. Jasper looked around his room, on the floor in a pile of clothes, games, and books he saw a game which gave him an idea. Jasper picked up an old fighting game released in the 90s called Tekken. You would pick your character from a variety of choices and each character would have a different type of martial art like Tae-Kwon-Do, Jiu Jitsu or karate and you'd fight to the death. One of the characters, Kuma, was even a bear. Jasper laughed at the thought of him trying to punch a bear or put it into a headlock "like that would work" he chuckled.

Jasper threw down the game and looked over to the cage where he had made a bed for Scoff, he then walked over to the window, grasped the handle and with a pain down his side he pushed it open, in the hope that Scoff would find his way back. Jasper turned to look at the mess in his room and started picking up all the books and games, tidying them back onto the shelves thinking about each character from those games and how they fought their enemies. A chiming noise sounded from his computer and the screen lit up. He saw a photo of Lucy and a name appear on the screen.

Dreamreaver Calling!

Uplifted by the sight of her Jasper put on his headset and with a wince of pain he pressed a button on the side of the headset to answer the call.

    "Hey Luce".

    "Hey, Jasp can we talk?"

    "Sure, what's up?" Said Jasper, settling into his chair.

    "Ha, what's up? I thought that would be pretty damn obvious".

    "Haha alright, alright how're you doing then?" Jasper said with a smile. "Other than hurting all over and being absolutely terrified, I'm great". Jasper could hear the worry in her voice but hearing her over his headset filled him with warmth.

"Yeah, I hear you, I've been thinking about how we could have handled that better and I can't come up with anything", Said Jasper.

"Me neither, I've been trying to get hold of Billie but he's not answering any calls. Spoke to his mum though, she said he'd locked himself in the garage".

"I'm not surprised, probably trying to just busy his mind so he doesn't have to think about what happened", Said Jasper.

"Jasper, I think he's going to take this hard. He is already blaming himself for what happened to Lee. He's just going to keep going over everything again and again until it drives him completely mental".

"I know, what can we do about it though?" Said Jasper.

"I guess all we can do is be there for him and try to encourage him, that's all really".

"Yeah, you're right". His headphones went quiet, and Jasper decided to change the subject to something a little lighter. You know, I've been thinking, what do you think Mr J will talk to us about tomorrow? Obviously about the bear, but the way he sent off everyone like that, it was a little strange don't you think? Like, what was actually wrong with it? Or maybe it wasn't actually a bear at all", Said Jasper.

"What? you think it was diseased? Or that it might be another mythical creature or something?".

"Well, yeah maybe. We found Scoff, didn't we? He's not exactly normal is he". Said Jasper.

"Yeah, you're right maybe he knows something about Scoff too. Do you think you'll tell him about the little guy?"

"I don't know, I doubt it. I care about him, I don't want anything bad to happen to him and he did kind of save all of our lives today too, so the last thing I want to do is put him in any kind of danger".

"I don't know, I think he can protect himself. Did you not see how he ripped that things eye out? It was so gross!" Said Lucy.

"Oh god don't remind me, even thinking about it makes me feel sick". They both laughed but it subsided quickly as they both pondered what had happened.

"So, what are you going to get up to this evening?" Jasper asked, trying to fill another silence. "I'm not sure, maybe play a game for a while, get my mind off things, you know".

"Yeah, sounds like a good idea, fancy an extra shield with you?"

"Always!" said Lucy excitedly. Then they both lost themselves in an alternate universe, fighting all sorts of monsters, gules and nasties unknown to this world.

**

In the early hours of the night Jasper stirred as a small fury creature curled up beside him and grumbled as it snuggled into his shoulder, with a large sigh it closed its eyes to sleep. Jasper recognising and ignoring the bin like smell, wrapped his arm around the creature and pulled him tight, Scoff's fur brushed against Jaspers chin. "Thank you", Said Jasper. Scoff made a quiet grumble in appreciation and the two drifted off into a dreamless sleep.

Chapter Ten: Total Manic

Jasper awoke to his alarm playing the 'quiet' musings of Wake Me Up Before You Go-Go by Wham. Which was received by a chorus of Urghhhs and no's! Before it was turned off and launched across the room. This ritual of throwing his phone was becoming increasingly more common, this was likely because Jasper had only recently changed his alarm to include the added Wham factor. He was also frequently being kept up, mainly by Scoff. After throwing his phone Jasper wrapped his arm around Scoff nestling him close in an attempt to gain another five minutes sleep. Scoff grumbled in annoyance as Jasper got comfortable. Five minutes later just as they were nodding off Jasper's alarm filled the room with infuriatingly buoyant go gos. Scoff wriggled from Jasper's arms in a rage and launched himself across the room towards the phone, chewing and kicking the phone, cat-like and furious. Jasper climbed out of bed, grabbed the phone from Scoff and turned off the alarm, this time for good.

"Must have pressed snooze. Good morning little buddy" said Jasper rubbing his eyes. Scoff scratched behind his ear with his foot and looked up to Jasper, his ear twitched like an angry butterfly. "I'm guessing you want some breakfast? We had a big old day yesterday. I'll shoot downstairs and get you some water and toast".

Pressing down the toaster with a metallic click, Jasper turned on the kettle and made himself a fresh coffee. He inhaled the South American brew, allowing the warm vapour to fill his lungs. Smiling he could already feel his body awaken, something that could only get better with a hot shower. He felt a nudge on his leg as Maxie the excitable spaniel sniffed at him curiously. Jasper watched as the spaniel's wet nose sniffed up and down his ankles. With one last sniff Maxie looked up to him and tilted his head in confusion. "What's up bud?" Jasper said squatting down to rub Maxie's head. Whatever was worrying Maxie before, was instantly forgotten as one of his favourite humans began stroking his back finding that perfect spot. Maxie then began kicking out his back leg frantically, as if his one leg were doing a solo one hundred metre sprint. Maxie's tongue splayed out of his mouth flapping back and forth as he panted. Jasper went back to stroking his head and his tail darted back and forth. Jasper smiled and thought of Scoff and wondered if he had that sweet spot too.

Grabbing the pile of toast, water and his coffee Jasper made his way upstairs. Opening the door, he could see Scoff was curled in a ball on his bed, sleeping soundly. Jasper walked over to the bed and sat down next to Scoff, sipping his coffee. "What are we going to do with you now bud? I've got to go to college. Well, I guess you could stay here again, if you want?" Scoff then rolled over onto his back and started rubbing his back on Jasper's bed, rolling back and forth making his strange garbling noises whilst waving his feet in the air. "Yeah, I think you'll be fine here", said Jasper smiling. Scoff looked over to Jasper, his tongue hanging out. Jasper grabbed a piece of toast and chucked it to Scoff, who caught it in an open maw and wolfed it down greedily, slapping his chops like a toddler with each chew. "You know what I think you'll be fine here. I'll leave the window open for you, so if you want to leave you can, but you don't have to at all. If you want to relax here, that's okay too. Just please don't trash my room", Said Jasper. He looked at Scoff rolling around on the bed garbling again and wondered if there was any hope of him staying here and relaxing. "I'm not sure if you have any concept of time but today is Friday, so I'll see what I can do because we might be able to get you back home to the moors this weekend. I'm not sure yet though, we'll have to see, but for now I've got to get to college".

Once ready Jasper typed a quick message to Billie and Lucy letting them know Scoff was safe and sound. Running downstairs he threw on his jacket, said goodbye to his mum, and with a wince of pain he shrugged on his paper round bag, then hopped on his bike and rode down the street. Distracted by thoughts of the bear Jasper shot through his paper round so fast it became a blur. He still had his morning interaction with Mr Albert, and even almost the exact same reaction with his cat Churchill, the angry feline always rubbing past his leg, with its passive aggressive ways then it nipped him on the shin. Generally, he could avoid Churchill, but he was becoming increasingly more distracted. Yesterday, his 'friend' had been rushed to hospital after getting attacked by a mutant bear so Jasper was not in the best of mindsets.

He had almost reached college when something occurred to him, if there was any news out of the ordinary, gossip would fly faster than nits in a kindergarten group hug. He spotted Lucy fumbling with the combination lock on her bike, and he cycled over.

"Hey Lucy, how's it going? Sorry I missed you gaming this morning, I was trying to work out what to do with Scoff for the day". Lucy finished locking her bike then lent on the railing.

"That's alright don't worry about it, I didn't really get a chance to play this morning either. I was out of it, I'm still knackered. How was Scoff? Did you manage to find a place for him to stay?"

"Yeah, he's doing great, little bugger fared the best of all of us against that bear. He's staying in my room again today, I'm not sure how long he'll actually be there for now though, I left the window open. Figured he wouldn't trash my room if he can get out easily". said Jasper sitting next to Lucy on the bike rack.

"Let's see if he actually stays there this time. I doubt he will from what I've heard about him, he's a little rascal. What if your mum opens the door again?"

"Oh, for Christ Sake, I didn't think about that. I must be tired", Jasper said slapping his face.

"I'm sure it'll be fine. He'll probably just run away again if someone tries to come in. Hey, you wouldn't have happened to notice every single kid here is already looking at us whispering". Said Lucy flicking her head to two girls walking past them. They'd clearly been talking about them but as soon as they saw Lucy look at them, they turned their heads and pretended they didn't even see Lucy and Jasper.

"Dammit I knew this would happen, at least we're all the people that survived the bear attack, that's pretty cool right?" Said Jasper trying to build his confidence. Lucy spotted a small kid walking over with his hood up, hiding his face.

"Whoop there he is!" She shouted.

"Shut up!" said Billie. "You'll draw attention".

"What do you mean? We're the people who survived a bear attack, that's cool right?". Said Jasper as he looked over to a couple of girls who smiled at him.

"Yeah, that's cool for you two but not for the kid who's getting blamed for the murder of Lee" said Billie hiding his face.

"What?! Murder? You didn't do anything like that! Who said that?" asked Jasper, drawing even more attention.

"That's not what Lillz is telling everyone, she's saying that I'm the reason the bear attacked Lee. If it wasn't for me, he wouldn't have got attacked. I had three texts from people this morning telling me how they wish Lee had pushed me in front of the bear".

"I don't understand how this has happened, we told everyone that Lee saved all our lives, how's that turned around? Wait a minute" Said Jasper with an air of understanding "Mollz, Lillz and Jordie ran off before they really saw anything that happened".

"And now they all think it's your fault". said Lucy.

"Thanks dream squad! What am I meant to do now?" said Billie, hiding his face from another group of people that were walking past.

"Murderer!" shouted one of the teens in the herd. More people began to gather around to get a look at Billie. Jasper heard a short girl wearing a cardigan and thick glasses say to a friend.

"How come he's not been arrested?" Her friend, a tall brunette girl with acne replied "I heard it's because he ran away. Pushed Lee into a bear to save his own skin". Suddenly furious Jasper turned to the crowd.

"Billie hasn't done anything wrong! He's not a murderer! If he was, do you really think he'd be here looking at you lot?" Shouted Jasper. The crowd began to split and murmur as two people emerged from its centre. *You have got to be kidding me* thought Jasper. Lillz stormed out of the crowd, closely followed by a very sheepish looking Mollz. Mollz looked like she hadn't slept for days, her hair was like a bramble bush tangled and messy. Lillz folded her arms and glared at Billie who was still attempting to hide his face. She turned to glare at Jasper, her eyes boring into his. He had a strange feeling that part of him had just disappeared back inside of himself.

"You were there Jasper, you saw it! Billie and Lee got into a fight when the bear attacked, Billie left Lee to die. Billie killed him! People if you don't believe me look at his face!" She shouted to the crowd, which was followed by more murmurs.

"Are you kidding me? You left him there, we stayed to help but you left! If anyone is to blame, it's you. If you

107

weren't such a coward maybe you could have done something about it. Now you can't, so don't blame Billie for your mistakes!". Jasper saw that he'd clearly hit a nerve as her face began to burn a dark shade of scarlet and a vein had started throbbing violently on the side of her forehead.

"Look at the proof, look at Billie's face!" She screamed. The crowd cowered at the outburst. "It's his fault! He's always had it out for Lee and now he's finally got what he wanted. Lee's gone and it's because of him!" she threw her accusing finger in the direction of Billie.

"That's enough! All of you get to class, now!" Everyone froze and turned to see Principal Buckman, a tall older woman with a greying bob haircut. Buckman was standing at the top of the steps wearing a black pencil skirt and blazer with her arms folded as she looked down on the crowd. "I said NOW!" She shouted and the whole crowd dispersed as quickly as they could. She stood to the side, letting all the teens pass until it got to Jasper, Lucy, and Billie. She reached out her knife-like palm which cut in front of Jasper. "Not you three" she said ushering them aside. "You three need to come with me". She then spotted Lillz attempting to sneak past the crowd with Mollz. "And you Lilly!" Miss Buckman shouted. Lillz huffed and dragged her heels over to Miss Buckman, leaving Mollz in the crowd. "Right the four of you. With me" she turned on her heels and stormed into the college. Lillz followed begrudgingly making sure she was in front of them. Lucy and Jasper looked to Billie sympathetically before following behind her.

The teens found themselves sitting in a large office in front of a grand finely polished mahogany table, with a placard which had Principal Buckman's name written upon it. Her desk was strictly managed, pens, some paperwork, and a green lamp that you'd only find in an old-fashioned bank, were all parallel to the angles of the desk. Mrs Buckman sat back in her chair, arms crossed and looked at the five awkward teenagers, staring at them individually in utter silence. All the teens fidgeted in their seats, her stare unsettling all of them. Mrs Buckman looked to Jasper, who crossed his arms and stared back at her, seemingly being the only one of the teenagers her glare was not penetrating. As she looked at him, she lifted her eyebrow seemingly amused by his insubordination.

"So, before I start, Billie will you remove that stupid hood, it's not raining, we're clearly inside and quite frankly you look like a prat". Billie looked up at her, and she frowned piercing her lips. Billie slowly lifted his hood and draped it around his shoulders. The right side of his face was swollen and bruised a dark purple with a yellow tinge around its circumference. Billie looked over to Lucy and Jasper. Jasper's defiant face dropped as he glanced over to Billie.

I'd not thought Lee'd hit him that hard he looked to Lucy who shared his same pained expression.

"Right, I hear that you four, as well as Jordie and Molly have had quite the night". Lillz burst out of her seat.

"Quite the night! Lee's dead and it's all because of him!". She shouted, jabbing her finger at Billie.

"Lilly, sit down". Said Miss Buckman so sternly Lillz sat automatically.

I need to learn that! thought Jasper. The principal looked to Lillz then the rest of the group.

"I wanted to let you know that Lee is in a stable condition. The bear damaged his back severely and the doctors are worried about infection. They have put him in an induced coma to help protect him, but the doctors say that with a bit of luck he will pull through". She paused for a moment and looked around the three again. "Lilly that means you can stop, telling everyone he's dead. And, if I hear of you telling anyone that Billie murdered him again,

109

you will be suspended, immediately". She looked at Lilly dead in the eyes "Is that understood?". Lilly looked at her hands intertwined still fidgeting uncontrollably.

"Understood" she said with the attitude of a petulant child.

"Good. Well, this has been a traumatic time for you all, so you are all welcome to go home and take today and the weekend to relax. I will see all of you Monday. You three, I still must have a word with you. I have told Molly and Jordie's tutors too and they have also been let off for the day, so Lilly you may want to see them". Lillz stared at Mrs Buckman bemused. "Well, Lilly. You are dismissed". Lillz hastily got out of her seat and walked out of the room, but not before glaring daggers at Billie.

"Right then, to you three. I've had a conversation with the police, and they tell me that you three were the last ones to see this bear alive and that you all claim that it was Lee that saved your lives". The three nodded to Miss Buckman agreeing with her statement. "Well, that's good to hear, he was on his last warning before being expelled. I never would have thought he would have done anything that heroic, but hearing you say that is very encouraging. Also don't worry I don't believe anything that Lilly has been telling everyone either". Billie gave a pained smile. "I've spoken to Jessie, sorry Mr J, and he said that he'd like a word with you before you go. As he spent the entire night chasing that bear, I have got him cover for the day. So, if you wouldn't mind swinging by the biology lab before leaving that would be much appreciated". the three teens looked at each other amazed.

"He was chasing it all night" said Jasper in amazement.

"Yes, but sadly they never managed to find it", said Miss Buckman. "You three have been very brave and incredibly lucky indeed. Take the next three days to relax and recuperate. Your A levels start in a couple of weeks, and I don't want this affecting your grades. You're good kids. For now, focus up and try to forget about what's happened. Now go on, go see Mr J. You're all dismissed". The three then stood up and began to walk out of the room whilst Lucy mouthed to Jasper.

"He was chasing it all night? He's completely mad!"
Upon leaving the principal's office they all shouted back "Thanks Mrs Buckman!" and out walked Jasper and Lucy followed by Billie who covered his face again with his hood.

The three teens were walking down an empty corridor towards the biology lab.

"I'm amazed you came into school Billie, you're a brave kid! I'm not sure if I'd do that with my face that beaten up", Said Jasper.

"I just wanted to be with you guys when you spoke to Mr J, but yeah this hurts, like a lot". Said Billie gently probing the tender swelling on his brow and cheek.

"Was that the bear or was it Lee?" said Lucy pointing at his bruised face.

"To be honest I'm not sure, definitely started with Lee but it could have been from the bear too. I have no idea, it's all a bit of a bad memory now".

"But didn't you guys not actually fight the bear?" said Jasper.

"Yes, we did, it hit me so hard it did this" said Billie pointing at his swollen eyebrow.

"Wait a minute. That wasn't the bear or Lee was it! That was you vaulting off your bike with that branch!" Said Jasper involuntarily bursting into hysterics.

"No! It was the bear" Objected Billie.

"Oh my god it was you!" said Lucy. Jasper and Lucy began laughing so hard that their sides began to hurt.

"That's why you won't show your face! You're embarrassed!" Laughed Lucy.

"Alright you two laugh it up. I'm still hurt you know!"

"If it was the bear, he'd be loving this!" said Jasper.

"Yeah, well it was just an unlucky fall alright. It could have happened to anyone". Said Billie crossing his arms.

Lucy and Jasper began to catch their breath and wipe away the tears as they walked up to the biology lab.

"So, Billie, what's worse? That mutant bear or some Hell Beasts?" laughed Jasper, but with a hint of seriousness.

"I would rather take on Hell Beasts any day, that thing was terrifying" Laughed Billie, relieved the conversation had moved on from his blunder.

"To be fair that thing looked like it could have been some kind of hell beast to me". Said Lucy.

"It all happened so fast I'm amazed I remember what it looked like", said Jasper.

"Are you kidding me? That thing scared the hell out of me. I'm not going to forget it for the rest of my life!", Said Lucy.

"I hear that", said Billie.

"What do you guys think Mr J wants to talk to us about? Do you think he wants to just get a more thorough description of the bear?" Asked Lucy.

"I'm not sure. He might just want to check if we're okay", Said Jasper.

"Ha! Does anyone mind if I say no?" laughed Billie.

"You may be battered a little but you're fine really, I think we're all a little battered aren't we Jasper" said Lucy Punching Jaspers arm. He recoiled in pain as he slammed her fist into a bruise like a bullseye.

"Yep" He cringed "We're definitely all hurting". Said Jasper rubbing his arm and scowling at Lucy, who smiled back playfully, and he couldn't help but return it. She always seemed to have a way of melting his mood no matter what happened.

All the other students were in class which left the corridor empty and silent. "I can't wait to hear what happened after we left. Do you think he found it?" Said Lucy.

Jasper looked at lucy. Her dark hair tied up in a loose ponytail with strands either side framing her face. It always seemed to amaze him how though she was shy she had moments of amazing confidence and energy. Billie knocked at the door of the Lab, snapping Jasper out of his daze. Mr J pulled a curtain open from a little square window in the door and peered through. Seeing it was the three teens he pulled the curtain closed and unlocked the door.

"Hello, you three come on in". Said Mr J swinging open the door "Wow, Billie what happened to your face. Was that Lee or the bear?" Billie scowled at Mr J who laughed as the three walked in. "You shouldn't make jokes Mr J he was born like that" Laughed Lucy who was joined by Jasper, Mr J and even Billie, but he was laughing much louder and maniacally than the others, then stopped abruptly and glared at all three of them.

"Hilarious".

Suddenly Billie let out a yelp and all three teens stopped in terror. Led on a tarp in the middle of the biology lab, in Haywood College was none other than the mutant bear. It lay there unmoving and massive with brown matted fur. Weeks old peeling scabs scattered its body, all the while boils leaking pink ooze gathered into a rancid broth underneath the creature. Mr J observed their reactions as Jasper walked forward cautiously.

"Jasper don't!" Said Lucy grabbing his arm. Jasper looked at her and gave her a reassuring smile and persisted on. He rounded the bear to its massive head, the dead cloudy white eye still stared deep into Jasper's soul. Looking around the head he then saw the dark red and grizzly gap where Scoff had torn the eye from its socket. Jasper gritted his teeth and closed his eyes as he noticed that the optic nerve still hung limply from the bear's empty socket. Lucy turned in horror to Mr J "Mr J, what's going on?" she said.

"Yeah, that's something I'd really like to know" said Billie, beginning to get angry. Mr J went over to Jasper who was now resting his hand on the side of the bear's giant maw.

"Jasper, what are you doing it could still be". said Lucy before she was cut off by Mr J. "Don't worry it's quite dead, I chased him down last night".

"But you ran off with the police in the wrong direction?" Said Jasper, noticing a large wound in the chest of the bear.

"Yes, well you see the 'Police' don't understand the", he paused with a cough and looked at them all. "Unnatural. So, I had to lead them away before, dealing with the issue myself".

"Unnatural? So, you've dealt with stuff like this before?" Said Lucy.

"Yes, yes, I have. After seeing you three last night, I thought it best to show you and explain exactly what you had seen up close. You see I've left people to their own devices after they've seen a monster like this before and well, let us just say it didn't go well".

"Wait, so you know what this is? And there's more?" Said Billie.

"Oh yes! Lots more, they are rare nowadays, but you just need to know where to look. A lot are also exceptionally good at blending in".

"Lots more?" said Billie falling to a seat next to him.

Jasper removed his hand from the bear. "It looks so calm now, what happened to it? What is it?".

"So, this is something we call a slogolyth, it's a beast that's been infected with Manic. But this one hasn't been infected long, it's still only got four limbs".

"Only four?" Billie gulped.

"What's Manic?" asked Jasper.

"Well, how to explain it, Manic is a kind of virus called Maniacus Unilateralis. It is remarkably similar to that of the Zombie virus, but you wouldn't believe it, but it's actually more of a parasite than a virus. Mad I know! It is most similar to the Ophiocordyceps Unilateralis fungus which tends to affect ants and other insects. You see what it does is attach onto its passing victim and with enzymes it breaks down the exoskeleton of the carrier, then it takes over its mind. The infected insect, which is usually an ant, will then climb to the top of a nearby stem and clamp its jaws onto the stem before the fungus bursts out its chest. However, the 'Manic' seemed to only affect exceedingly rare mythical beasts. That is until the past hundred years or so where the virus has begun infecting other animals! Fascinating isn't it". The three teens looked at Mr J in utter disbelief. Jasper felt his stomach drop as he looked down to his hand where he'd just touched the bear. Mr J noticed the concerned look on Jasper's face "It's so rare, I've not seen a case like this in years, don't worry Jasper there's never been a case of a human with Manic. You'll be fine". Jasper quickly wiped his hand on his trousers and smiled at Lucy before looking away utterly horrified.

"Yeah fascinating" said Billie staring wide eyed at a spec of dirt on the floor.

Jasper turned to Mr J, "you said that there were loads more? But then you said that these are exceedingly rare. What exactly is there loads more off?".

"Now that is a brilliant question! And for that I think the three of you should sit down. That's the spirit Billie" he said as Billie looked up in dismay from his seat. Lucy and Jasper walked over to Billie and gave each other worried glances before sitting down. Mr J looked at the bewildered duo and Billie who was white as a sheet. "You know what? You three look like you could use a drink. Cuppa tea anyone?".

"Erm, yes please?" said Lucy, she looked at Billie who seemed like he was about the throw up. "I think we'll all have one thanks", said Lucy.

"Sure, I'll be right back" he then disappeared off through some double doors into a back room.

"Guys you don't think this", Billie paused "Manic can affect us, do you?".

"I doubt it" said Jasper, "Mr J never would have brought us here if it could affect us. Besides, he said it couldn't affect humans".

Lucy looked over to Jasper "Yeah I'm with Billie though, I'd still like to double check, this got weird as hell and is no one going to mention our teacher is a whack job?" she said over the sound of the kettle. "Whack job?! I resent that!" shouted Mr J from the back room.

"Whack job with stupidly good hearing" Lucy muttered.
"I don't think he's a whack job", said Jasper sitting forward to address the two. "He just clearly knows a hell of a lot more about this stuff than we do, I want to know what he's got to say. He's got to know something about Scoff for sure, he clearly knows about all this. We need to see what else he knows".

"I just want to chunder" said Billie, removing his hood to get some more air.

They all sat back in their seats as Mr J re-entered the room carrying two cups of tea in each hand. "I hope you don't mind cow juice because I gave us all milk and one, I'm not normally one for sugar but to be honest I think we all need it". he smiled politely handing each of them a steaming mug. He then turned around, walked round the corpse, and sat on his desk behind the slogolith, placing his mug next to him. "Well, I'm not really sure where to start. Okay, so you know all the monsters in myths and legends, yes? Well, the majority of them are true". He paused to watch the expressions of the trio, to his surprise they did not react, so he pressed on. "Okay? So yes, mythical creatures are real. Trolls, griffins and even the Baba Yaga now that guy really is a real piece of work. Other people call him the boogeyman but I feel like Baba Yaga suits him much better. Did you know that the Baba Yaga scares the hell out of kids for fun? The other beasts just eat people and animals for food to survive. That guy just tries to see how much he can make them scream. Creepy if you ask me. If they don't react the way he wants, he eats them. He's very good at scaring people though, I've not heard of him eating anyone in a while. Lucy are you alright?" asked Mr J, "you're looking a little pale. Drink some tea, it'll make you feel better". Jasper looked over to Lucy, she'd gone white as a sheet, and he noticed a bead of sweat trickle down Lucy's forehead as her trembling hands lifted the mug to her lips.

"I'll move on from that then" and Mr J continued, "it appears that the three of you have just spotted your first mythical creature, well sort off. Most people would have just seen a bear attacking people last night however, you three have clearly had brushes with Mythical creatures before which is why you could see the Manic. Manic for some strange reason only makes itself apparent to people that have had brushes with mythical beasts. That or it's gone so far through its transformation it's no longer recognisable as an animal, then yes normal people see it too. So, in its own weird way it turns normal creatures into mythical beasts. Not like a dog into a griffin but more like a dog into a strange mutant dog". Mr J looked at the confused, glazed look on the teenagers faces. "Okay maybe I've not explained this well. So, a mythical beast is not only something from history and legend, but it can also be a creature that is extremely out of the ordinary. A perfect example of this would be the Slogolyth, a creature that has been infected with the Manic and has begun to transform into something, different". He looked down to the bear in front of him. Now I know a bear escaped from a zoo last week, I expect that this is the very same bear. It probably got infected whilst it was in the zoo, then broke out at night in a fit of rage. Luckily for the zookeeper's it was at night. There's been a couple of occasions where animals in early infection in this country have killed keepers, and they've been put down. But for this guy, he managed to break out, and the parasite took over his body. I was worried when you kids explained him to me because it sounded like he'd gone further through the process. It appears it's still fairly early on though, only the pusy boil stage at the minute". he said sipping at his tea.

"Pusy boil stage? What stage is after that?" Asked Jasper, it appeared that he was the only one that could even move at this point, as Lucy's and Billies mouths seemed to be frozen open.

"Oh yes! I'm glad you asked. The next stage varies from animal to animal, but a lot of the time the guts fall out and they start sprouting other limbs, appendages, tentacles stuff like that. But like I said it's very rare indeed. This guy", he said nudging the beast with his foot. "This could have been a real doozy, as it was, he only needed a skewer

118

and that sorted him right out. I will incinerate him once we're done here, I just wanted to make sure you three were aware of the situation and your minds could be put to rest that it was dead". said Mr J adjusting his glasses.

"Well, I feel 'so' much safer" said Billie not trying to hide his sarcasm.

"Yeah, me too" agreed Lucy equally sarcastic.

Mr J frowned, "For me, I had two choices, either tell you the truth or leave it to you and in my experience the latter doesn't go well. The two last students I saw that had similar experiences have both gone". He looked at the two and waved a finger around his ear. "A little mad. One stays in his house all day wearing a tin foil hat and the other is stuck in a mental institution. So, I figured what the hell third time lucky and at least you three have each other to lean on. So, I feel I've been talking for ages, have you three got any questions for me? I'm sure you have". The three looked at each other. Lucy turned back to him.

"So, what other mythical creatures live around here?" asked Lucy.

"Well, that's easy, the most common around the world are pixies, they're little buggers. You know when you lose your keys or your phone. Even when you are trying to find something that's not important, but you really need it at that moment in time. That was probably a Pixie. Annoying little buggers but they're all over the place, we'll never get rid of them. It is almost impossible to see them because they're completely see through. I worked with a group called M.I.T.H a while back to try to find a pixie that was planting Bombs all over the UK. Naturally the government blamed it on the Middle East, another perfect excuse for them to get more oil and the public ate that lie right up didn't they. Anyway, I'm getting side-tracked. So yes, around here you have Pixies, there is a troll not too far away but she is lovely, a real sweetheart. Wouldn't hurt a fly! On purpose. Then you have the Bogarts but they're on the moors and no one's seen them for years, oh and you can't forget the werewolves. But again, they are rare as hell and thank god, I dealt with one in Spain a while back that was not pretty, nearly killed an entire village. To be honest, we don't have many in the UK, we're quite lucky".

"So, when you say you dealt with a werewolf, you mean killed? How did you do it? Was it with silver? like in the movies or is it a kind of shoot it with anything kind of thing?" Said Lucy. The colour returned to her face as she listened in amazement to Mr Js adventures.

"Well, shoot anything enough it will die, so it's always good to have a gun with you if you're hunting something dangerous, even if it is only normal bullets. That being said the movies are damn good at getting these things right, silver does the trick much faster than bullets would. Could take eight or more shots to take one out normally, but with a clean silver sword to the chest it'll go down much more efficiently. To be honest that is the best way to take out most beasties, just something about silver that quite literally makes their blood boil".

Billie took his eyes off the beast on the floor with interest catching him too. "So, you're saying that all mythical beasts are true? Does that mean Bigfoot is real too?".

"Ha sadly no, there was a M.I.T.H investigation a while back and it turned out that it was only a very hairy lunatic running around the California red woods. He almost fooled them too he was so hairy, a real modern day neanderthal". Mr J rubbed the stubble of his chin deep in thought "I can't quite remember his name but I think it was Leonard something, Leonard Buck maybe? I can't remember. He lives in Arizona now though".

Billie rubbed his face trying to get his head around everything he was being told. "So, what about Hell Beasts? Are they real? Please don't tell me they're real". Mr J put both hands behind him leaning back on the desk thinking with a heavy frown.

"Hell beasts, never heard of those before. I don't think they are". he then threw himself forward and put his hands on his knees. "Then again, I've not seen everything yet!" he laughed.

"Bogarts?" Asked Jasper. Both Billie and Lucy looked at him.

"What about them?" asked Mr J.

"You mentioned them before. What are they? I've never heard of them before. Are they like the slogolyth or are they similar to pixies?" Jasper asked. Billie and Lucy's eyes both shifted to Mr J curiously, who looked at them and gave a big smile.

"My, my Bogarts are nothing like anything else I've ever seen and complete opposites to slogolyths, they're little green terrors. They'll eat family pets, kids, anything they can get their hands on really. Considering how small they are they do have some ferocious appetites. You know their mouths can open wider than their entire body, and unhinge their jaws like a python? I saw one a while back on the moors, he'd eaten an entire deer, whole! Just like an anaconda. Poor little guy was trying to attack me because I wouldn't stop laughing at him. I couldn't help it. He was so heavy and full he couldn't even move! It was just his tiny arms and legs scrabbling at the ground as he tried to get me" Laughed Mr J wiping a tear from his eye.

"So, what did you do with him after you found him?" asked Jasper worried about the answer.
Mr J tried to hold back his laughter "Nothing, he wasn't a contract. So, I left the little fatty be and carried on with my hike".

Lucy picked up on something that he'd just said. "Contact? Are there contracts on mythical beasts?" she asked curiously.

"Oh yeah! There always has been. Think of them as bounties. Sometimes it's a capture, sometimes it's a kill. I don't tend to do them too much. The pay is great but not good enough for risking your life every day. I generally only do them when they are a little too close to home, or if someone asks me to help directly. I'm happy teaching biology. Nice and safe". He smiled. "So how are you three feeling now? All finished your tea?" The trio looked down into their empty mugs and nodded. He then stood up and collected their mugs.

"So, what are we supposed to do now?" Asked Billie giving Mr J his mug.

"What do you mean? You carry on with your life. But just be thankful that you are not one of the ignorant ones and be happy that you're still alive. Just don't go around telling people about it, they'll think you're mad. That and M.I.T.H will probably hunt you down, they don't like people spreading panic. Ha, never know you might end up on the contract list, it does happen from time to time".

Lucy looked to the slogolyth then back to Mr J "That Parasite, Manic, was it? Can that transfer to humans too or is it just animals".

Mr J turned to the slogolyth "Just animals, I've never heard of a case of it reaching humans. Don't worry you will all be alright" he smiled. "So, I think it's best that you three head home. I know it's a lot to take on, but you've got a day off and the weekend. So, take that time to relax and process everything. Now I've got to process this guy, then head out to the morgue to get it incinerated. So, if any of you three have any questions please feel free to ask. You know where I am. Oh yeah!" Mr J then went over to his desk, tore three post it notes and wrote down a collection of numbers on them. "Here's my number in case any of you need anything. Feel free to call me anytime with anything Myth or Monster related. If it's about Biology that will have to wait until class".

The three began grabbing their bags to leave the room, bewildered, confused and with quite a bit on their minds. Just as they were leaving the room, Mr J spoke "Oh and Jasper at some point we're going to have to go through your drawings. You know, it is funny. That's one of the reasons I decided to tell you all about this in the first place. Any way off you go, I've lots to do and you've all got lots to think about I'm sure, see you all Monday". Said Mr J shutting the door and it made an audible click as it locked.

The three walked down the corridor deep in thought. Billie looked over to Jasper and Lucy "How is he going to get that bear, wait no, slogolith out of the biology lab? No, how did he get it in the biology lab? He was telling us so much in there, but I just kept getting fixated on it".

Lucy laughed, "Of course you'd get fixated on that Billie. Mythical creatures are real, I suppose that also means dragons are real too?"

"Or were real" said Billie. "I can't imagine they would have survived this long without being spotted. They're huge, remember and don't forget they can breathe fire". Billie then looked over to Jasper, "what was he talking about your drawings?" asked Billie.

Jasper frowned, thinking. "Well, a few days ago, he caught me drawing in class. I can't even remember what I was drawing now. You guys know what I'm like. I'll just sit drawing creatures for hours". Said Jasper.

"That's strange, I'm sure you'll find out soon. Well, as we've got three days off, I suppose we should try and get Scoff back home?" Said Lucy shouldering her bag.

"Yeah, it would be great but, how are we meant to get to the moors? We're a good one hundred miles away from them. I can't drive either so that makes getting there fun". Said Jasper, pushing open the doors to the front of the college.

"That's true, we could take the train?" Said Lucy.

The three walked down the steps of the college to their bikes. It did make Jasper wonder, how on earth Scoff got to Haywood in the first place. It was over a hundred miles away from the Moors. Jasper thumbed the lock on his bike, and it clicked with the correct combination. Wrapping the chain around his bike, he lifted his leg over and sat.

"We could cycle?" Jasper said laughing.

"Over my dead body!" Said Lucy jumping onto her bike.

"Yeah, the train seems like the only option. Hey, do you guys want to come to mine? My mums out with Johnny so I've got a free house. It would be good to relax and come up with a plan? Maybe even get some snacks on the go".

"Music, mythical beasts and loads of snacks sounds like the perfect plan to me, what about you Billie?" said Lucy with a smile.

"Sorry, guys I think you might have to go without me on this one. I'm not sure if I'm up for it, you know?" he said walking away from the two teens, "I'll maybe see you both on Monday though yeah?"

Lucy and Jasper looked at each other a little shocked. "Billie are you sure? We might end up seeing something amazing. Who knows there might be loads of them" said Jasper attempting to lure Billie in, but he wasn't budging.

"Nah sorry guys". Billie said as he walked throwing his hood up to hide his face.

"Well, I guess it's just me and you then Jasp", said Lucy. Jasper's face dropped at the thought of already losing his best friend on such an adventure.

"Yeah, I suppose so. I guess the bear and what happened to Lee was a little too much for him". Said Jasper looking to Lucy for reassurance. "He did get a little beaten up". She placed her hand on his shoulder. "Hey, we've only just found out about these creatures, do you really think that he would miss every adventure? I have a feeling there will be a lot more where this came from, and he'll definitely join us in the future" Lucy said resting her hand on his shoulder.

Jasper smiled, "Yeah, it's about time we got some real adventure ey! Alright let's head to mine and we can start planning".

Chapter Eleven: The Plan

"Scoff it's alright, I'm just going to pop this around your neck, and you'll be fine". Said Jasper as he lowered the slip lead towards Scoff. Scoffs eyes darted from the slip lead to Jasper and back again. Centimetres away from Scoff, Jasper dropped the lead over his head. Scoff hopped to his right and the lead fell limp to the floor. Jasper frowned and launched himself at Scoff. Scoff made a startled grumble and dove onto the crate, to the windowsill, then onto the bed. All the while Jasper was right on his tiny tail.

"I'm doing this for your own good Scoff. Get back here!"
Scoff hopped onto the desk, picked up the computer mouse and launched it at Jasper. Jasper flinched and raised his arms as the mouse snagged on its cable and bounced right back hitting Scoff. Jasper swung out his arms frantically trying to grab Scoff, who again and again jumped just before Jasper was about to catch him. Jasper picked up the slip lead and threw the loop towards the crate where he thought Scoff would be next. To his delight Scoff jumped right in the way of the lead and it fell loosely around his neck. Scoff, desperate and a little frightened, jumped off the crate and onto the floor running at Jasper, the loop tightened.

The sun was shone through the windows causing the light to scatter as specks of dust floated through the sun rays. Lucy sat cross-legged on the floor of Jasper's living room next to a mound of snacks. Maxie was already curiously investigating, sniffing as his tail darted from side to side. Lucy was unloading her bag, pulling out an A4 Pad of lined paper and a few pens. She flicked through it to find an empty page. Grabbing her favourite pen, the one which clinked to different colours. She clicked it to green and drew a cloud in the centre of the page. Inside the cloud she wrote Scoff. Suddenly there was a crash from upstairs causing Maxie to jump. Lucy looked to the ceiling curious.

"Jasper? Are you alright up there?"

At that moment there was a sound like that of a herd of elephants charging down the stairs. Maxie stepped in front of Lucy's legs, his tail pointing out straight as he stared at the door. Suddenly, the living room door flung open. Scoff burst in and tried to run into the room tiny claws outstretched but was yanked backwards by the lead held by Jasper. Maxie's eyes narrowed at the mythical intruder, and he began barking relentlessly at Scoff.

"Hold on bud you can't just dive at everyone you see. Sometimes, you must greet them. They'll be much more inclined to be friendly" said Jasper holding Scoff back. "Let's introduce you two slowly, okay? Maxie come'on, who's this ey?" he said, putting on a gentle encouraging voice. Scoff looked at Maxie then up at Jasper lifting one eyebrow, Jasper saw the expression and could read it instantly. It was as if Scoff was saying, really? This guy?

"Alright you two, gently, gently. It's alright Maxie he's ok". Maxie edged each paw little by little, moving ever closer. The barking had ceased but it was replaced with a low, nervous growl as Maxie approached, his tail now firmly between his legs. "It's alright. Who's this Scoff?" Jasper said as the two creatures met almost nose to nose. The tension seemed to lift in the room as Maxie's tail wagged cautiously as he began to sniff all over Scoff, first around his neck and ears then down his body. Scoff looked up to Jasper with confused eyes, his eyes instantly widened in horror as Maxie shoved his nose firmly into Scoffs rear end. Maxie then bounced away in approval of Scoff and his tail began to resume its usual unrelenting wag. He then began jumping from side to side dropping his head, egging Scoff on. Scoff dropped to all fours and lifted his bum into the air and dropped his head to the ground, mimicking Maxie's movements.

"Here we go…"

Jasper reached down to the lead on Scoff and gently removed it from his head. Scoff then pounced at Maxie, who dove out of the way, turned and dove back at Scoff. Scoff rolled from Maxie's faint attack, and hid behind the legs of the dining room table. Maxie then sprinted after Scoff and the two began running circles around the table, taking it in turns chasing each other. Jasper's eyes darted around following the duo, but just the sight of them running around and around made his eyes blur and his head dizzy.

"Well, that went better than planned", said Jasper as he walked over to Lucy, leaving the two balls of energy to their games. "Nice we've got crisps, cookies, coke and these two are getting along. I'm all kinds of happy". He picked up a packet of cookies, the packet rustled as he opened them. He offered one to Lucy who unhesitatingly took a cookie from the packet and nibbled at one side.

"I'm surprised he let you put that lead on him" Lucy chuckled with bits of cookie unknowingly falling to her top. "I've started a little brainstorm of what we need to do to get Scoff back home and keep him safe", she said looking at the pad in front of her.

"Awesome! What have you got so far?" Jasper said, picking a cookie from the packet and taking a bite.

Lucy gave Jasper an embarrassed look, then showed him the page "So at the moment I've written, Scoff" she said laughing. "I've only just started". Jasper laughed.

"No worries let's do this. Obviously, we need to get him to the Moors. So, we need to work out how we're going to get there and how much it will cost. Then we need to work out how on earth we find the Bogarts when we are there. I mean, I've watched a lot of adventure shows, so I know a bit about tracking, but I wouldn't say I'm a tracker by any stretch, so I doubt that would help". Lucy wrote frantically, branching off each section for them to expand on later.

"We can't forget we actually need to eat on this little adventure too. What do you think about us bringing Hiking bags and a tent? Then we can crash on the moors for the night, before having to come back". Said Lucy.

"Wow, you want to go all out roughing it. That is a great idea and best of all it's free. This would be so much easier if Billie were coming. He could help carry stuff and if we bumped into anything technical, he would be the one to do it". said Jasper, whilst also wondering if they'd end up bringing just one tent to, 'save on space'.

"Yeah, it's a real shame he's not coming, we could really do with his help. Worst of all he won't get to see the other bogarts. He's going to hate himself". Said Lucy.

"It's his decision, we can't force him. We asked him if he wanted to come".

"I know, I know, I just feel bad. So anyway, how are we actually going to find these bogarts when we get to the moors?"

"Well, actually, I had a great plan for that, we just need to follow our lead". Said Jasper smugly.

Lucy raised an eyebrow "And what 'lead' would that be?"

"So, remember Billie told us about the sheep getting attacked on the moors? I read an article on my paper round about this farmer's flock getting attacked. It said it was near the Priddacombe Mounds near a place called Mt Pleasant. So, I was thinking, if the sheep are getting attacked in that area, then that's where the bogarts must be. They at least would have had to have been there to kill the sheep anyway. If we bring Scoff there, I'm sure Scoff could catch the trail of the other bogarts. Other than that, all I can think of is walking aimlessly around the moors until we find something".

"Sounds like a plan", Said Lucy "I'll write it down". She then began scribbling notes about the farmer on her mind map.

"Hey Luce, I had a thought. Earlier when Mr J was telling us about other creatures and monsters, well, he said that all three of us must have seen mythical creatures before because the early stages of Manic can only be seen by people who've seen mythical beasts. It occurred to me that you and Billie met Scoff after seeing the slogolyth, so you guys must have both seen mythical creatures before otherwise you would have just seen an ordinary bear. So, do you remember what creature it was you saw?" Said Jasper curiously.

Lucy signed regrettably "I knew you were going to ask that eventually. I had the same thought when he said that because I could not remember ever seeing any mythical beast. Because you know, one would think you would remember something like that. I was racking my brains trying to work out what on earth it was I had seen, but nothing came to mind. That's when Mr J mentioned the Baba Yaga, he terrorized me for years when I was a kid, he'd visit me every night. It was like he delighted, in terrifying me. The first time I saw him I remember being around six. He crept into my room whilst I was asleep, he must have knocked into one of my shelves because it fell off the wall. Books fell everywhere, which is what woke me up, I saw his dark image and asked him what he was doing. I had just watched Alien and his ghostly form was nothing compared to that thing, plus I thought it was a dream, so I had no reason to be scared. He instantly screamed in my face. I seem to remember saying something like "that was rude" or something equally innoxious. He was thrown by that and asked me why I wasn't scared. I said it was because this was a dream, and no one needs to fear dreams, plus Alien was way scarier. Anyway, he said something about this not being a dream and that he was going to become my worst nightmare. He then vanished into thin air, and I carried on sleeping" said Lucy deep in thought.

"That doesn't sound too bad?" Said Jasper.

"Yeah, that was just the beginning, I then slept well for a couple of weeks before he came back again. But each time he'd terrify me in a different way, some days he'd scream in my face, his long sharp teeth engulfing my nightmare. Other times he would put something dark over my face and hold me down in utter silence, I could feel his cold presence in the room and feel his cold hands holding my neck and arms down like he had four arms. When I couldn't take anymore, he'd pull down whatever was suffocating me just below my eyes and stare at me with his giant unblinking milky dead eyes. I'd scream and scream but make no noise. Every night he'd steal my voice before waking me, so each night I was totally helpless. After this, I was terrified about going to sleep and I had this go on for months. Eventually he obviously thought he'd made his point clear because he never came back. Thank god he didn't because I was in a horrible state every day. It is probably the whole reason I'm withdrawn now. He ripped every bit of confidence from me and took my dreams for years, even after he'd left. I haven't had a good dream since. When I do dream, I just see those dead eyes staring into my soul, they're not vivid like they used to be, and I don't dream much anymore. But when Mr J said that, it scared the hell out of me. The fact that it was actually real, everything, every night, I still remember his horrifying screams".

"That's awful! I'm glad you screamed the next time". Said Jasper.

"What?" Lucy said confused by the strange response.

"Mr J said that the Baba Yaga eats the children that don't scream, so you're lucky to be alive. He clearly knew it was his fault at the start for you not screaming, then he made sure you really feared him before he left you be".

Lucy frowned "Yeah I suppose you're right".

"Yeah, you probably knocked his confidence a lot, that's probably why he eats the kids that don't scream. It hurts his gigantic ego" Jasper laughed.

"Ha yeah, he must have a pretty big ego to react like that" said Lucy with a struggled smile. "Anyway, I wonder what creature Billie has seen, obviously Scoff was yours".

"That's a good point, knowing Billie it was probably a leprechaun or something else completely ridiculous". A brilliant idea came to Jasper because his voice changed to complete excitement. "I bet it was a hell beast! He's always going on about them".

Smiling Lucy looked to Jasper "We're getting side-tracked, we need to work out all the details for the weekend before we run out of time".

"You're right. Let's focus up. I've got some old ration packs that my dad left, those things never go off, so we can always eat those".

The two continued for hours working out the entire weekend, whilst eating copious amounts of junk and laughing the afternoon away. Jasper and Lucy had been talking for so long, the two bundles of energy had curled themselves up on the sofa together in an entangled mess of fur and claws. Lucy smiled as she watched their little fury bodies rise and fall with each breath as they slept. Occasionally Maxie and Scoff would open their eyes with a glare after being disturbed by the sounds of rustling packets or by Lucy and Jasper laughing.

Jaspers legs began to ache from sitting cross legged on the floor for so long. He stretched out his legs, feeling the tension ease across his knees and thighs. His knees made a loud clicking sound which made them both laugh. He then leant back on the bottom of the sofa, looking at Lucy.

"So, Jordie hey?" Said Jasper.

"What about him?" She said folding her arms and raising an eyebrow.

"Well before everything happened, you guys were getting on pretty well, weren't you?"

"We were until Billie got himself socked in the face" She laughed. "I just don't know how he gets himself into these situations, he's always getting beaten up by someone".

"He just doesn't quite know how to talk to ordinary people" said Jasper.

"Do we not count as people?"

"Not ordinary people, no, we take the piss out of each other all the time. We're used to it, other people aren't. They might not realise he's actually joking. Hey! Nice try, you and Jordie. Come on, is it because he's a cool skater dude?" said Jasper in a mocking tone.

Lucy laughed looking away from Jasper and she began to fiddle with her hands. Her dark hair was down just over her shoulders. Her elysian green eyes studied each nail as her thumb rubbed gently over the tips of her fingers. The song on the speakers finished playing and the room took an awkward silence. Though only a couple of seconds past, the moment before the next track felt like an eternity. The beat of the next chillstep tune began, it was a new mix by a DJ he knew they both loved called Suicide Sheep. Jasper noticed her stretched out foot started to tap to the beat of the new song, and she looked up to him.

"Jordie and I had a kind of little thing last year. You know I did kind of like him being a 'cool skater dude'". She copied his mocking tone. "But when the bear came, I couldn't believe he just left like that, he shot off like I wasn't even there. I mean I know we all ran at the start, but I didn't even see him look back. When we got back, even this morning it was like I didn't even exist. That or he was too much of a coward to talk to me. He just walked straight past and didn't even ask if I was okay".

Jasper could feel the mood change and he shuffled in his seat adjusting to the new environment. He knew that what he was about to say would make him hate himself for a very long time. Jasper looked down to his hands slightly nervous then back to Lucy.

"He was just trying to look after himself. I hate to say it, but he did also shout for everyone to run. He's probably killing himself now over not coming back, which is likely why he's not spoken to you. If he'd come back, he would have left Molly and Lillz somewhere up the track too. If it were the other way around, I'm not sure if I could have left you and Billie. You never know what could have happened with you two and I wouldn't be there to help. I love you guys and I'd never want anything bad to happen to either of you". Jasper could feel the soppy tone taking over and didn't want things to get emotional and changed his approach. "But let's not think about what happened to Billie's face that was his fault, I didn't want that to happen either" Lucy giggled.

Jasper and Lucy's eyes locked and they both broke into embarrassed uncontrollable smiles, instantly they both looked away. Jasper composed himself and pushed to his feet with a groan. lifting his arms to the ceiling, his spine popped as he twisted his body, giving it a good stretch. Both Scoff and Maxie noticed him reanimating to life and they lifted their heads to attention, Maxie in the hope of a walk and Scoff probably in the hope of a squirrel, cat or any other equally grim snack.

"Well, I think we've got our plan. Let's get moving, shall we? I've got all of the camping stuff here, we'll need to pack lite because we will be walking a lot. If you go and grab your bits, I'll get the stuff ready here. Meet here first thing in the morning then we can head straight off. How does that sound?"

Lucy jumped to her feet stretching out her equally achy legs. Scoff and Maxie immediately got up stretching their bodies too. "Sounds like a plan to me, I'm sure my parents won't mind. I'll just say it's for the Duke of Edinburgh and I forgot to tell them or something.

"Yeah! That's brilliant. I'll tell Mum the same. Then our stories will match. I'll make sure Scoff looks the part like we talked about. We can't get that bit wrong".

"I dread to think how this is going to work".

The next morning Jasper woke up doing his normal routine of coffee and toast before lugging all his hiking stuff downstairs. He'd packed all the hiking essentials, rations, roll mat, sleeping bag and clothes. He'd prepared so much as to be wearing full hiking clothes. Cargo trousers, and a black thermal top comprised his outdoorsy outfit, topped with hiking boots. Jasper walked past a full body mirror on the landing and looked at himself. "Well, it's not every day you look like you're meant to be living on a desert island". he said looking at his trousers. He started to imagine himself swimming in the ocean shouting, *Wilson!*

The doorbell rang and he darted downstairs, Maxie had already beaten him to the door and looked up to Jasper with his tongue splayed out and that stupid signature spaniel smile. Jasper opened the door to see Billie stood there face like a kebab, dark and sheepish.

"Billie? What are you doing here?" Said Jasper.

"Hey Jasp, sorry for leaving like that yesterday. I was a little overwhelmed. With being accused of murder, finding out that mythical creatures are definitely real and" he paused looking at his feet "you know, just seeing that slogolith thing again. It well, proper messed me up. Mind if I come in?"

Maxie stood at the threshold of the door tail wagging, almost exploding with excitement to meet the new person at the door. Jasper looked to the sky and pursed his lips to one side theatrically mulling things over, then stepped aside opening the door wider.

"Ummmmm, of course you can! Come in! Want a coffee? I just put on a fresh pot".
Billie smiled and stepped into the house.

"I can always have a coffee".

Billie squatted in Jasper's kitchen stroking Maxie who was already led on his back submitting to the newcomer. Billie removed his hand from Maxie's belly to take a cup of steaming coffee from Jasper. Maxie glared jealousy at the cup of coffee that was now receiving Billie's attention. Defeated, Maxie walked out of the room head down, sulking. Resting his back on the kitchen side Billie took a sip of the coffee.

"Where's your Mum and Johnny?"

"They went off earlier to a garden centre or something. I think mum wanted more herbs for the garden. Have you spoken to Lucy about the plan for the weekend?"

"Yeah, so I might have packed my stuff already and it also might be outside. I wasn't sure if you'd want me to come with you guys after I left yesterday, so I didn't bring it straight inside". Jasper laughed.

"Of course, I want you to come! It would not be the same without you. You're the bow to our arrows".

"The Salt to your vinegar?"

"The Bacon to our egg"

"The shield to your sword"

"The cream to our tea"

"Wow that one sounded weird", said Billie.

"Yeah, super weird! I got a little carried away" said Jasper, a little embarrassed and they both laughed.

"So, where's Scoff? I hear he's getting on well with your doggo".

Jasper laughed "you're kidding, you can't hear them?"

Billie now only just noticed a loud grumbling, growling noise coming from the living room and he poked his head around to see Scoff and Maxie rolling around the floor play fighting. Each of them at each other's throats like it was life or death, but neither putting any pressure on any of their ferocious attacks. Billie smiled.

"Well maybe I'm deaf as well as bruised".

"I'm packed here, so if you've got everything you need..." Jasper was interrupted by the doorbell. "That'll be Lucy" Walking out of the kitchen he shut the battle of the furs in the living room and went to the front door. Swinging it open, he saw Lucy. Her hair tied up in a ponytail exposing her neck and shoulders. She was the spitting image of Jasper wearing cargo trousers, boots and a black thermal.

"Well, that's embarrassing", said Lucy eyeing Jasper.

Billie rounded behind Jasper to see Lucy. "I clearly missed the memo about the uniform" he laughed.

"Hold on!" she burst between the two of them, Jasper and Billie both getting knocked back by her large rucksack. She threw it down, clicked open the top and rummaged through. "That's better", She said as she ran into the bathroom carrying another top.

"She looks like Lara Croft", said Billie looking at Jasper, who appeared to be staring into a world of his own. Billie imagined that the world involved a pistol wielding adventurer.

Two minutes later she re-appeared wearing a low-cut white thermal and stood in front of the pair of idiots. "Better?" asked Lucy.

Jasper snapped out of his trance, "yep better, totally better".

Lucy walked into the kitchen, followed by the idiots and poured herself a cup of coffee. She could hear the battle of the paws in the other room and took a sip of her drink.

"Those two still going at it?" Jasper drained the rest of his mug. Preying it wouldn't bring on the caffeine sweats.

"Yeah, they've been play fighting all morning"

"I think Scoff has begun to really love it here, he and Maxie get on really well". Said Lucy

"I'm going to miss him for sure, he's like one of the family already", said Jasper.

The three stood around drinking coffee and discussing the plans for the weekend. After they'd finished their coffees, Jasper roused the group, and they gathered their hiking gear and locked the house. Then the group headed off to the train station, ready, caffeinated and in high spirits, even with the added risk of Scoff being seen as he bounced along fences beside them. Jasper wanted to give Scoff as much freedom as he could before he did something he knew Scoff would never forgive him for.

Chapter Twelve: Unplanned Parenthood

It was a bright clear morning at the station, barely a cloud in the sky. A fresh spring chill washed over the teens like a cold shower. The station had many platforms but was almost completely empty, except from the three college students who stood there, hiking sacks by their sides. Lucy was wearing a soft black fleece, both Billie and Jasper were wearing t-shirts, Jaspers was a long sleeve which he rolled up. Lucy and Jasper were discussing their tactics for defeating the rage crawler, whilst Billie shivered uncontrollably.

"I just love playing with a shield, the artwork is just always amazing on them, sometimes with emblems, dragons or lions. Then you get the sword with it too, but it's really the shield that sells it for me", Said Jasper.

"The shields do look awesome; I like the agility of the rogues. Running, shooting their arrows. You can't even touch them. Billie, just put a jumper on" said Lucy laughing after Billie made a loud shuddering noise.

"No! I don't need one. I'm fine. Jaspers not wearing a jumper, so I don't need one either", Said Billie.

"Yeah, but I'm carrying this bundle of joy, he's keeping me nice and warm, aren't you my beautiful boy", Said Jasper, nuzzling Scoff's nose, which poked out of a bundle of blankets which surrounded Scoff. Scoff grumbled and tried to wriggle out of his comfy cage. "Now, now little buddy it'll be alright. The train journey won't be that long then you'll be right out of there, okay?". Billie looked at Jasper nuzzling the fury babe and huffed.

"Right, I'm getting a jumper on, I can't take any more of this. Especially with the weird coochy-coo rubbish. You two are making me want to barf". Jasper and Lucy leant into one another making faces, which was immediately followed by a sickening chorus of: "Where's my little sasquatch, awwww there he is".

"Who's a good boy hey?"

"Awwww look at your beautiful face"

"Hello"

"Hey"

"Heya"

Lucy then began sticking her tongue out at the baby and began blowing raspberries. Billie fumbled through his backpack in search of his jumper. Pulling it out of his bag, he pulled the drawstring, then clipped up the top making sure it was secure. He then put his arms through the jumper and lifted it over his head then pulled it down to his waist. Feeling the cool fabric on his skin he immediately felt the chill disappear.

"You two are just disgusting and so is your weird fury baby".

An old lady dressed in a cream long Jacket had slowly and merrily crept up behind Jasper and Lucy. She rounded behind them startling the two.

"Hello there", she said with a warm loving smile, shuffling from side to side with her walking stick. "Who have we got here?" Jasper turned to the old lady and forced a smile.

"This is our boy, little Jacko", Said Jasper, hesitatingly showing Scoff to the old lady, who was already reaching out her hand to greet little Jacko.

The old lady's hand suddenly recoiled as she spotted Jacko's green fur and big golden eyes, "oh!" she began to laugh. "A fuzzy little fella isn't he", she said wide-eyed and laughing. Her laugh was so shocked jasper could even see her uvula through her worn down pensioner teeth.

Lucy smiled and gently patted the bundle of blankets, "oh he's our little sweetheart" again she patted the blankets and was immediately greeted with a little growl from the bundle.

Jasper began to bounce him up and down "Oh little guy, I'm sorry" He said to the old lady, "he's probably just hungry".

Billie was amazed by watching the interactions between the Bogart and the humans. But not so amazed that he was going to miss such an incredible opportunity to trap Lucy and Jasper.

"Awwww little guy, he's not eaten in hours. He must be starving" he paused and looked at the mother. "Lucy?"

Jasper realising the hole that they'd just dug, had to stifle his laughter which was already becoming too much to handle. Lucy still with her hand on the blankets, closed her eyes and stifled a grin then looked to Billie, who was wearing the smile of a chimp that's just succeeded in throwing a large poo in your soup.

"He's just eaten", said Lucy through gritted teeth as she took little grumbly Jacko off Jasper and walked away rocking him from side to side.

The old lady looked at Jasper "he's just lovely isn't he" she said with a smile so big it closed her eyes. She then hobbled off with her walking stick to the other side of the platform.

Jasper sniggered and looked over to Billie who was still wearing a grin so proud, you might have thought he'd won the lottery.

"I'm so glad you're on this trip with us, you're an absolute nightmare", said Jasper laughing.

"Yeah, I'm glad I came too", Billie said, still smiling.

"Yeah, stupidly glad!" said Lucy sarcastically as she re-joined the two.

A loud squealing made the three cringe. Down the tracks a large train followed by three garish green and yellow carriages slowed to pull up to the station. The squealing continued as the train found its destination, it stopped abruptly with a steaming hissing noise as pressure was released. A calm almost robotic female voice called over the Tannoy system.

"The train, for the southwestern rail service for Cornwall, stopping at: Yeovil, Taunton, Exeter...". the voice continued reeling off stops. The teens hefted up their bags and stepped onto the train, each being sure to 'mind the gap'. They made their way onto the carriage and lugged their bags into a baggage holding area at the front of the carriage. Making their way to their seats they read the numbers on each chair as they went down, noticing that each seat was empty. They found their dusty seats, next to a table and made themselves as comfortable as they could on such an old rickety train. Two wardens were talking outside the train wearing orange high vis jackets. One of the men looked at his watch then blew his whistle before they split up and stepped into the train. It jolted as it began to move on its westward journey away from the station.

Jasper gazed through the dirty mud-covered window, watching the blur of trees and countryside pass them by. Listening to music through tiny headphones Jasper's mind wandered. Looking down to the ball of fur in his lap he thought about the past week, bumping into Scoff, encountering the bear and the conversation with Mr J. He looked over to Billie on the seat opposite, fast asleep and drooling like a baby. He then looked to Lucy next to him who was trying to stay awake, but he could tell her eyes were getting heavy and she was beginning to nod off too. He felt the brake pads press against the disks of the train and they were coming to a stop. Slowly and with an ear-piercing squeal the train pulled up to a station. Grey people with blank expressions stood there staring into space, going about their ordinary day to day, nine to five jobs. Jasper couldn't help but wonder how each of those people got themselves into that situation.

"You know, I think that through everything that has happened, we're so lucky. Look at those people out there, living the humdrum of everyday life" he glanced down at Scoff fast asleep in his lap "we've got something really incredible here, we were dying for adventure, diving into games to get our fix. But we've got an amazing adventure right here. Getting this guy home, keeping him safe". Jasper looked at Lucy. Her eyes were shut, and her head tilted unconsciously to one side, she was fast asleep. Jasper smiled looking at his friends. He went quiet again and pressed his head against the window next to him and closed his eyes.

Scoff woke to a grumble in his stomach, his large yellow eyes individually blinked brightly, and he peered around. Jasper and the others were fast asleep, Billie snoring loudly a bit of drool slowly making its way down to his top. People were sleeping all around the carriage. Scoff looked out the window, the train had pulled to a stop. Outside the window, sat on a fence was a cat cleaning itself. It licked its paw with its little pink tongue then repeatedly wiped its face. Scoff eyed the cat. His large tongue licked his lips and he wriggled one arm free from the quilted cage. With his free claw, he pulled the blanket from his front, unwrapping himself from the cotton cradle. Scoff stopped suddenly and became motionless on his back, legs in the air like a dead insect as Jasper stirred in his sleep. Jasper tasted the air then settled again and rested his head on Lucy's shoulder. Lucy too was fast asleep. Scoff then looked back to the cat, licking itself unaware it was being watched. Scoff then climbed off Jasper and with claws grasping the fabric of the seat he began to climb up to the window. Reaching the latch of the window, Scoff pulled, and the window opened with a clunk. The cat instantly stopped licking itself and it spotted Scoff glaring at it through the open window. Suddenly the train lurched into action throwing Scoff from the top of the seat and into the lap of a sleeping fiery-haired woman. He landed on his back in her legs and looked up at her innocently. Opening her eyes, she saw the green toothy, yellow-eyed monster in her lap and let out an ear-piercing scream so loud it put the squeaking breaks of the train to shame. Instantly all the passengers in the carriage ducked their heads into their hands. Billie jumped out of his seat, Lucy's eyes blinked to focus, and she threw her hands to her ears. Jasper flailed in his seat, the scream making him throw blankets everywhere. Scoff yelled back at her with a scared garbled cry. The two screamed at each other in terror, then she began shouting.

"What is it? Getaway!" Jasper realising Scoff was missing clambered over Lucy who threw herself back as arms and legs crawled over her. Jasper got to his feet and turned to the screaming woman, her arms up as she tried to get as far away from the creature on her lap as possible. Scoff saw Jasper appear from behind the seat, got to his feet and dove into the relative safety of Jaspers arms who caught him like a rugby ball. At that moment, a balding slightly pudgy ticket attendant slid open the door and turned his back to the carriage to shut it again. Billie spotting the ticket attendant threw a blanket to Jasper who wrapped Scoff up as quickly as possible. Lucy slid to the window seat and Jasper quickly sat down into the seat next to her and proceeded to put Scoff to his chest bouncing him up and down calmingly.

The ticket attendant heard the commotion from the fiery-haired woman and ran over to her attention.

"Mam are you okay?" said the attendant.

"The, the, the baby" she looked at him wide eyed, her bottom lip trembling as she tried to process what she just saw, "green, with y-y-yellow eyes", she muttered.

144

The fiery haired woman looked up with wild eyes to the attendant, her hair standing on end like a petrified ginger cat. The attendant looked to the bundle of blankets in Jasper's arms then to Lucy who leant forward and made a gesture waving a finger around her ear with an eyebrow raised. The attendants' eyes shifted to Billie who looked to the attendant with accusing eyes and lifted his thumb and pinky of one hand and began to do a drinking motion tilting his hand back and forth, before nodding his head. The Attendant understood, the woman was nuts and completely drunk, he nodded and turned to the woman.

"Mam, do you want to come with me to the front carriage. It's nice and quite there, perfect for someone like you".

"No there was a monster, I swear! The baby, it's, it's not a baby.

"I'm sure it's not, but you know where there are no monsters? At the front".

The woman nodded, shaking as she got to her feet and he put his arm around her as they made their way down the carriage. The woman looked back to see the yellow eyes staring at her from over the seat, she screamed again and began to whimper. Jasper quickly hid Scoff. The attendant looked back and saw Billie making the same hand signal as Lucy had, waving his finger around his ear. The attendant signed.

"Come on mam, let's get you to the front". The other passengers looked on to the crazy wild-haired woman in confusion as she was escorted out of the carriage.

An elderly man turned from his seat to look at the three. "Heavy drinker", said Billie looking at the man. The elderly man nodded and turned back around.

Relieved Jasper bounced Scoff unconsciously resuming his fatherly role. Billie released a breath he didn't realise he was holding and let his body slump on the chair.

"That was close guys, too damn close", said Billie.

"I hear that. It scared the hell out of me". Lucy said with the kind of smile that you would only get if you had just had a brush with death and are overwhelmed with relief that you can't help but smile.

"Guys, guys, I think this is our stop!" said Jasper bobbing Scoff. Scoffs stomach then made a loud rumbling noise which startled Jasper who looked down. He spotted Scoffs hungry eyes, the large golden globes looking up at him. "Bud, I think we need to get you some food, I'll get you something as soon as we get off the train alright bud?". Scoff grumbled in annoyance.

A tannoy sounded through the train "Next stop! Bodmin General station". At that moment people from all over the carriage that had arrived whilst they slept stirred to life.

"Okay guys let's get out of here, nice and slow". All three slowly began to move into action, picking up their stuff then moving to the front of the carriage to grab their bags. The door slid open with a hiss and the three stepped out onto an old-fashioned stone platform. The cream eaves curved and bounced from one end of the platform to the other. All along the platform hung hanging baskets full to the brim of brightly coloured pelargoniums, the ground dark beneath them as drips of water occasionally patted the ground. Billie looked to the end of the platform where a waist-high tacky ceramic train conductor stared at him with a manic smile.

"We're not in Kansas anymore. This place gives me the creeps", said Billie.

Lucy looked to the beautifully planted baskets "are you kidding me? This place is lovely. Look at the little conductor at the end of the platform, he's so cute".

"Cute? That thing's creepy! It's like one of those dogs you see at supermarkets. The little statues they always

146

have in the entrance asking for money with their eyes all wonky. I'd give it money just to get rid of it".

"So does everything scare you or is it just inanimate objects and anything that moves?"
Billie scowled at Lucy unaware that one of the hanging baskets was dripping water on his shoulder.

"Billie, you might want to move. The hanging bask…" Billie cut her off.

"Oh yeah! The flowers are coming to get me now are they! I'm not scared of everything, urghhh what's that?" He said feeling a splashing against one side of his face and backing away from the flowers.

"I think they've just been watered" Said Lucy.

"Urghhh why didn't you tell me? My shoulders soaked". Said Billie.
Lucy face palmed. Billie looked down the end of the platform and he saw that the red-haired lady was shaking as she was being helped off the train by the conductor.

"Wow, Scoff really did a number on her didn't he Jasper. Jasper?" Said Billie. He looked around to see Jasper disappearing towards the exit.

Jasper, ignoring both Billie and Lucy had walked off the train and made straight for the exit, Rucksack over his shoulder and Scoff in his arms. Scoff was beginning to wriggle in his arms. He had the horrible feeling that Scoff could detonate at any moment. Billie and Lucy hurried after him, their bags almost falling off as they ran.

"Jasper slow down!" Billie shouted.
Jasper swung open a small picket fence at the side of the station and ran down some steps to the main street. Billie and Lucy caught up to him looking a little dishevelled.

"Sorry guys I had to get out of there as soon as I could. This little guy is hungry, and if I've learned anything with him staying with me the past couple of days, is that he's a nightmare when he's hungry". Jasper looked around the street. Through passing cars, Jasper spotted a butcher just down the road. "Guys follow me, I've got an idea".

Chapter Thirteen: Let's have a Butchers?

A bright white light from fluorescent tubes illuminated an immaculate white room. Dark red meat of numerous animal corpses filled the fridges. A large pale man stood at the back of the shop, with a knife so big Lurtz would have issues carrying it. He slammed the large knife into the ribs of a once large animal, now reduced to meat. The bones made an audible crunch as the shards of bone and grizzle slid against the butcher's knife. The large man turned to see three teenagers rush into the shop.

"Good morning, now how can I help you three?" said the large man through his thick moustache. Jasper looked at the man in front of him, his eyes then wondered around the fridges filled with meat and fish. Billie's face fogged the glass as he stared at a large fisheye, which he could have sworn was staring back at him. The bundle of blankets on Jasper's chest began to make a sniffing sound as Scoff caught the scent of meat.

"I'd like some meat please!" Said Jasper with the most natural smile he could muster, which ended up looking extremely forced.

"Ha! Some meat?" chuckled the butcher. "Well, you've come to the right place. I hope you won't mind me asking, but what kind of meat can I do you for?" he said, his strong Cornish accent evident. Scoff began to wriggle frantically in the blankets and Jasper had to turn away from the man just to keep Scoff hidden. Scoff's arm managed to free itself and he grabbed onto it, shoving it back into the blankets. He turned back to the man smiling.

"You know some meat, anything really?" Said Jasper struggling to keep Scoff contained.

"Are you alright there young sir?" said the large man trying to look over Jaspers shoulder to the struggling child.

Lucy cut in front of Jasper and confronted the man. "We'd like a bag of meat, we don't really mind what it is, see it's for our pet lizard, he'll eat anything" she paused, "and I mean anything".

"Oh well, you know I do have a load of offcuts, which generally will just get thrown away. For some reason, people don't tend to eat it. See now me personally I don't mind. But that there average Joe won't touch the stuff" he disappeared into the back room. Then returned carrying a transparent bag filled with red and white animal parts. He lifted the bag and dropped it on the counter with a squelch. "Ear you can have that for free" he then looked to Jasper, who was still struggling with Scoff. "He's a strong'n that little one isn't he", said the man.

Lucy looked over to Jasper struggling with Scoff then back to the butcher. "You have absolutely no idea. Thank you so much for this, it's a massive help" she said hefting up the bag of meat. "I hope you have a wonderful day", said Lucy as the three left the butchers.

He watched the three leave as the child wriggled frantically in Jasper's arms "Aye and you three", said the butcher. He lifted his meaty hand and rubbed at his chin, "quite the kid". He then turned back to the counter, lifted his massive knife and slammed it into another chunk of flesh.

"It's great he gave us all that for free", Said Billie. His face turned to the other two with a wry smile "shame it smelt so 'offal'" he sniggered. Jasper laughed and instantly became more serious.

"We need to get somewhere a little more secluded, and fast. I can't keep this guy under control for much longer. He's wriggling all over the place". He spotted a small, wooded alleyway not far from them. "Look over there!" the three then made their way over to the alley. They were extremely lucky no one was walking by as they failed to look inconspicuous. Blankets fell everywhere as Scoff struggled with Jasper, Lucy carried a bag of meat and Billie just ran behind them frantically picking up blankets.

The alley was walled on one side with a slope that had a row of trees on the other. The sun poked through them with a warm light that dappled along the wall. Jasper looked around making sure the coast was clear.

"Okay, this will do".

He bent down and Scoff splayed out of the blankets, instantly jumping to two feet, turning to Jasper and making an angry garbling shout. Jasper's stomach clenched as he felt Scoffs eyes bore into his. Lucy handed the bag to Jasper who took it and squatted down in front of Scoff.

"Hey bud, I'm really sorry about keeping you in those blankets, don't worry you won't be in them for much longer I promise". He then reached into the bag and the meat squelched as he put his hand into the squelching pile to pull out a strand of red and white flesh. Scoffs demeaner changed and his lips smacked together as he saw Jasper remove a piece of meat and fat from the bag. Jasper threw the meat to scoff who caught and swallowed it happily. Jasper reached into the bag again and threw Scoff some more.

Lucy looked at her phone, checking the bus times. "Guys we're going to have to get a move on, the bus taking us to the farm is leaving in ten minutes".

"No worries, we'll leave just after this guy has finished eating. I don't want him freaking out again. Halfway through the bag Jasper stopped feeding Scoff and handed the bag to Billie who took it reluctantly. Jasper looked at the fluff ball, who released a joyous burp and sat with a tiny thud. "Alright buddy, we're going to have to wrap you up again, it's about an hour then you'll be right back out, Okay?" he said picking up Scoff, who grumbled wearily.

The three made their way around the corner to see their bus already waiting on the road. The door closed with a hiss as the last passenger walked on. Frantically they all ran, their rucksacks bouncing from side to side. Billie waving the bag of meat around as he ran. As they reached the bus, Lucy knocked frantically on the door. The driver, a stubbly man in his fifties, looked at them with tired eyes. Unblinking he re-opened the door, Jasper and Lucy ran straight through the door and onto the back of the bus, the stubbled man looked back at them about to object when Billie stood in front of him happily.

"Three tickets to the moors please", he said with a smile on his face. The stubbled man looked at the beaten-up teen in front of him.

"That'll be nine-pound sixty", he sighed.

"Not a problem at all good sir" Billie splatted the bag of meat on the driver's counter and rummaged in his pockets. The man looked at the meat, mouth open in disbelief. Then looked back up to Billie who handed him a ten-pound note. "Thanks! Keep the change", said Billie as he cheerily swiped the meat bag from the counter and disappeared to the back of the bus. Parking himself on the back seat he looked to Jasper and Lucy. "Almost there! I have to admit I'm pretty excited", said Billie, smiling at the other two.

"Don't get too excited, we've got loads of walking to do yet. We might not even find them for a couple of days. That and we never know what the farmers going to be like", Said Jasper.

Lucy leaned forward "I'm pretty excited too. I really hope Scoff can catch their scent. If he can't, we might end up wandering around aimlessly for days".

Jasper Smiled to Lucy. "Have some faith, it will be fine. He's like a bloodhound, as soon as he catches the scent of food, he won't stop till he gets his hand on it. When he catches the scent of the other bogarts I'm sure it'll be the same. Worst comes to the worst we could just walk as far as we can into the moors away from any roads. If they're around it's likely that they'll be as far away from humans as they can, right? Otherwise, they would have been found by now".

Lucy nodded "Makes sense. So first we'll see the farmer, if that doesn't work, we'll head straight to the most secluded part of the moors and if we find more bogarts on the way we'll say goodbye to Scoff and leave him with them. If we don't find any other bogarts there, what will we do?"

"I guess we'll just camp out there and keep searching before heading home on Sunday. Mr J said that the bogarts definitely live there so it might be that we have to just leave him there?" Said Jasper. He knew he didn't want to just leave him on the moors by himself, and knew he wanted to get him back to his own species but there was a part of him that had begun to really love Scoff and Jasper knew he was going to miss him.

Lucy looked to Scoff in his arms who looked at her with golden eyes.

"It would be a shame if we had to leave him on the moors by himself".

The bus slowed to give way to an oncoming car before accelerating again and pulling the teens back to their seats. Jasper looked down to Scoff, the thought of leaving him weighing heavily on his mind. The bus emerged from the town and drove on into rolling hills, where trees became sparse and only sheep and horses roamed. Jasper looked back to the town which was already disappearing into the distance. It was like a line was drawn in the land and on one side was the town, trees, houses, shops, and people, on the other was vast heathland, gorse, heather and the bogarts.

Twenty minutes later Lucy spotted a sign for Priddacombe Downs, and they began passing sporadic fields surrounded by unique Cornish hedges. What makes 'Cornish hedges' unique is that they aren't exactly hedges at all. They are in fact walls which like most walls are part stone, but these are part earth sculpture and part planter. The walls are a ramshackle mess of stones piled on top of each other with soil filling the gaps. It's in these soil gaps where the plants and flowers burst out adding a dash of colour to the Cornish hedge row. Lucy lifted her head peering through the front window searching for the indicator she needed. There it was. They were fast approaching a small stone bus shelter not much bigger than a bathtub. Reaching up she pressed her thumb to the yellow stop button and a pleasant bell dinged around the bus. The bus began to slow to a stop, it hissed as the pressure was released from the air brake system.

Billie and Lucy got straight out of their seats and Jasper froze staring down the bus, the door seemed so far away. His heart raced in his chest; he was potentially about to abandon Scoff. The idea made him sick to his stomach, he'd never abandoned anything and even though Scoff was from here and it was better for him, it still felt to him like he was his dad. Abandoning his wife and children, his responsibilities. He thought that if Scoff were a fox or a badger that he wouldn't feel like this, the issue wasn't that he was just releasing it back into the wild, he understood that. It was the fact that Scoff had saved his life, stayed with his family, he even got on so well with Maxie, he was a part of the family. Jasper felt a lump start to appear in his throat and he looked down to Scoff, who looked back to him with his curious golden eyes. Lucy turned to see Jasper unmoving on the back seat.

"Come on Jasper lets go, we've got to get moving!" said Lucy waving her hand encouragingly.

Jasper swallowed the lump in his throat and pushed ahead. He walked down the bus his body feeling stiff, and alien. He reached the door, instantly his skin tightened as he felt the cold breeze bite at his cheeks. Walking down each step, he felt the wind wrap around his body pulling him out of the bus and onto the moor. The muddy gravel crunched under his boots, and he squinted as the wind and light forced his eyes to adjust. The bus made a loud sigh as its doors folded shut and it moved away heading to its next stop. Jasper turned to watch the woeful bus drive into the distance. He then turned in line with Billie and Lucy to see the farmers home surrounded by Cornish hedges.

"Well, looks like we're one step closer to your family" said Jasper looking at the golden globes hidden in the blankets in his arms. "Now I guess we just need to find out what this farmer knows". Jasper took a deep breath then stepped forward and headed towards the gate.

Chapter Fourteen: Beautiful Destruction

The white old English farmhouse was surrounded by fields and was neatly boxed in by the Cornish hedgerows. Just outside the front door was a garden full of vibrance and colour, anyone could clearly see that it had an extraordinary amount of time and energy put into it. Bright orange dahlias and plush pink marigolds filled the flower beds as fuzzy kneed bees buzzed around them, filling their pollen baskets with the bright yellow dust then happily flying away to get their next hoard.

Lucy, Billie and Jasper who was still holding Scoff, hopped over the wooden gate at the front of the cottage and made their way through the garden. The garden was like a waist-high maze of flowers and hedges, so much so it occurred to Billie that if he was any shorter, he might get lost. Jasper looked around and found a well-trimmed hedge which he could hide from the house. Crouching behind it he placed Scoff on the floor and unravelled him from the blankets, the little green monster rolled out, landed on his bum like a teddy bear and instantly looked to his left where a dahlia hung close to his nose. He sniffed at the flower before grabbing the delicate head, tearing it from its stem and throwing it on the floor.

"Well, that was a little unnecessary?" said Lucy watching Scoff.
Scoff then dropped his back into the flower and began wriggling and garbling as he rubbed his back all over the flower, crushing its scent into his fur. He kicked with each twist of his body.

"Okay stay here little buddy, we're just going to go to talk to the farmer. We won't be too long". Said Jasper.

"So, he will just rub himself on anything? Scoff you used to have standards, can't believe your rubbing on flowers instead of rubbish. You disgust me!" Said Billie. Lucy and Jasper both smiled.

"He'll be fine here by himself, won't he?" Asked Lucy.

"Yeah, he'll be fine. Won't you Scoff?" Said Jasper. Scoff promptly ignored him and continued to rub his whole body all over the flattened flower.

"Here goes nothing", said Jasper and the three left Scoff and headed to the front door of the farmhouse.

They approached the large heavy wooden door. The door was a dark stained wood with large black hinges that stretched across the door. Jasper reached out to the door knocker. The knocker was painted black iron, with a boar head holding a large iron handle in its mouth. Grabbing the iron handle Jasper wrapped at the door three times.

"This place is beautiful, I've never seen anything like it", Said Lucy.

The three looked at each other as they could hear someone moving behind the door and they heard the voice of an old woman.

"I'll be one minute, gosh darn it where'd I put that key". There was more of a clatter behind the door "Oh there it is".

They heard the woman insert the key into the door and with a click, it opened. The old lady pulled the heavy door open revealing the three teenagers.

"Hello there, how can I help you three", Said the old woman. Her hair was a swirl of silvery curls, she was short with a cream cardigan that wrapped around her shoulders. Jasper realised his stupidity that he hadn't even considered how many farms would actually be in this area, he swore there couldn't be that many, he remembered having a little look when he and Lucy were discussing their plan. He thought and hoped that there were only around

157

five. He resolved that if this wasn't the one then they'd just have to move onto the next, and the next until they found it.

"Hi, we were just walking in the area and wondered if you knew anything about the sheep that have been going missing around here?" Said Jasper

Her face darkened. "Not you too, my husband has been hounded enough by reporters and locals thinking he's gone mad". Said the old lady about to shut the door.

Lucy stepped forward "No, no, no we're not reporters, we were just walking in the area and spotted a dead sheep not far from here and hoped you might know something about it. I have to be honest, after seeing it, I feel a little queasy".

"Oh no! Really? Not again. You know it's been happening so much recently" said the old lady opening the door again. "Come on in, tell me all about it" The old lady stepped towards Lucy and put her arm around her leading her into the house. "Shut the door behind you", She said to Billie and Jasper with a warm smile.

"That was brilliant", said Billie under his breath to Jasper as he walked into the house, clearly impressed by Lucy's quick thinking. Jasper took one last look back at Scoff who was still rolling around on the pancake-like flowers before following Billie into the house and shutting the large wooden door.

The low-ceilinged living room had dark wooden beams that streaked across the painted white ceiling that both Jasper and Lucy had to duck for. Inside was a sofa which faced the garden and to its left were two armchairs which faced the TV in the corner of the room. In the centre was a mahogany and glass table. The old woman shuffled into the living room carrying a shaking tray with four empty cups, a small jug of milk, a pot of tea and a small bowl of sugar with curved sides that cradled the spoon.

"Oh, let me help you with that", Said Billie, standing and taking the tray from the lady and placing it onto the table.

"Thank you, my child", Said the old lady, letting Billie take the tray. She then planted herself into one of the armchairs next to Lucy who had also taken up residence in the other. The old Lady reached over and held Lucy's hand. "What's your name dear? Mine is Mary, Mary Barric. Tell me your name then you must tell me what happened". Said Mary.

"Oh, and dear I like mine with milk and one", said Mary with a little glare to Billie, who gave a confused look to Jasper.

"I'll have milk and one too thanks Billie", Said Jasper smirking.

"Oh yes, same for me thank you Billie", Said Lucy, the sight of the fictional dead sheep clearly getting too much for her.

Reluctantly Billie stood up and started to make the tea. He lifted the lid to the teapot and peered into it.

"My name is Lucy, that there is Jasper and making the tea is Billie". They both gave a smile and a little wave.

"Lovely to meet you all. So dear tell me what happened".

Lucy sighed.

"Oh, but it is awful".

"That's fine my girl it's been happening a lot around here, just tell me what happened".

Lucy masterfully choked back tears.

"Well, we were walking up from that lovely little station in Bodmin, then you know through that little wooded area. Then onto the moors because the area around here is just delightful. We came over a beautiful little stream and there it was... dead".

"Oh, my dear that is awful". Said Mary.

Billie was just about to pour the tea into the cup when Mary turned.

"What do you think you're doing?" Said Mary abruptly. Billie froze.

"Milk first then tea. I don't know where you're from but we're not animals here. Milk always goes first. Didn't your mother teach you anything?" Said Mary.

"Oh yes of course how could I forget", said Billie gritting his teeth.

Lucy stifled a laugh as Mary looked back to her.

"The sheep my dear, did it have any markings? If it did, we might be able to work out if it was one of ours".

Lucy paused thinking.

"Oh no I couldn't look at it, it was just so terrible", Said Lucy.

"What about you?" She shot a look to Jasper and suddenly he inhaled some of the tea Billie had just given him. Coughing, he answered.

"I don't know. I think it was too much for us, I'm not one for blood. Makes me queasy",

She looked at Billie.

"Me too, terribly queasy indeed".

"You town folk are a bunch of soggy towels. I bet you don't even know where your meat comes from". Said Mary.

Billie sat next to Jasper and muttered "Pretty sure I know where chicken and fish come from".

"So, Mary, what has been happening to the sheep around here? I think I saw your husband on the news" Asked Lucy politely sipping her tea.

"Oh, it is horrible, it's been happening so much recently. I don't know what it is but from what Monty says. Monty is my husband". She leaned in close and said under her voice "See now what he says is that there's some sort of creature roaming around out there killing our sheep".

160

"Like a dog?" asked Billie.

"What!? No not like a dog you foolish boy, you think some dog could rattle me and my dear husband?" She said furiously. After that outburst Billie looked sheepish and kept his mouth shut. "No, you see my husband thinks it's some sort of creature, like that of a monster".

"Really? Oh my, that is awful" said Lucy pressing both hands on her chest faking surprise.

"Oh yes, it is. It's been killing all around here too, not just our sheep but other farmers sheep too". Lucy was making Mary more animated with every minute. It was as if no one had believed Mary since this had happened and the stories were just pouring out of her.

Billie was listening intently to Mary's story of the first dead sheep she found killed a couple of weeks ago when Billie saw something move outside the window, his eyes widened in panic.

"God that is awful. So do you have any idea what this monster looks like?" asked Lucy.

At that Billie nudged Jasper with his foot who moved his foot away, ignored him and continued to listen to Mary's story.

"Well, you see we've had loads of attacks now, but they always seem to happen in the dead of night. So, we've not actually seen what is doing the killing. Whatever is doing it, leaves the sheep in a terrible mess, blood everywhere. It doesn't always eat the sheep either which I thought was strange for a hunting animal".

Jasper contemplated the idea of Scoff leaving food and thought back to all the times' Scoff's almost killed for food. But he did find it strange that the bogarts were leaving the dead sheep. Mr J had told them a while back about a bogart that had swallowed a deer whole then became so fat that it couldn't even move. It was strange that they'd be so messy, he'd never seen Scoff like that with his food. Then again, he did rip out the eye of the Slogolyth.

Jasper felt a hard prod in his ribs, and he turned to Billie who was staring at him.

"What?" whispered Jasper impatiently.

Billie said nothing but nodded his head to the window. Jasper's eyes took on the same bemused stare as Billies. Outside the window, he saw Scoff jumping and rolling through the flowers. Again, and again, he bounced up in full view of the window trying to catch a bee whilst covered in dahlia petals.

"What do we do?" whispered Billie.

Jasper looked over to Lucy and Mary then back to Scoff who had begun tearing up flowers and throwing them at the bee.

"So, you see it's been exceedingly difficult for us here. We have had so many of our sheep killed that Monty is out night and day trying to hunt for the creature. Sadly, he's had no luck. I have just been so worried the only thing keeping me going is my garden. Whilst he's out I just use it to keep my mind off things. It does give you such a sense of achievement seeing it all done as well". Said Mary.

"It really is a lovely garden. We all thought so when we walked up the drive, didn't we guys"

Billie and Jasper turned their heads around to look at Mary as they tried to hide their dismay.

"Yep wonderful", Said Jasper.

"Lovely" said Billie.

"Very nice" said Jasper

"I loved the orange and pink ones", Said Billie.

Lucy could see them both sweating and raised an eyebrow. Mary smiled.

"Oh, they are lovely, aren't they? They're called dahlias and they are definitely my favourite. Not too easy to look after and when they blossom, they are beautiful".

At that moment Jasper saw Scoff launch himself into the air after the bee with a mouth full of dahlias.

"Uh-oh", said Billie.

Jasper shot him a look, trying to shut him up but then realised that although he was looking out the window, he wasn't looking at Scoff. Jasper turned to look where Billie was staring, and he felt a pit in his stomach as he spotted a cloud of dust rising into the air. A black land rover was making its way down the dirt track towards the farm.

"I do love seeing bees buzzing around all the flowers". said Mary. Abruptly Jasper stood up from the couch.

"It has been lovely talking to you Mary but I'm afraid we have to leave. Thank you so much for your hospitality".

"That's right it's, it's been lovely" said Billie standing up and darting out of the door.

"Lucy, we have to go". Said Jasper pulling at her arm.

"What, why?" she said, starting to stand up.

"Because it just occurred to me that we left our dog at home too long, he's probably starving" said Jasper with a wide-eyed conspiratorial look. Taking his hint Lucy stood and turned to Mary who was already beginning to stand a little confused.

"I'm so sorry Mary, I completely forgot too. Thank you so much for your hospitality and telling us all about what happened, it sounds like you've had a real hard time at least you've had your garden to keep you going".

"Thank you dear, you know if any of you are in the area again, please feel free to pop in".

"Aww thank you". Said Lucy and they embraced each other in a hug.

At that moment outside the window Scoff, now covered in pink and orange, bounced up into the air and with a garbled yell and snapped repeatedly at a bumblebee buzzing over the decimated flowerbed.

"Oh my god!" said Lucy seeing the fury fruit salad flying past the window.

"What? what is it?" Said Mary trying to release herself from the hug, but Lucy just held her tighter.

"Oh! You are just so kind and generous", Said Lucy gritting her teeth as Scoff bounced up again but this time spitting dahlias at the bumblebee.

"Lucy, we have to go", said Jasper.

"Okay, okay. Mary, stay strong and no matter what happens you can always start over. Okay?" said Lucy releasing the hug and resting her hands on Mary's arms.

"Yes, of course. Are you three alright? You're not in trouble, are you?"

"Not yet no", said Jasper hurrying out of the room.

Billie opened the front door to see flowers scattering the path and lawn. He then saw Scoff who was bouncing up and down in the middle of a flattened flower bed trying to catch another bee which was circling over his head. The land rover pulled up to the farm and the drivers' door opened. Billie felt his neck shrink and his shoulders tense as he saw Mary's husband step from the land rover wearing flat cap, khaki trousers and a green fleece. Farmer Barrack looked on in horror at his wife's destroyed garden.

"Mary! What the hell happened?!"

"Bye", Said Lucy as she ran from the living room and to the front door. Shocked Mary slowly followed her, hobbling as fast as she could. Jasper bumped into Billie and looked to the garden. Plants had been uprooted and launched all over. All the flowers had been beheaded and their beautiful petals were now scattering the floor. In the centre of one of the flower beds Scoff stood looking glumly into the sky as the bee had enough with him and had flown away.

"Scoff!" shouted Jasper.

The farmer turned to Jasper and Billie fury in his eyes. He then looked over to the colourful fury mess in the centre of his garden and his eyes widened in horror. He began backing away to the land rover.

"Mary! Mary! It's the monster! Mary, it's in the garden!"

Lucy bumped into Jasper and Billie to see the carnage in the garden and see farmer Barric running to the boot of his land rover. With a creak and a thud, he hastily opened it and reaching in he brought out a large Remington shotgun. Jasper spotted the farmer hastily loading shells into the weapon.

"Scoff!" Jasper shouted and he sprinted into the garden. The farmer cocked the shotgun and took aim at the creature. Scoff looked at Jasper, tongue happily splayed out to one side of his mouth. a loud crack came from the shotgun. Jasper stumbled at the sound. His legs flailed like he was moving too fast for them to keep up. Leaning forward he scooped up Scoff like a rugby ball and ran to the other side of the garden stopping briefly by one of the Cornish hedgerows. He turned to the farmer whose shotgun was in a deadlock between himself and Billie. Billie was only around two-thirds of the size of the farmer but was putting up a good fight. Likely because he'd taken the farmer by surprise. The shotgun fired again into the air.

"Oh my god Billie!" shouted Lucy as she ran from the cottage. Jasper and Scoff saw Billies struggle with the farmer end abruptly, as Lucy vaulted the garden gate like a cat launching herself at the farmer. Her fist clenched, she hit the farmer square in the jaw with a devastating right hook, knocking him to the ground. Landing on two feet she panted then after a moment a searing pain swelled in her knuckles.

"Ahhh my hand!" She shouted.

Billie stood holding the shotgun as the farmer rolled around on the ground holding his face.

"You broke my jaw! You broke my bloody jaw!" Screamed the farmer. Well, that is what they all thought he said anyway, it did sound very slurred.

"Guys! We've got to get out of here!" shouted Jasper as he and Scoff vaulted the Cornish hedgerow. Billie looked at Jasper then to the shotgun in his hands. Feeling the cold steel weighing heavy in his hands he threw it in some gorse next to the Land Rover and sprinted over to the house with Lucy. Grabbing theirs and Jasper's bag they ran through the garden. Mary came to the front door of the house to see her beautiful dahlias scattered across her decimated garden.

"What, what, what happened?" She said in almost a whisper as she bent down to pick up a tiny petal which had landed on her doorstep. Rubbing it between her fingers she saw with tears in her eyes the teenagers running through the garden jumping the hedgerow. Her mouth was left open in sorrow and dismay as Lucy called back to her.

"I'm so sorry Mary, this was never meant to happen, but we believe you about the monster! Don't ever listen to anyone saying it's not true" Said Lucy as she vaulted the hedge throwing Jasper's bag to him. "Don't leave this behind again!" She shouted at Jasper berating him.

"Oh, I'm sorry I forgot about a bag, I was a little preoccupied with saving Scoff from getting his head blown off!" Said Jasper as he grabbed it.

"That's enough! Let's just get the hell out of here!" shouted Billie. They all began to run as fast as they could through the gorse not realising that Scoff was not with them.

166

Scoff stood on the hedgerow covered in pollen and squashed petals and looked at the distraught old woman on the porch of the cottage. Tilting his head, he noticed that in her hands she was rubbing a petal between her fingers. With a little bum wiggle, he darted off the wall and ran over to the woman. Mary stood staring at Scoff trembling. She began to step backwards away from the bogart until her back hit the doorframe and she gasped.

"G, g, get away from me" She stammered.
At her words Scoff halted on all fours only a few meters away from her. With a sigh, he ran to a flower bed, picked up a single dahlia and put it in his mouth like a rose. He then scurried over to her, stood on two legs and gave her a bow as he placed the flower on the porch in front of Mary. Her terrified expression turned to one more like that of confusion as the little critter placed the flower in front of her. Her eyes then followed the creature as it scarpered over the hedge after the teenagers. She reached down and picked up the flower. Rolling the stem between her fingers she looked at the strange pollen covered creature then back to the flower. Her and Monty weren't going crazy, monsters were real. She then heard a moan coming from the garden gate as she saw Monty push it open, one hand holding his face.

"Those bloody kids, are you alright?" He moaned.
Mary's face then changed again to one of worry.

"Monty! Oh my, what happened?" said the old lady as she hurried over to her husband.

"That was too bloody close guys!" Said Jasper as he ran to a stop, trying to catch his breath.

"Yeah, too damn close", Said Billie coming to a stop just after Jasper. Lucy came up last just behind Jasper and Billie.

"Hey Luce, good thinking earlier saying about the sheep", said Jasper with a bit of a grimace as he tried to stretch out a stitch. "If you didn't say that I don't think she ever would have told us about what's been happening. Also, I think you and Billie saved my life back there. Billie if you didn't grab that gun, I'd be a goner right now and Luce you sucker-punched that guy into next Sunday! Thank you, I owe you both my life and I think Scoff probably does too".

"Don't worry about it", Said Billie waving his hand as if it were nothing.

"Well looks like you'll just have to owe me one", said Lucy as she poked him in the ribs. Jasper flinched and grinned. Lucy then took her rucksack off her back and pulled out a map of the moors. She began scanning over it "So if I remember rightly, we should be around here" she pointed to a section of land not too far from some little squares which Jasper assumed must have been the farm.

"As there have been so many attacks around here, they've got to be close by. I think we should head further into the moors but in line with the farm to the road. Fingers crossed Scoff should have caught the scent of the other bogarts by then and he'll help point us in the right direction" said Jasper pointing to a green hill surrounded by gradient lines further into the moors.

"Hey, where is the little guy?" The three then began looking around them, when they heard panting as Scoff bounced up the path to them. Jasper bent down to greet the creature when it jumped up into his arms and twisted making himself comfortable. "Ha! Hey there buddy, it's good to see you too". Jasper smiled down to Scoff. Gritting his teeth he turned to Billie and Lucy "I reckon we head to that little hill, if we don't find any trail by then we should make camp for the night".

"It is getting pretty late, we should get going", Said Billie. Jasper looked at the sun fairly low in the sky and he remembered something that he'd seen watching on a survival program when he was younger. Placing down

Scoff, he stretched out his arms towards the sun one hand above the other. He then with his hands horizontal faced his palms towards himself and counted how many fingers were between the horizon and the sun. The sun was just above both of Jasper's hands.

"Billie's right we've only got around two and half hours left until the sun hits the horizon", Said Jasper placing his hands on his hips.

Lucy raised an eyebrow "Okay Bear Grylls".

"I could have told you that" said Billie pointing at his watch that said six-thirty.

"What?" Jasper shrugged.

Chapter Fifteen: Assault Gorse of Daggers and Thorns

The once warm setting sun had been covered by a dark curtain as increased winds drew stormy clouds overhead. The three walked through winding trails of bog and gorse that whipped around slashing left and right. Every few meters there would be new deep sections of bog, which though perfectly clear had a grim yellowy brown tinge, that made Jasper wonder if it was even water at all. Scoff walked on all fours close to Jasper, his large golden globes now like golden slits, his eyes scouring every bush and trail they crossed. The wind pulled Scoffs fur like an ocean's current pulling it in all directions. He walked fast but low to the ground, and not with his usual bouncy pace. Scoff had brushed past so many bushes and jumped in so many puddles his coat had even lost its colourful pollen from the farmer's garden. Lucy held the map and compass, confidently she was in front of the group walking them to the small hill indicated on the map. Billie, Scoff and Jasper were all hanging back, following Lucy's lead and observing their thorny surroundings.

"I just don't get how there's so much of the stuff? Why is it so sharp? I mean what's the point? No pun intended" said Billie as the thorns again poked through his trousers, stabbing his legs.

"Stop whining Billie", said Lucy "I'm trying to concentrate".

"Urgghhh, I mean look at this" Billie lifted his trouser leg exposing tiny red lines all over his ankles as he hopped alongside Jasper.

"Ouch! Yeah, at least your legs are matching your face now" Jasper smirked. Billie instantly scowled at Jasper. "To be fair though, it looks like the bruising has gone down a little. I bet it doesn't feel anywhere near as bad as it did". Said Jasper walking along trying to avoid each boggy section of the path. Billie prodded at his face, feeling the swollen muscle.

"Yeah, it doesn't actually feel as bad as it did, still swollen though".

Japer looked down watching Scoff. His demeanour had changed and was now completely different to the little terror he knew. It was like he was a different animal altogether. Scoff seemed on edge and Jasper could have sworn he saw fear there. Normally he'd be climbing all over him or so far ahead they'd be running to catch up, but now he was quiet and timid.

"Guys I think somethings wrong". Said Jasper.

"What do you mean?" Asked Lucy.

"Somethings wrong with Scoff, he's not acting like himself. Look at him he's on edge", Said Jasper.

Lucy looked over to Scoff "I'm sure it's just because he's back in his home, he's probably just confused because he doesn't understand how he got back".

Jasper hopped over a bog and ran beside Lucy and spoke conspiratorially to her, "but don't you think he'd be happy to be home. Watch any video with an animal being released back into the wild and they go completely nuts with excitement. Ever seen a fox get re-introduced to the wild? They shoot off and bounce around all over the place".

Billie shouted over to Lucy and Jasper "Urgh, guys I think you'd better look at this!"

Jasper and Lucy looked over to see Billie almost completely hidden by gorse.

"Billie, what are you doing?" Shouted Lucy through the heavy wind.

Billie huffed impatiently, "just come here!"

Jasper jumped over some boggy patches to Billie, Lucy was following close behind folding up the map and putting it in her backpack. Jaspers eyes widened and Lucy threw her hands over her mouth. In front of the teens lead on its side was a moorland pony, its strong body lifeless on the soft ground. Jasper squatted observing the body, he placed his hand on the animal's hind leg. Pressing firmly, he felt through the fur to the animals' skin, it felt cool to the touch. Sighing, he placed his hand on his knee and walked around to the animal's large head. Squatting again he observed the neck of the animal, it's trachea had been torn out and blood was still seeping into the bog next to it. The blood didn't turn the water red instantly, it first was wispy like a drop of milk in an unstirred tea, settling to the bottom. Jasper examined the eyes of the animal, lifeless but not yet cloudy. Lucy watched Scoff as he Padded his claws over the body of the Pony and sniffed at the gaping wound in the pony's neck, she could not help but walk away to try and hold in the contents of her stomach. Billie looked at Jasper concerned.

"Jasper, I'm worried, you don't think this was a bogart, do you?" Said Billie.

"It's been all over the news, animal attacks on the moors, I was so sure it was the bogarts. But look at this, its throats torn cleanout, there is no way a bogart could have done that to a pony, to a sheep maybe, but not like this". He looked to the bulk of the Pony and saw five bloody gouges on its shoulders. "Look at those indents there, they almost look like claw marks, and not claw marks from something small like Scoff".

"If it's not from a bogart then what's it from?" Asked Billie his eyes darting between Jasper and the dead animal.

"I don't know" Jasper said, but he was already forming a surprisingly good idea in his head. "Whatever it was that did this, isn't far away though, this happened recently. What I don't understand is why the thing that did this didn't eat it after it killed it". Jasper looked at Scoff and a memory came back to him.

"Guys", he said a little louder to also grab Lucy's attention, who was standing back trying to not look at the downed animal. "A while back, Mr J was telling us about animal rehabilitation in class. He said that he knew a guy that spent weeks slaving away cleaning birds that were caught in an oil spill. There were guillemots, razorbills and even puffins, whilst they were cleaning them, he had to bandage his arms, they fought back so hard biting his arms whenever they got a chance. When they were rehabilitating them, these little wild birds were hard as nails. When they were better, he took them back out to their natural habitat in a cardboard box. Then at the edge of a cliff face where they live he'd open the box and as soon as they could see the sea they'd fly out, free as a bird". Billie and Lucy looked at Jasper not yet understanding his reference.

"One day he was releasing a puffin, but when he opened the box, the puffin sat on the edge. Suddenly it turned around frantically trying to get back into the box, trying to stay with him". Jasper looked up to Lucy and Billie "The animal had to go back into the wild, so he picked up the struggling animal and threw it to sea. It flew for its life, but moments later a peregrine falcon swooped down and instantly killed the puffin". Lucy and Billie stared at him in silence. "What if Scoff never wanted to come back? What if he was driven from here by something else and we've just brought him back to whatever it is he's running from? What if we're bringing him to his falcon?"

Scoff stopped suddenly, eyes darted around wide open, his large antenna-like ears searching the surroundings. He sniffed at the air, then dove from the pony, splashing in a puddle before running around the gorse and up the track towards a bare windswept tree at the top of the hill. Jasper threw his bag to the ground and ran as fast as he could to catch up to Scoff.

"Scoff stop!" he shouted as he ran splashing through puddles.

Billie and Lucy shared worried glances and quickly followed suit dropping their bags to the ground and running after Jasper. Scoff bounded as fast as his legs could carry him covering meters with each stride. In front of him below a bare, leafless, windswept tree was a collection of large mossy boulders surrounded by gorse. In the centre of the boulders was a small cave opening. Jasper caught a glimpse of Scoff as he disappeared down into the cave mouth. Jasper ran after him and then came to an abrupt stop. At the foot of the entrance, he saw a large paw print heading into the cave. He stood up straight and took a deep breath. Placing one hand onto the cold wet stone he slid down into the cramped cave. The cave wasn't completely dark, gaps in between the gorse and heather ceiling let slithers of light illuminating the dark. Jasper slid down five meters before the cave opened into an area full of mossy boulders and tree roots. Jasper looked closely around the room, dark roots crisscrossed covering the walls, he stepped closer placing his hand on the moss, it was wet and cold. Pulling his hand back, he examined it under the light rubbing his fingers together. They were covered in a thick wet red substance.

Jasper heard a snuffling from around a boulder and he took a step forward. His foot pressed on something soft, lifting it he looked down to see the severed arm of something green, with fur, dark and thick with blood. Trembling his vision began to blur as the realisation of what he was walking into hit him and he rubbed his eyes. Rounding the boulder, he dropped to his knees, his arms limp. Scoff was led in between three green fury bodies, he nuzzled at the head of one of the bodies and its head rolled turning to Jasper, its lifeless golden filled with accusation. Scoff turned to look at Jasper. With teary eyes, Scoff buried his head into the fur of the body in front of him. Jasper's palms dropped to the floor, and he felt the fur of something beneath it. Lifting his hand, he saw the small gangly body of a baby bogart, its body splayed limply on the floor. Teeth marks had punctured the baby's leg and shoulder, its head arched at a strange unnatural angle, its neck clearly broken.

Jasper looked up to Scoff, tears streaming down his face. Scoff was still crying into the body of another bogart. He lifted one knee, placing his foot on the ground and with as much effort as he could muster, he pushed himself up and walked broken over the bodies of dead bogarts to Scoff, then again fell to the ground. Scoff growled at Jasper defensively. Jasper reached a hand forward and pressed it to Scoffs shoulder where he could see a tiny scar had formed from where the car had hit him. Jasper choked and struggled to inhale, a lump was firmly stuck in his throat and his eyes streamed. Scoff began to move slowly pushing himself from the pile of bodies, Jasper reached out to him with both hands, as you would to a hurt child. Scoff crawled onto Jasper's lap and Jasper embraced him tight, his stomach lurching as they cried.

"I'm sorry, I'm so, so sorry Scoff".

For that moment everything was silent in the cave except for the dripping of water from moss. Jasper heard something out of place, a soft crack of a stick came from in front of Jasper, and he stayed perfectly still as if he hadn't heard a thing. He opened his eyes as slowly as he could, blinking through the tears. He saw something large hidden in the dark at the side of the cave, its green catlike eyes staring at him. He noticed that its shoulders began to rotate like a cat, ready to pounce.

"Jasper are you okay?" Lucy shouted from the end of the tunnel.

Startled, the beast's immensely strong legs kicked off the wet stone as it pounced at Jasper and Scoff, its eyes wild and claws outstretched. Jasper dropped to his side just out of the way with Scoff held tight in his arms. The huge black beast dove off the wall and again flew at Jasper who threw Scoff towards the exit of the cave. It slammed both its claws into Jasper's shoulders as he tried to stand. Jasper and the creature were sent hurtling back into a wall of the cave. Jaspers back hit the wall hard, suddenly followed by a crack of his skull as it hit the cave wall. The creature instantly opened its huge almost crocodile-like maw wide. Scoff rolled to his back and scrambled backwards, staring in horror at the strange creature, cat-like but with an elongated head and jaw, a remnant nightmare. Jaspers outstretched hand fumbled around the ground for anything to help him, but he reached around in vain until his fingertips felt something cold. The creature's head lurched forward, almost engulfing Jasper's head before he slammed a rock into the side of its head. Jasper screamed out in pain as the bloodied claws tore themselves away from Jasper's shoulders releasing him from the wall. The blow to the creature's head caused it to waver and fall to one side. Gritting his teeth through the pain in his shoulders Jasper pushed himself off the ground and ran as fast as he could to the exit of the cave. He stopped suddenly as the large cat-like form darted in front of him cutting off his escape. It snarled as its gums pulled back like a wolf, exposing its grotesquely long snout and large canines. Saliva dripped from its hellish jaws as it stepped on a corpse of a Bogart. Jasper steeled his resolve and his grip tightened on the rock. The beast went silent, and it turned to see Scoff scramble up the slope and out of the cave running from the beast. Its claws dug into the ground, and it pushed itself around to give chase to its tiny prey.

Billie and Lucy stood outside the cave with sorry expressions.

"Jasper, are you ok?" Shouted Lucy becoming a little impatient. At that moment an enormous roar came from the cave and both Billie and Lucy felt their bowels loosen at the sound. They looked at each other with eyes wide with terror. They were miles away from anyone or anything. They had no help, no backup, and no escape. Lucy came to an awful realisation. What were they even thinking? Coming where there had been so many deaths, Billie began frantically searching the gorse for a branch or any other kind of weapon.

"In this sea of thorns, how is there nothing here to use as a weapon?" he shouted frustrated. A low growl echoed from the cave and Lucy searched frantically for a weapon. She spotted something and picked up the only the thing she could, a large moss-covered rock. Scoff darted out of the cave, terrified and covered in blood. She had almost launched the rock at him but pulled short. A large muzzle appeared from the entrance clawing itself up and out of the cave, she slammed the rock into the creature's face. It flinched, but then turned its attention to her snapping its teeth as its claws dug into the ground. Its maw opened wide as its claws found purchase but just as it was about to pounce its jaws suddenly snapped shut and lurched backwards. Inside the cave Jasper had dropped his rock, grabbed onto the tail of the creature, and began pulling as hard as he could. It clawed frantically at the walls trying to grasp onto anything it could. But then slipped and went tumbling down the tunnel. Jasper jumped aside letting it pass, a claw swiped out and ripped at his arm. Screaming in pain he grabbed his arm and tried to drag himself up the tunnel. Billie caught sight of Jaspers hand trying to drag himself out of the cave and he jumped at it holding it tight. Just then Lucy jumped to Billie's aid, and they dragged Jasper out of the cave.

Jasper fell on his back, blood drenching his top. he looked down to the blood on his shirt then lifting his hands he noticed they were covered in black fur and a strange pink mucus like substance.

"Lucy quick!" Shouted Billie running over to a boulder to one side of the cave. Billie and Lucy both pressed against the boulder above the tunnel as a blood-curdling snarl echoed from the cave. Billie and Lucy pushed their feet firmly into the ground and the boulder went tumbling down into the cave. The snarling continued and they looked around panicking with nothing else to do. They both ran to a larger boulder on the other side of the entrance and pushed hard against it. Lucy's knuckles were white, and she screamed with all her effort, pushing her legs down through the ground until the boulder began to move. They both heaved it again and the boulder rocked, then to their relief, it rolled lodging itself tight inside the entrance of the cave blocking in the creature.

Billie cried out frantically grabbing Jasper's arm dragging him off the ground. "What the hell was that thing?"

Jasper stared at the tunnel entrance, "I have absolutely no idea. Let's get the hell out of here!" he shouted. All three of them grabbed their bags and sprinted as fast as they could from the cave with Scoff far ahead of them. Jasper looked back as a claw burst from the cave's ceiling and the beast began to tear itself free from the cave. The beast emerged, its muscled shoulders rippling as it tore itself free. Jasper spotted that the strange panther-like creature had sections of fur missing from its shoulders, exposing flesh and muscle. He looked down to the fur residue on his hands in horror and continued running as fast as he could.

The creature stared at them. Bracing its claws into the ground it then lurched its body forward and released a deafening, raspy howl. The group heard the unholy noise and their stomachs churned as they ran for their lives. Its howl ceased and the creature looked at the group distastefully then with utter disregard of the distraction in front of it the creature turned, jumped off the cave and disappeared into the gorse.

Now that the lifeless tree and the cave were long out of sight, the teens came to a reluctant but necessary stop. Scoff ran back to the teens and tugged at Jaspers trousers, ushering him to keep running.

"Scoff, I can't". He tried to catch his breath. His throat burned from the exertion. "Guys let's keep moving", He said coughing "even if it's just as a walk. The further we can get away from that thing the better". Billie and Lucy nodded in agreement, both struggling to catch their breath, then continued walking through the never-ending gorse.

"I'm not sure about you guys, but that thing looked pretty hell beasty to me", said Billie his face had lost all colour.

Lucy looked to Billie and Jasper "I'm with Billie, that thing was terrifying. It was like some cat, wolf, hybrid, thing" She looked over to Jasper who had blood covering his shoulders. She jumped to his side "Jasper your hurt!" she tried to gently hold him still, but he shrugged her off.

"I'm fine, we'll sort me out when we're all safe. We can't do anything here" he said, outright refusing to stop.

"You're bleeding?"

"It doesn't matter, we can sort it when we're safe", he said, with a sternness she'd never heard in his voice before. She stopped for a moment watching him walking away, then ran to his side.

"Alright but as soon as we get far enough away from here, I'm making sure you're alright", said Lucy.

"Alright" Jasper smiled painfully as his rucksack rubbed against his shoulders.

The night was beginning to roll in and the four had continued to walk uninterrupted, for a long while. They were beginning to tire. Stubborn as Jasper was, his movements were becoming sluggish, and he was beginning to slow. Billie looked to the other two.

"I'm not sure about you guys but I'm not staying in a tent tonight, not a hope in hell! Not with that thing running around", said Billie.

Jasper was becoming pale, and Lucy put her arm around his waist supporting him.

"I'm... alright", Jasper said hazily.

"I know you're alright, I just wanted to put my arm around you". She said holding Jasper up, keeping him moving. She looked at Billie, without saying a word. He also put his arm around Jasper. Without saying a word, they both came to the same conclusion, they needed to get Jasper to a hospital and fast.

Finally, the group managed to get themselves to a road, but where they were they had absolutely no idea. With them running for their lives and Jasper now barely conscious, Lucy hadn't even had a chance to look at the map. She reached into her pocket and checked her phone, there was no signal. Sighing she put the phone back into her pocket. In the distance, she spotted what looked to be lights shining from a small house nestled in a small woodland.

"Billie look!" She pointed to the house. He nodded and grimaced as he adjusted his grip on Jasper. The group walked slowly to the light, Billie and Lucy both supporting Jasper as much as they could. Getting closer to the house they began to see more and more trees. Billie began to feel an immense relief as they got closer and closer to the building, that was until he began to get a horrible sinking feeling as intermittent between the trees were graves. Rows and rows of them. In the dark he could not tell how many there were but there were way too many for this to be any normal kind of house.

"Lucy, have you seen the graves?" he said looking around Jaspers sagging head.

"Yes, but it doesn't matter we need to get him safe. This is our only option" she said. Ignoring Billie's hesitation, they stepped up to the door of the morgue.

Chapter Sixteen: The Mortuary

Reaching the door to the morgue Lucy raised her arm and knocked on the door three times. They waited patiently for a moment, there was no response. She knocked again.

"Please we need help! Our friend was attacked". Still no answer. Impatient she made a fist and began wrapping it against the door again and again until she heard a voice.

"Alright, alright! I'm coming!" said the voice from inside the house. A small circular light appeared in the centre of the door, "My he is in a sorry state", said the voice. Billie and Lucy looked at each other, then back to a small lens in the centre of the door.

"Please, we need help" Lucy pleaded.

There was an enormous wrenching sound then the door made a tiny click. The handle twisted and the door swung open. In the doorway was a balding older man with grey wispy hair, with a look like that of a reverend. He stepped back waving them in. They did as they were told and shuffled into the house holding Jasper. The old man pushed his entire body weight into the door, and it slowly creaked shut. He then grabbed a huge lever attached to a mechanism like what you might find on a ship or submarine and began turning it until multiple bolts clicked into place. Billie and Lucy looked at the old man astonished, the old man turned to them and shrugged.

"What? You can't ever be too careful". Said the older man. "Right let's get that sorry mess sorted", said the old man waving at Jasper. "This way! Come on don't dilly dally!" The old man then disappeared into another room. Helplessly they followed and took Jasper through to a small plain room with a camp bed at the back and a rack of towels and sheets on the side. Billie and Lucy walked Jasper's barely conscious body over to a camp bed and laid him down. The old man walked over to the bed carrying some scissors.

"Right, you two, out of the way. What was his name again?" asked the old man. The two parted for the priestly man, who knelt next to Jasper beginning to cut into his blood-soaked shirt.

"His names Jasper. I'm Lucy and this is Billie", said Lucy.

"Good to meet you Lucy and Billie, my names Atticus. Shame we could not meet in better circumstances. Okay, Jasper, I'm just going to remove your top to have a little look at what we're dealing with". Said the old man knowing full well he wouldn't get a response out of the unconscious teenager.

Removing Jaspers top Atticus examined the wounds, five claw marks punctured each shoulder, and he had another slash across his arm. He turned to look at Lucy and frowned. "Well Lucy, the flow of blood has already slowed a lot and from the looks of things, young Jasper here is lucky to be alive. All the wounds he has sustained are fairly and I say 'fairly' superficial. Whatever did this hit hard into his shoulders and went deep into his muscle" he prodded each wound with his finger, causing a small amount of blood to seep from the wounds. "Luckily though no arteries were punctured otherwise this would be quite a different story. The best thing for me to do now is clean up these wounds and do some stitches. He'll need some rest, but he should pull through".

The night drew on as Atticus worked to mend Jaspers wounds. Hours went by and Lucy and Billie were both slumped against a wall almost nodding off.

"Hey, Billie!" said Lucy grabbing his attention. Billie rubbed at his eyes.

"Huh? Yeah, what's up" asked the tired teenager.

"That thing that got Jasper wasn't a bogart. It was huge, like some kind of mutant panther". Said Lucy

"Don't remind me, I don't think I'm ever going to get the sight of that thing clawing up that cave. Did you see its bloody claws? They were like the slogolyths, just one hell of a lot quicker!"

"I've never even heard of creatures like this before and since Jasper found Scoff, we've seen three. That can't be a coincidence can it?"

"I hear that, I was thinking the same thing. I can't even imagine what would have brought them here though. I didn't even know they were real until a couple of days ago".

Abruptly the old man shot up from Jaspers side. "Right! We're done here". Lucy and Billie jumped alerted by his sudden movement. "Now you two. I think we need to have a little talk", said the old man. "I'll put the kettle on".

Lucy and Billie were sitting in a small clinical looking reception area, awkward and anxious. The old man walked back through some double doors carrying three mugs of tea. The doors swung shut and he handed a tea to both of them. He pulled a chair up and sat opposite. Atticus looked from one teenager to the other. "So, why didn't you call an ambulance?" Lucy and Billie looked at each other. Billie looked at Atticus and just as he opened his mouth to say something he stopped himself and looked to Lucy who now had her eyes locked to the ground. Billie then closed his mouth and bit the inside of his cheek.

"Do you know what did this to your friend?" Said the old man folding his arms.

Billie without a moment's hesitation said to the old man "it was some kind of mythical creature, like a panther crossed with a huge bull terrier and a wolf. It killed a load of bogarts, yes bogarts they're mythical creatures too and we're good friends with one". Billie had clearly had enough and just wanted some answers. The old man's mouth dropped open in shock. Lucy reached over and backhanded Billie who flinched.

"What? That is what you were about to say right? Mythical creatures are real, and our lives are a lie?"

Atticus frowned "Urm well sort of yes, yes I was. How'd you?" Lucy interrupted him.

"We had a similar conversation with Mr J from Haywood college. We were attacked by a Slogolyth last week". The old man's eyebrows rose.

"So, this Mr J told you everything, did he? Did he tell you about what mortuaries are also for?" said Atticus crossing his arms with a smug look on his face.

Jasper pale, topless and covered in bandages stumbled into the room and flopped into the seat next to Lucy who handed him her tea. He thanked her and sipped it tentatively. "They're for the incineration of deceased mythical creatures. Mortuaries also supply the bounties for troublesome mythical creatures". The old man's mouth again dropped open in shock, it also looked like one of his eyebrows was trying to run off his forehead with frustration.

"You know I've not had the chance to break that news to anyone in so long! The least you could have done was play along for a while. We don't get many mythical creatures around anymore. Wait you three are friends with a bogart?" asked the old man.

Billie grabbed his rucksack and unclipped the top. Scoff rolled out with his head in the bag of meat, completely unfazed by everything that was going on around him. "Yeah, he's a bundle of fun".
Jasper sipped at the tea again then coughed weakly.

"So, we know that the creature that attacked us was mythical but what was it exactly?" Asked Jasper his voice raspy.

The old man smiled at being able to tell these smart-arse teenagers something. He leant forward and put on a voice as if he was about to tell a great tale "The creature that you encountered on the moors, is a monster that has roamed these parts for generations. It hunts and feeds on the odd animal here and there but never goes for anything bigger than a lamb. That's why it's generally always gone unnoticed and that's how it's also stayed off the bounty list for so long. It is quick, quiet and deadly as a tiger. It's called" he paused for effect and leant in captivating the teens. "The Hell Beast of Bodmin Moor". Billie's head fell to his hands. "It roams all the moors but was found here first so we named it. It used to be called the Beast of Bodmin, but that didn't quite have the same ring to it as" he paused again for effect "Hell Beast of Bodmin Moor".

Lucy looked to Billie then back to the old man, "you said it only attacked lambs and small animals, but we found something very different. It had torn out the throat out of a pony and" She looked to Scoff preoccupied with licking the now empty bag of meat. "It had slaughtered an entire group of bogarts", whispered Lucy. Jasper looked to Scoff solemnly. Scoff removed the bag of meat from his head and his long tongue licked across his entire face removing every last chunk of meat. He then bounced over to Jasper, climbed up his leg and laid down in his lap. The old man looked at Scoff and rubbed a hand over his bald head.

"Well, if that was the group on the hill with the dead tree. That would mean that" he looked at Scoff a little pained "That he's the last of the bogarts". The three teens looked at Scoff with sad expressions. The old man sighed rubbing his forehead "The beast, never was like this before. Recently it has just gone mad, violent, attacking anything and everything. Its grown too. Which is why it has gone onto the bounty list, normally we'd never bother with something like that. It's gone too far now though. You three are the first humans its attacked, I think. I'll inform M.I.T.H and they'll up the bounty tonight, that should get more qualified hunters involved. I just don't know what's got over him, he never used to be like that. He was always timid, only killed what he had to, to survive. Almost all mythical creatures are like that, it's how they stay in myth and legend".

Jasper looked to the old man "I think I know what made the creature become more violent". The group turned to Jasper "it was the Manic. When I grabbed the tail. Its fur came off in my hand with an oozing pinky substance. Then when I looked back at it when we were running, I noticed sores on its shoulders, it looked similar to the slogolyth. But obviously not a bear".

The old man nodded "that would explain its change in behaviour. Manic is very rare though, it's strange that you've even witnessed it once let alone twice in the past week. What's even more strange is that you've lived to tell the tale and twice at that. You three are some kind of lucky". He looked at Billie's face then to the bandages covering Jaspers shoulders and arm and he blew at his tea "Well, kind of lucky" he muttered before taking a sip. "Well as you four are still alive, it can't be too far through its transformation. So, the sooner it gets taken care of, the better. I think what's best to do for now is for all of us to get some sleep, especially you Jasper. I get groups of people arriving here in the night more often than you would think, so I've already got some beds made up. You can all stay here the night. Don't worry, it's perfectly safe. This place is like Fort Knox, not even a fully grown slogolyth could get in here. The three nodded appreciatively to the old man, who stood up to show them to their room for the night. "Now I'm sorry but you'll have to share the room, but I'm sure you'll be alright with that won't you?" he said not really caring about the answer "that's unless you'd want to sleep on an uncomfortable camp bed?" he suggested.

Opening the door there was a room with three bunk beds similar to that of a hostel. The teens sat respectively on the bottom of each bed and Jasper turned to the old man.

"Thank you, not just for looking after me but letting us sleep here too".

The old man smiled. "That's not a problem, it's the least I could do, now you three get some rest", he said pulling the door shut.

Billie fell back onto the bed, crossing his legs and putting his arms behind his head.

"A proper bed! I know I only slept in one last night, but this feels so good! It's even better than the one at home".

Lucy sat on the side of her bed and bounced, feeling the soft white quilt between her fingers. "It's much better than a roll mat", she said.

Jasper looked at his bandages, "I hope I don't get blood on the sheets". He said laughing, but completely serious at the same time. Scoff bounced onto a grey blanket at the foot of Jaspers bed. He clawed like a cat at the blanket making himself comfortable before curling up into a ball.

"Here, let me help" said Lucy standing. She walked over to her bag and pulled out a blue towel. "It's not as comfy as the sheets, but at least laying on this you won't get blood everywhere". She laid it down under the quilt and flattened it. "They're perfect", she patted the towel, took a step back and turned almost bumping into a Jasper. Looking down she saw the lines where his abs met his waist and looked up seeing the scratches and bruises on his chest. She smiled embarrassed. They both muttered "sorry" she sidestepped him, and he awkwardly sidestepped around her. He automatically reached up to scratch his head, instantly his shoulders screamed in pain, and he winced dropping his arm and Lucy reached out to steady him.

"Are you alright?" she said holding him.

He laughed "Yeah, I'm Good. Just a bit sore is all" he said before looking into her eyes.

Scoff groaned impatiently.

"Yeah, I hear that Scoff!" Said Billie "Grown! Get a room you two!"

They both pushed each other away, each turning a bright shade of red and got into their beds.

"Urgh what? With *Vandlehammer*, gross! What a dweeb!" said Lucy grabbing the quilt and rolling over.

"Like Dreamweaver's, any better, what a nerd!" said Jasper attempting to roll over mimicking her but stopped abruptly as his shoulder and arm screamed.

Billie closed his eyes and chuckled "you two are the worst". Before a pillow flew across the room hitting him square in the face. "Hey! Alright, I give".

The three teens drifted off to sleep as Scoff rolled around the foot of the bed attempting to get comfortable. The old man looked through the peephole of the door to ensure the three teens slept soundly, then he walked over to the desk to the front of the mortuary and put down a fresh cup of tea. Putting his hands either side of his chair he groaned, as he lowered himself down onto it. He winced in pain as he banged his knee against the shotgun under the desk. With a grumbled sigh he picked up the tea and sipped loudly at it before placing it down and reaching over to his phone. The swirling cord of the phone bounced as he pressed the dated thing to his ear and pressed one button, the phone automatically beeped several times in his ear before a voice answered.

"Mythical, Investigations of Terrible Homicide". said a heavy male voice from down the phone.

The old man put his mug on the table in front of him and leant back on his seat.

Atticus rubbed at his forehead "There's been another attack".

Chapter Seventeen: What was your First?

It was pitch black in the windowless room where Jasper, Lucy, Billie and Scoff all slept. Jasper rolled around in his sleep, the bandages squeezing tight on to the claw marks over his shoulders. Covered in sweat he rolled to his back, then again to his side. He was muttering in his sleep the same words over and over again.

"Hell beast, Human... Mother... Manic..." he shot up breathing heavily. His hands back white-knuckled, clenched to Lucy's towel behind him. Looking around he could see the faint outline of Lucy and Billie fast asleep. As he looked down to Scoff he saw the little creature staring up at him with his golden globes. Scoff grumbled as Jasper patted his head. His fingers ruffled through Scoffs green fur and Jasper itched the top of his head. "Sorry if I woke you little guy". The bedsprings creaked as Jasper led back and winced. As he wiped the sweat from his face with the towel and rolled over again. He could just catch the outline of Lucy sleeping, her face was calm and soft, squashed happily against one of the soft pillows. Smiling at her content, he closed his eyes and drifted back into sleep.

Jasper opened his eyes to see Scoffs golden globes, staring only inches away from his face.

"Buddy? are you alright?" said Jasper confused.
Scoff, happy he was awake, bounced off Jasper's chest and jumped up and down next to him in excitement. Jasper sat up rubbing his eyes as he observed his surroundings. He was in a large, wooded forest, beautiful and green. All the trees were a vibrant green covered in soft moss. The sun's rays shone through the trees and tiny harmless seeds appeared as they floated through them, then disappeared again as soon as they passed into shadow.

Jasper pushed himself to his feet as Scoff spotted some butterflies on some flowers at the base of a tree. Scoff bounded over to them and just like he did in the farmers garden he dove at them claws flailing trying to catch one. The flutter took flight, flying up and out of the canopy revealing a large owl staring at Jasper from a branch in the tree. Though they were submerged within the feathers of its body, Jasper could tell that its wings were clearly vast just by looking at the size of the bird. Feathery horns lead down to large deep orange eyes that blinked individually inspecting Jasper. He looked back to the owl curiously, something changed in the owl, and it shivered, ruffling its feathers. Blinking its eyes individually it settled again, its feathers resuming their position. It looked at Jasper with an intense stare as if the bird's eyes were drawing Jasper in. Jasper looked around as everything went silent in the forest, he then looked back to the owl who still stared deep into his soul. The owl then blinked both eyes simultaneously and the world around Jasper changed instantly. All the mossy ground vanished, replaced by a dry and desolate Mars like plain, that went on for miles. A few trees were still visible but were now black and scorched. The air around him had also changed from a humid forest air full of life to a thin, dusty, and coarse air that drew the moisture from his throat. Scoff chasing butterflies, fell to the ground as the butterflies disappeared. Scoff then dropped to all fours close to the ground, backing away he darted over to Jasper and climbed up his back and onto his bandaged shoulders. Jasper looked back to the owl which now looked rugged and was covered in sores, sections of the bird's feathers were missing from its body and a pink ooze drained from its leg onto the branch it was perched upon. Its eyes had also changed, one eye still had that deep orange, but the other was milky and scarred. The Owl again ruffled his feathers and looked to Jasper with that same intense stare judging his every movement. The owl shifted its eyes to look at Scoff, who was standing perched on Jasper's shoulder holding onto his head for support. Something caught Jasper's eye in the distance, he saw a teenager collapsed on his knees. The world jolted again flashing between the ancient, wooded forest and the barren landscape.

"Hey!" Jasper shouted, his voice echoed and was lost in the vast desert. There was no reply, Jasper was about to run to the person in the distance when the owl again ruffled its feathers catching Jasper's attention. Blinking its eyes individually the owl looked at Jasper, then with that same intense stare it blinked both of its eyes and Jasper's world went black.

Jasper awoke again with a jolt, both he and Scoff sat up confused and disorientated. Scoff turned and looked around the room blinking frantically, ensuring it was really there. Jasper looked to Scoff who looked back, curiously they stared at each other. Jasper thought it was strange, it was almost as if Scoff had woken up at the exact same time as him. He looked at Scoff and wondered if he had just had the same experience. There was a knock at the door and Jasper quickly forgot about the dream as the reality of the situation sunk in.

"Come in", Jasper said, rubbing his eyes. Billie and Lucy stirred.

"Sorry to wake you all, but it's ten in the morning. You've all been asleep for a good ten hours. This room can be a little confusing not having any windows. I've made coffee for you all and there's someone here who'd like to see you" said the old man.

"Thanks. We'll just get ready and be right out" said Jasper getting out of bed.

"How are you feeling? Any better?" asked Atticus.

Jasper rubbed his eyes, then scratched the back of his head and felt a sharp pain across his shoulders and back.

He winced and lowered his arm. "Yeah, much better", he said gritting his teeth.

"At least you got some rest, some coffee will do you good. I'll see you all in just a moment".

The old man nodded, turned on the light and shut the door.

Billie groaned, removing the covers and swung his legs from the bed, putting his elbows to his knees he rubbed at his face. "God I'm tired", said Billie rubbing his eyes.

Lucy rolled over hiding her face in the quilt. "No! Why is it the day already?" she cried into the quilt.

Jasper stood up out of bed and stretched out his back with his arms stretched out as far as he could. Feeling his shoulders loosen a little but the stretch was cut short by a burning sensation in his shoulders. He loosened his body then knelt to his bag. Rummaging through he pulled out a plain white t-shirt, and cargo trousers. He stretched the top over his head carefully over the bandages. Just as Jasper was about to put his trousers on, he looked at Lucy who still had her head buried in the quilt. Momentarily embarrassed he threw the trousers back into his bag. His checked PJ bottoms would just have to do for now.

Jasper opened the door of the room and walked over to a small bathroom. After relieving himself, he turned to the sink to wash his hands, looking up he saw himself in the mirror, his brown copper hair was straw-like, dry, and messy. His face was marked with scratches that criss-crossed one cheek and his forehead. He filled his hands with water washing the dirt and blood from his face and neck. Flashes of decapitated bogart bodies filled his vision each time he splashed water to his face, then a flash of the beast's putrid green eyes filled his vision. Placing his hands on the sink, he relaxed his breathing. He looked up to the mirror and caught his breath as alien eyes looked back at him, one a deep orange and one a milky grey colour.

Shaking his head, he splashed his face again and looked back to his plain brown eyes. Dropping his head, he sighed as he rubbed his face. His brain felt like it was trying to break out of his skull. Turning around he dried his hands and walked into the mortuary.

Jasper walked through a small corridor, past the storage cupboard where he'd been bandaged and towards the reception. As he swung the door open, he saw a man talking to Atticus with a serious expression, he was holding a cup of white coffee. Jasper thought the coffee would have obviously had one sugar in it because he would have needed it. Spotting Jasper, Mr J's face lit up.

"Jasper!" he said bursting from his seat. "It's good to see you" he quickly went over to Jasper and embraced him in a hug. Jasper winced in pain, letting out an involuntary yelp. "Oh yes, I'm so sorry! You're hurt. Sit down, sit down". he said pulling up a chair and giving him a coffee. "I've heard you've had quite an adventure. You must tell me all about it. Before you ask, don't worry the coffee has one sugar, I thought you'd need it". Jasper smiled at his upbeat and positive attitude.

"How did you even know we were here?" Asked Jasper with a smile.

"Well, you wouldn't believe it, I only just got around to dropping off that slogolyth, it was really starting to stink. This is the closest M.I.T.H bounty collection mortuary to us. They used to be all over the place but not anymore, now you've got to travel quite a way. When I came in this morning, I saw Atticus here cleaning up some bloody bandages. So obviously I was curious, and he told me about three teenagers who were out and about fighting the Beast of Bodmin"

Atticus interrupted *"The Hell Beast of Bodmin Moor"*. They both laughed.

"Yes, the Hell Beast, I bet Billie loves that". Said Mr J. His expression went suddenly solemn "I also heard about the bogarts. I was sorry to hear that, they've been having trouble for years. But I heard that they'd finally managed to start populating again, which was brilliant but the fact that they've just been completely wiped out, is a sorry blow indeed". At that moment Scoff burst through the door, bounded over to Jasper and jumped onto his back. Jasper winced in pain and put Scoff onto his lap.

"Hey bud" said Jasper, wincing then stroking Scoff.

Mr J looked to Atticus then back to Jasper. "You didn't tell me about him?" he said accusingly to them both.

Jasper put on an apologetic smile, "Sorry, he's actually been with me a while".

Mr J nodded understanding "well that explains why you could all see the manic in that bear when it attacked you all".

"Actually, Lucy and Billie hadn't met him at that point. He was the first mythical creature I'd ever seen though".

Mr J raised his eyebrows whilst sipping his tea. Swallowing he said, "so what was it Billie and Lucy had seen?"

Jasper leant forward "Well I don't know what Billie has seen, but I know that Lucy was tormented by the Baba Yaga for a long time when she was a child. Sounded pretty terrifying from what she told me".

Atticus shivered "yeah he was my first too, terrifying! He visited me only once though, thank God. I woke up to what felt like he was screaming into my soul, I couldn't move my entire body, and with his two-inch long sharp teeth leant over my face screaming. He is a horrible git".

"I thank god he never visited me when I was a kid" agreed Mr J with a shiver.

Coughing, Jasper laughed "It sounds horrifying, I'm glad I never met him either". Jasper looked to Mr J "I hope you don't mind me asking Mr J, what was your first encounter?" Asked Jasper.

Both Atticus and Mr J went completely silent. Atticus looked to Mr J empathetically, then turned back to Jasper "Maybe that's for another time?"

"No, it's alright", said Mr J and his expression turned sour. "It was a wyvern". Jasper's eyes widened.

"That's like a dragon, right?" asked Jasper.

Atticus turned to Jasper. "It's similar to a dragon though dragons have four legs, typically a wyvern has two legs and two claws on its wings that it uses as legs". Atticus and Jasper turned back to Mr J who continued.

"Back in my twenties, I used to give guided tours, taking climbing expeditions all over the world. I'd often go with my friend Hunter from Uni, we decided that we wanted to battle something that no one had dared to before. You know, something really stupid. We wanted to tackle the western side of Everest. The group I took up there were great", he smiled reminiscing. "There was Hunter and his sister Hellen, it was hilarious those two were always in competition trying to outdo one another. She was nowhere near a natural climber as hunter was, but she tried so hard doing climb, after climb, after climb until she made herself his equal. There were also two others which I didn't know too well, Lucy and Bo. They were friends with Hellen, but they came with us on every training climb, so I soon trusted them enough to join us. We'd spent two months trying to get up the western side of the mountain. That's how long it normally takes to do the entire mountain up and down on any other route. But this was the western side, no one had ever tried it before, it's so perilous. But we in our arrogance thought we could do it. Halfway up we were hit by a horrendous storm, which almost knocked us off the mountain itself, so we took shelter in a cave. We thought it

197

was strange that there was a cave there, but none of us were complaining. We were simply happy to be out of the storm. Later once we'd warmed up, Sara, ever the curious one, wanted to explore the cave. Hunter and I were sceptical at first but eventually, we agreed, and we went in. It wasn't long before we came across what I now know to be wyvern eggs. We were all amazed, at the strange orbs encased in ice and that's when it attacked. The wyvern tore through all of us like we were ants that had to be squashed. I tried to fight back but was flung through a tunnel, which then collapsed and gave me this". he lifted his glasses and his fridge which just covered his forehead to reveal a large scar above his eyebrow. "I never saw any of the others again". Said Mr J draining the last of his coffee.

Jasper looked to his teacher with newfound respect. "How did you manage to get back down?"

"I climbed", he said as if it was the most obvious thing in the world. "I woke up in the cave freezing to death with a cracked skull and blood down my face, so I did the only thing I could. I climbed down by myself, I'd already seen my friends die and I was certain I was about to die too, so I had to try. I'd almost got to base camp when I fell. I don't know how far but next thing I knew I was in a hospital. According to the nurse, a group of sherpas had found me and brought me off the mountain. I was one of the lucky ones, most people just get left there to die, but I'd managed to get myself close enough to the camp that they could save me. Apparently, they were keeping me warm and alive in a tent for a week before the storm subsided. They then flew me out by helicopter, and I spent the best part of two months in a hospital recovering before I was strong enough to come home".

Jasper was trying to focus on the story but was finding it hard to concentrate with his head pounding. He took another sip of coffee. "What did you do then?" Jasper asked.

"Well, I did what any sane person would do, I went completely mental" He laughed. "I'd been attacked and seen all of my friends get killed by a mythical beast. What would anyone else do? Wasn't long after I got back to the UK that I was visited by M.I.T.H and I met Atticus here" said Mr J slapping Atticus's shoulder. "Atticus taught me all about mythical creatures. I've been teaching biology and hunting down the bad ones ever since".

"I'm sorry Mr J that sounds horrendous. But, just saying, you surviving that. You're a badass!" said Jasper as a bead of sweat ran down his brow.

Mr J laughed. "You sound like your head's not right".

The door behind Jasper swung open, with Lucy and Billie rubbing their eyes. Their legs heavy like it was five in the morning, Lucy's eyes shifted from her rubbing palms to Mr J.

"Mr J!" They both shouted.

"What are you doing here?" said Lucy running to a seat in the reception area, followed by Billie.

"It's great to see you all and good to hear you are all safe. I've heard about the monster on the moors, and I think it's about time we have another catch up".

Suddenly Jasper felt himself becoming overwhelmed by a strange hot sensation that felt like it was engulfing his entire body. The back of his tongue tingled, and he felt his mouth begin to salivate. Trying to distract himself from the strange sensation he slurred "Mr Js first mythical beast was a dragon!"

Billie and Lucy's faces lit up in excitement at the new development and looked at Mr J, their mouths wide open.

"A dragon! That's incredible!" Said Billie. "You've got to tell us what happened!"

Atticus turned to Jasper "it was a wyvern, not a dragon. I told you that already". Jasper's eyes began to roll. "Jasper? Are you okay?"

Jasper's face turned pale with a slight shade of green. "Sorry" he said drunkenly, his hearing completely morphing into something alien and echoey "I meant wyvernnnn". Jasper's cup slid from his fingers and shattered on the ground, his head rolled, and his entire body became limp. Scoff dove from his lap as Jasper came crashing down from the chair, landing in a heap on the floor.

"Jasper!" Everyone instantly stood from their seats and Lucy ran to Jasper's side. He had landed face-first. Putting her hands around his shoulders she rolled him to his back. His lips moved, muttering something. Mr J ran to his side.

"Jasper! Jasper! Can you hear me? Wait! What's he saying" Asked Mr J.

"I don't know I can't hear. He's burning up" she lifted her hand and placed it against his face.

Atticus took Mr J by his shoulder. "We need to get him to the other room now". Mr J nodded and looked to Billie who gave a worried smile then nodded. Mr J slid his arms under Jaspers shoulders, then under his arms. Billie went to the other side lifting his feet. Together they looked at each other and counted to three.

"One, two, three" then struggling to keep their hold on his sweat covered body, they carried him as carefully as they could to the little room where Atticus had bandaged him just the day before. Laying him down Lucy went to his side again and with tears in her eyes she called out.

"Jasper, can you hear me. Jasper! Jasper!"

Chapter Eighteen: The Murky Grey of Deep Orange

The world was damp, dark, and humid. Jasper could faintly hear someone calling his name, but it was so warped, he couldn't make out who it was. He thought that maybe it was Lucy, but he couldn't make out what she was saying. His eyes, though still blurry, were becoming brighter and he could just start making out the green of trees above him. His vision cleared and the sound of Lucy's voice completely disappeared as a tiny seed attached to a long stem floated across his vision. As he sat up, he saw the ancient forest, with its beautiful mossy floor and sun rays just peeking through the trees. He rested his hand on the floor pressing the damp moss, it softened compressing until he released his hand, it expanded again, resuming its natural position. He watched as butterflies fluttered overhead. He looked around for Scoff, but he was nowhere to be seen, then he looked to the branch where he saw the Owl, again it was there. Perched on the branch staring at him, blinking. He pushed himself to his feet and looked at the large bird, who tilted its head curiously to him. The birds intense stare began to irritate Jasper, so he turned away. He noticed that to the right of the bird was a trail surrounded by moss and rocks. Looking back to the bird, he gave a single wave with two fingers before taking his first steps into the ancient forest. The Owl turned its head watching him leave before blinking its eyes individually, its right eye becoming cloudy as it did.

Jasper was walking through dense brush, pushing ferns and vines to clear his way. He noticed that although his arm still had the bandage on it did not hurt anymore and neither did his shoulders. Pleasantly surprised he continued pushing through the woods, observing everything that he passed. Jasper was becoming very aware that he was alone, he'd had Scoff with him almost every day for the best part of a week and this was the first time in ages he actually felt alone, isolated from everyone. He refused to let it get to him, so he powered through.

"I've been by myself for years, I can deal with being alone for a while now", he muttered to himself. He noticed that every hundred meters or so, the owl would reappear staring at him curiously. Jasper couldn't help but think that the owl was not only staring at him, but he swore that occasionally its tiny black tongue poked out and licked its beak. *Creepy freaking owl.* He quickly disregarded the thing and pressed on. It occurred to Jasper that he had absolutely no concept of time here, the sun hadn't moved the entire time he was there. It felt like he'd been walking for hours, and his feet were beginning to ache. He spotted a clearing ahead and noticed a teen with a large build and dark curly hair. The teen was collapsed on his knees, motionless. Jasper ran over pushing his way through ferns and jumping over branches. "Hey! Hey, are you okay?" Asked Jasper.

The teen looked up with defeated eyes. "Jasper?"

Seeing the teens brutish face and blue grey eyes. Jasper stopped suddenly in utter amazement barely believing his own eyes. "Lee?"

***

Lucy and Billie were sat by Jasper who was unconscious on the bed, with a glisten of sweat covering his brow. Lucy was holding his clammy hand in hers rubbing it with her thumb.

"He's going to be okay. I know it. This is Jasper he'll be alright" said Billie trying to reassure her and himself. She looked over to him.

"I hope so. He always wanted life to have more adventure, more excitement. Well, Jasp you've found it now".

Billie exhaled a chuckle, "Yeah that excitements got him good now. He keeps muttering something, do you know what he's saying?"

Lucy looked to him "No, I can't hear it clearly. I've heard a couple of words. He said Gaia, Lee and I think I heard him say Roga, but that makes no sense. So, I don't know really, none of it makes sense". Billie and Lucy both turned to the door as they heard Mr J and Atticus arguing.

"Why didn't you say before!" Shouted Mr J furious.

Billie and Lucy crept closer to the door to listen to the conversation. Lucy found an opening in the door and could see both Atticus and Mr J in the corridor.

Atticus flustered and pleaded to Mr J "I'd been sworn to secrecy and to only report to M.I.T.H. They told me, they'd handle it. But that was weeks ago, it's been the third attack in two weeks. So, I had to tell you".

"Yeah, and now three people have been attacked and the last of a species has almost been wiped out! Atticus, you should have told me sooner. You know I would have done something about this".

"These aren't the first Jessie. It's beginning to happen everywhere. And you don't know this beast. You can't take it by surprise look at what happened to Jasper".

"Has anyone contracted it?" Asked Mr J

"The manic? No, no one's contracted it and survived, but it's mutating somehow, it never even affected humans before", Said Atticus.

"Jasper!" Said Mr J his face falling, and he ran to the door. Lucy jumped back as the door flung open and Mr J stopped as he saw the two teens stood in front of him. "Out of the way!" he ordered as he barged past them. He knelt beside Jasper looking at his pale green face. He then

203

looked, down to his arm which had been clawed by the beast, lifting it he unravelled the bandages. He noticed that the wound was healing nicely, and the flesh was already knitting together forming hefty but weeping scabs. Mr J dropped his head in relief. His heart still raced from the panic that Jasper could have been infected. He lifted his head to look to Jasper and he noticed the bandage by his collar. Poking through the bandage barely visible was a couple of dark veins. Mr J turned to look to Lucy who had rushed beside him.

He looked to the shelf next to Jasper where the scissors still laid from when his top had been removed before. "Pass me those scissors" he ordered.

Lucy grabbed the scissors and passed them to Mr J who instantly began cutting Jaspers top from his body. Lucy watched as Jasper's chest gradually rose and fell. His skin was pale, with a green tint as the fever had begun to take over. Mr J looked again to Lucy with a serious expression.

"Brace yourself", said Mr J.

He lifted the scissors and began cutting the bandages up the centre of Jasper's chest, revealing dark green veins which spidered out from each claw wound covering his shoulders and spreading over his chest and neck. Lucy gasped, throwing her hands to her face. Shocked Billie put his arm around Lucy comforting both of them.

Mr J threw down the scissors in anger and stormed out of the room barging past Atticus.

"Jessie wait!" Said Atticus.

"Wait for what? For the monster to kill someone else. You and I both know there is nothing we can do for him now. You did this! If you had told me sooner, I could have done something. Now look. Look at that boy there. He is going to die because you did nothing. I'm not going to stand around and let this happen to someone else".

"What are you going to do?" asked Atticus.

"I'm going to end this nightmare now!" Said Mr J.

"Wait". Said Billie appearing next to Mr J. Billie looked to Jasper then to Mr J. "I'm coming with you. This thing did this to Jasper. I'm not letting that happen to anyone else. I have to help, for Jasper".

Shocked, Mr J looked at Atticus, "I'll look after the boy, there's nothing any of you can do here now". Said Atticus trying in vain to reassure Mr J.

"I'm coming too". Said Lucy standing and joining Billie.

Mr J looked at her confused. "Don't you want to stay here with Jasper?"

She looked to Jasper, motionless on the camp bed. Then to Billie and they nodded steeling themselves "Atticus said it himself, there's nothing any of us can do here. The best thing for us to do is help you". She said, wiping a tear from her cheek.

Mr J looked at the two determined teens, staring at them and judging their resolve. "Alright, but you two are nuts and you're definitely not going like that". Billie and Lucy looked at each other confused.

***

Jasper could feel the air being squeezed from his lungs. With each breath, he could feel the grip getting tighter and tighter. He opened his mouth to try to talk.

"Lee, you're choking me", gasped Jasper, he was being embraced in the biggest hug of his life.

"Sorry, Jasper I thought I was alone here". Lee released his grip "I feel like I've been here for months. I'd finally given up, I thought I was going to be lost forever. But if you're here you must know a way out. You do know a way out, don't you?"

Jasper looked around the wooded forest, he then looked up to the Owl, which stared down observing the two. Jasper turned back to Lee "I might know a way, but I'm not sure. What happened, how did we both get here?"

"Thank God! The last thing I remember was us fighting by the sewers, then next thing I know, I'm stuck in this place". Said Lee gesturing around him. Jasper stepped back from Lee.

"Don't you remember what happened? When me and you were fighting, we got attacked by a bear?" said Jasper.

"I think so", said Lee deep in thought. His eyes took a darker turn and he pressed two fingers to his forehead. "I remember seeing something, it was coming out of the tunnel".

Jasper laughed awkwardly. "Yeah, and you shouted at it". Jasper stopped to look to Lee, who was staring at the ground deep in thought. Which Jasper thought was odd he'd never seen Lee deep in thought before, in fact, he wasn't even sure he'd seen him thinking.

"The bear hit me, didn't it?" Said Lee, as more of a statement than a question. He was beginning to recall the attack.

"It did". Said Jasper. "I won't go into too much detail, but from what I last heard. I'm sorry Lee, you've been in a coma for almost a week in Haywood hospital".

"How am I in a coma? I've been walking around here for months?" said Lee.

"When the Monster attacked, everyone managed to get away, but it went for you first. It got you pretty bad. Once the ambulance got there, they weren't sure if you'd make it, but you survived".

"So, if everyone got away and I'm in a coma how come you're here?" Asked Lee.

"That, I'm still trying to work out myself". Jasper wanted to tell him about the Manic and Scoff, but hesitated, after some quick contemplation he decided to hold that side of the story for now. "After the bear attack, we went to find out what was doing the attacks on the moors. Whilst we were there, the creature found us first. That's when I got attacked, it clawed my shoulders and my arm. The creature had a disease", said Jasper.

Lee turned from Jasper and walked over to a fallen tree at the side of the clearing. Sitting down on the moss-covered tree he felt the damp through his trousers, he sighed and looked to the ground.

"So, I'm in a coma and I got attacked by a diseased bear. How do you know it was diseased? It looked ordinarily terrifying to me".

He spoke softly as he walked over and sat next to Lee. "The disease is called Manic, it only affects animals but it's kind of like a Zombie virus, it turns animals into complete psychos. Most people can't see the virus and just see an ordinary creature. I know this is going to sound mad, but I figure we're in some weird ancient dream world right now. You can only see the Manic if you've had a run-in with a mythical creature. Something like a troll, werewolf, naga or even the Baba Yaga". *Well, there goes not telling him.*

At the mention of the Baba Yaga, the large feathery horned owl across the clearing tilted its head to them, ruffled its feathers and shuffled its fist-sized claws on the branch. As it settled it glared again at Jasper, then shifted its glance to Lee and squinted a little. Lee frowned at the large bird and turned to Jasper with a look of desperation that Jasper had never seen before on the brute's face.

"Lillz, is Lillz alright?" pleaded Lee.

"Yeah, she's alright. She's visited you a few times from what I hear. Hell, she thought you'd even died at one point and managed to turn the entire school against Billie for murdering you".

Lee pressed his lips together with a pained smile, clearly missing her. Trying to hide his emotions he shifted his eyes angrily over to the large owl.

"That things, been following me around ever since I got here". He frowned, showing his anger at the bird. "It just stares at me with that same stupid expression". At that Lee reached down and picked up a rock. He rolled it around his hand, feeling the sharp jagged edges and weight of the hard stone. "I've tried attacking it, tried chasing it off but nothing works, it just watches" Lee then lifted his meaty fist and launched the rock directly at the owl. The rock went clear through the bird's head and disappeared rustling through the branches behind it. The bird looked back to Lee unblinking and squawked angrily from the other side of the clearing. "See, nothing". Said Lee defeated. "I've been here for months, and he's taunted me every step of the way". Jasper looked over to the bird then looked back down and they both sat in silence for a while, both deep in their thoughts.

Suddenly an idea came to Jasper "I'm dreaming. That's what this all is, I'm dreaming, I was here before, but it was a dream. I woke up, all we need to do is wake up".

"Wake up? Don't you think I've tried that? I'd be happy to slap you if you think that would work though?" said Lee with a hopeful look. Lee could see Jasper mulling it over for a moment, so Lee rolled up his fist and slammed it into Jasper's shoulder causing him to rock to the side in pain.

"Ouch! Alright, alright I'm not asleep. I can definitely still hurt here too", said Jasper rubbing his arm. Jasper looked back to the bird and pushed himself off the fallen tree.

"What are you doing?" Asked Lee.

"I just want to check something", said Jasper rubbing his arm.

Jasper tentatively walked over to the bird which looked down on him with judgemental eyes. Jasper squatted down and searched the ground, rubbing his fingers through the dirt and grabbed a handful of small rocks and twigs. He then looked up at the bird and threw a rock, which like Lees passed straight through it. Taken aback the bird squawked at Jasper angrily.

"Where are we?" Asked Jasper, to the bird.

"What are you doing?" asked Lee.

Jasper glared at the bird, which glared back with angry eyes.

"Look I know you're not just a bird, so tell me. Where are we?" Jasper commanded launching another rock,

Annoyed, the bird moved down the branch furthering itself from Jasper.

"Where are we!" Jasper shouted, launching his last rock.

The irritated Owl squawked again at Jasper and ruffled its feathers. Lee stood back behind Jasper watching the interaction between the two of them, he then saw Jasper grab another hand full of rocks and dirt from the ground and he continued launching rocks and dirt at the annoyed bird.

"Alright, if you won't tell me where we are, tell me who you are", Jasper said calmly before throwing a continuous barrage of rocks and soil at the bird. The bird wasn't getting hit by any of the projectiles as they were passing straight through, however the bird's mood was visibly becoming more agitated. "Look I know this is annoying you, so I won't stop until you tell me what's going on here". Said Jasper continuing the never-ending barrage. Lee spotted the effect Jasper was having on the bird and ran over to join him. Picking up a handful of dirt and rocks then too began to launch projectiles at the bird. The bird flinched continuously until enough was enough, it threw itself forward and released an enormous screech which threw Jasper and Lee from their feet. Both landing on their backs they looked up to see the great owl become larger and larger in size. Flapping its wings, it wrapped them around itself, concealing its body. The Feathers of the creature fell into black of the creature's cloak which emerged from within the winged cocoon. From the shoulders of the creature emerged a bald, gaunt head with large cloudy eyes. The eyes glared at Jasper with utter disdain as the creature clicked through two-inch long sharp teeth. The world faded around them growing dark. The trees began to melt into a dark sludge, releasing tar like bubbles as they formed large gelatinous puddles. The dark-cloaked creature glared intently at Jasper and hissed his name through its long-elongated teeth. "Jasper" it hissed. Jasper did not reply but the creature persisted "Jasper!" it hissed again.

"What does it want from me? It won't stop saying my name". Said Lee

Jasper realised that the creature must have been talking to them both individually. Jasper began to shuffle himself back as the creature floated towards him, its breathing was coarse and laboured. Jasper noticed Lee was shuffling away from him and was looking up at something that wasn't there.

"What do you want from me?" Lee cried to nothing. Jasper looked up to the creature floating over him.

Jasper shouted to Lee. "Lee it's not really there it can't hurt you".

The creature turned to Lee, then with a lopsided demonic grin, it turned back lifting its long gangly hand with nails dagger-like and dark. "Can't I?" the creature hissed as it stabbed its claw into Jasper's shoulder. Jasper cried out in pain as each dirty black talon pierced his skin, puncturing deep into his shoulder. With a demonic grin the

Baba Yaga sneered "You called for me Jasper, and now, I'm here".

Chapter Nineteen: Soaked in What?

It was morning and the sun cut beautifully through the trees laying upon a slight mist in the woodland. The ground was wet from rain that must have fallen during the night. Lucy and Billie followed Mr J to his car outside. The old grey 164 Alfa Romeo was parked on the gravel outside the mortuary. The Romeos wheel arches were rusted, it was clearly the kind of car you would expect to backfire with a loud repetitive pop as soon as you accelerated hard. Attached to the back of a car was a large metal horse box. The teens didn't even need to even ask what Mr J needed that for, as red stains could be seen seeping from the gaps. Their boots crunched on the gravel with each step, as Mr J walked the teens around to the boot of the car.

"What a junk heap!" said Billie.

"Junkheap?" said Mr J as he stroked his hand down the side of the car, his fingertips gliding over the paint. "This is my beautiful girl, Vinessa. She's saved my bacon more than once you know, with a V6 2.0 engine she goes like nobody's business". Mr J made his way to the back of the car and pulled the trailer plug.

"Is that fast?" Asked Lucy quietly.

"Is that fast? Does the queen wear stockings for Prince Philip?" he pulled the leaver releasing the trailer from the car. "Yes, it's fast! Now give me a hand with this". All three pushed the tailer away from the car and parked it next to the main building of the mortuary.

"Excellent!" Mr J clapped his hands together like they were covered in dust. "Right, you two. With me." He turned on his heels and made his way back to the car.

Mr J grabbed the latch of the boot, and it clicked open. Staring into the boot he rummaged around searching through and around bags.

"Ah-ha! Right, take this". A bow landed in Billie's hands, and he caught it clumsily.

"What's this?" Asked Billie holding the complicated bow with confused eyes.

"That my boy is a compound bow, years old and an absolute beauty. It's even been blessed by shamans in the Congo".

"It's definitely old". Said Billie looking at the cables distastefully. "Wait blessed by what in the who now?"

"Shaman in the Congo. Mythical creatures are real Billie. Keep up".

Another weapon came flying at Lucy, she caught the long shaft of a spear with a silver tip. Feeling the weapons weight, she threw it from hand to hand, finding its centre of balance. She looked at it with a disturbed manner, then looked over to Billie who was looking distastefully at the compound bow. Billie looked over to Lucy's Spear with envious eyes. He walked over to her holding the bow out with two hands. She smiled, taking the bow, and offered him the spear which he took eagerly.

"I'd much rather the bow anyway", Said Lucy happily.

Billie held the enormous spear with both hands and began Jabbing the air around him.

"Yeah, much better!" Said Billie approvingly. Jabbing left and right Billie shouted at Mr J between breaths. "So, this spear, who blessed this? Was it some priest from the Vatican or was it from a tribe in the Amazon rainforest?"

"That, I made in my garage and the wood has been soaked for ten days in tiger urine. Now don't break it".

Billie stopped jabbing with the spear and looked back to Lucy with the bow. She spotted his longing look at her blessed bow and took a step away. He looked back to his weapon and gave it a sniff.

Mr J looked at the two and raised an eyebrow. Reaching back into the car, he pulled out a large belt with a Rapier sheathed inside. Mr J thumbed the buckle and pulled the belt tight. He wrapped his fingers around the hilt of the rapier. The ornate silver guard crisscrossed above the shoulder of the blade and swirled up around his hand to the pommel. Tightening his grip he pulled the sword from its scabbard, making a satisfying sharpening ting as the sword left its sheath. Mr J sliced left and right with an audible whip with each slash. He then stood up straight, the blade mirroring his stance vertically in front of him. The blade slashed to one side, swung up and disappeared back into the scabbard. Billie looked back at his spear and frowned.

"Well, that's just not fair", He said as if Mr J had just drawn a flush and Billie only had a meagre pair. Mr J stepped over to him.

"These are all I have to hand and hey that's what I used to take out the other slogolyth. Spears are really handy, they've got great reach, you can take out the enemy before they even get close to you. Just don't let them get too close, that's what the pointy end is used for. Always keep your distance and you'll be fine. Same for you Lucy, keep your distance" He looked to the bow in her hands. "Do you know how to use one of those?" said Mr J. Lucy smirked and walked over to the boot of the car where she took out a quiver of arrows. Standing in front of Billie and Mr J she searched her surroundings before she spotted a tree stump around twenty meters away. Grasping her left hand tight onto the grip, she nocked an arrow to the bowstring. She then slowly lifted the bow, slowed her breathing, and drew the bowstring tight. Her thumb pressed gently to her cheek and her right eye looked down the shaft towards the stump. She exhaled releasing the string. Shards of bark shattered as the arrow slammed directly into the centre of the stump. She broke into a smile and looked over to Billie whose mouth had dropped open.

"I'm going to die". He said looking back to his spear.

"Very nice Lucy!" said Mr J approvingly. "Right, you're both going to want some protection too", said Mr J pulling out some vests and pads from the boot. "I'm sorry these are fitted for me but it's better than not having anything, you should be able to tighten the straps on the pads".

Billie took one of the vests. It was made of a thick Kevlar with pads across the chest, back and arms. Billie lifted it over his head, and it fell heavily onto his body. It sagged below his waist and the sleeves came over his hands.

"This thing's huge!" said Billie, looking like a child wearing his dad's clothes.

"Yeah, that is a little big. Hold on" Mr J stepped over to Billie and began jerking him around as he pulled the straps tight around his torso, fitting it snugly. "I'll just have to tuck in these straps then we should be golden. There, how does that feel now?"

Billie rotated his arms and through a few jabs in front of him. "It's a little restricting but it's better than not having it".

Lucy had already adorned in her Kevlar vest and was tightening the straps around her chest. She noticed that it fit well, tightening around the waist but she found the chest was very tight, it was clearly meant for a man. She rolled up the sleeves and removed the elbow pads, enabling more movement in her arms. She lifted the bow again and tested her movements pulling the bowstring whilst loosening her shoulders.

Billie planted the butt of the spear into the ground and looked to the rapier sheathed in Mr J's belt. "So, these weapons, are they all silver?" Billie asked.

"Of a type yes. If they were silver on their own, they'd be weak, however, the metal in the spear tip, the arrows and this sword are all made with a silver alloy. It's essentially a kind of silver steel. Very, very expensive and hard to make but it's the best way to take out a lot of mythical beasts. So, Lucy, do your best to not use too many arrows, remember I am just on a teacher's salary". She looked over to the tree stump and ran over to retrieve the arrow. "Well done, retrieve as many as you can after the battle too. I don't want to be out of pocket after this fight".

Atticus watched through old eyes as Mr J, Lucy and Billie finished adorning their armour and collected up their weapons. Lucy said something about a shotgun and had hopped in the front passenger seat and Billie reluctantly got in the back of the Romeo. Atticus looked over to Mr J who walked over to him and placed a reassuring hand on his shoulder.

"Look after Jasper, we'll sort this slogolyth and be right back, okay?" said Mr J. Atticus nodded and looked to the teens eager to fight against the creature that attacked them.

"Are you sure they're ready for something like this?" questioned Atticus.

"Nope, but when are you ready for something like this. You know I've killed slogolyths before, fingers crossed they won't even get their hands dirty. Gave them a spear and a bow, should keep them out of trouble whilst I take the beast out. It'll also keep them away from what's going to happen here".

"There's nothing we can do now, it's up to him. Best those two aren't here to see it".

Mr J looked through a window to Scoff who stood outside the utility room where Jasper slept. "That little guy hasn't left Jasper's side has he".

Atticus gave a weak smile "Yeah, seems like the little critter has taken a liking to young Jasper.

Mr J looked back to Lucy and Billie waiting in the car. "We'd better get a move on. We'll go to where they last saw the beast and go from there, we should be back before nightfall". Atticus nodded. Mr J squeezed his shoulder, "Atticus, when he turns. You know what to do". The old man's head gave a solemn nod and Mr J gave a forced smile devoid of joy. He turned and walked to the car. The door slammed shut, the ignition lit, and the car revved roaring like a leopard before the wheels spun kicking up stones and it shot down the track towards the beast.

Atticus shut the door to the mortuary, sliding the giant bolts shut. He then turned and walked back over to the reception desk where he saw his cold cup of coffee. Not wanting it to go to waste he sat lifted the cup to his lips and drank deeply. He placed the cup on the desk and wiped his mouth. His eyes caught sight of the shotgun and the reality of what he must do began to weigh heavily on him. Scoff appeared from around the corner. He looked at Atticus curiously then ran over and pulled at his trouser leg. He then bounced off around the corner and back into the utility room.

"What do you want, little guy?" Said Atticus following Scoff. Rounding the corner, he saw Scoff at the foot of the bed where Jasper lay. Jasper was shaking in the bed muttering to himself. Atticus walked over to Jasper and knelt down to try and listen to what Jasper was saying. He listened closely but couldn't catch anything through the muttering before his whole body stopped moving and Jasper became completely still. His muttering became quiet, and Atticus put his ear close to Jasper, then clear as a morning breeze Jasper spoke.

"Baba Yaga"

Atticus's eyes widened in horror, and he jumped to his feet, to see Jasper's eyes wide open but were milky white. Suddenly Jasper's shoulder was thrust back into the bed and eyes wide he screamed out in pain.

***

The creature stabbed his claws deep into Jasper's shoulder and he screamed in pain. The creature pulled out his claws gushing a spattering of blood on the floor. Jasper rolled away from the demented creature and jumped to his feet grasping his shoulder. He gritted his teeth and looked to Lee who was cowering on the floor. Running over, he grabbed Lee's arm.

"Lee, we have to run!" Jasper shouted, dragging Lee to his feet. Lee kicked at the ground, scrambling up as fast as he could, the two ran out of the clearing and down a wooded track.

"Jasper" the creature hissed in his ear. "You can't run, I control this place". Jasper turned to see the creature's head next to his, his rotten humid breath filling Jasper's nostrils. Jasper flung out his good arm, but the creature just stopped in mid-air laughing maniacally through elongated teeth. Jasper and Lee ran as fast as they could, trees melting and dripping all around them. Their feet splatted and squelched through the ever-growing slop from the melting trees and foliage. The tar-like slop was becoming heavier and heavier. Jaspers muscles were beginning to burn with each step. Lee grimaced as he pushed through the treacled trees, struggling with each step he took. Realising they weren't going to get away Jasper stopped and grabbed Lee.

"What is it?" said Lee gasping for breath.

"It's the Baba Yaga", Said Jasper. "It controls dreams, it can change and do anything it wants here". The Baba Yaga had morphed again and began flying beside them in its owl form. Bits of flesh and feathers dropped from its body with each flap of its wings.

"So, there's nothing we can do?" said Lee, panicking.

"At least we're certain this is a dream, which means there must be a way to wake up". Jasper waded through the sludge, going through every conversation he'd ever had with Lucy, Mr J or Atticus about the Baba Yaga. Every different attack and method he used to attack and disable his victims and anyway he could to get out of the dream. It was useless every time they'd mentioned him, he'd attacked until his victims were terrified or killed. But that was only to kids, and they were clearly terrified now, why the hell was it attacking them? Jasper's mind reeled trying to find a way out of the dream.

Jasper and Lee stopped suddenly as the putrid sludge below them began to shift and move. The great horned owl landed on a dead wiry tree in front of them, its eyes now both cloudy and dead stared at Jasper and Lee. Slithers of flesh and skin hung from the creature's fist like claws as it clung its vice like grip onto the branch.

"Why are you trying to run? I just want to play" the creature hissed. Looking at the owls dead milky eyes and its body blistered with chunks of feathers missing it finally hit Jasper.

Jasper held his shoulder and looked over to Lee, who was breathing heavily in front of him. "Lee, remember I said this was the Baba Yaga, well it turns out I was sort of right. It looks like we're in more trouble than I thought".

"What the hell? How could we be in any more trouble than we are in now?" Said Lee becoming angry.

"Well, remember I told you that, that bear that attacked us outside the sewers was infected with some kind of disease".

"Yeah, you said it was called Manic or something?"

"Yeah well, I think the Baba Yaga has been infected with manic too". Said Jasper gritting his teeth.

At that moment the Baba Yaga screamed, its wings flew out and a pink slime flung through the disintegrating trees. The sludge below Jasper and Lee began to move faster. It was thickening, forming a large mound in between Jasper, Lee and the Baba Yaga. The tar-like blob in front of them began convulsing as limbs sprouted out of the blob. From within the womb-like membrane a muzzle of a bear's skull pressed against its side, its canines' bit at the wombs membrane before tearing it open. Jasper and Lee felt their legs falter as the mutated bear roared in pain, the slime forming its cloudy eyes and mutated face. Its body was furless. Sludge flew in all directions as its claws hit the floor and it burst out of its womb-like state. The creature's chest heaved as it took its first struggling breaths from birth, its breath visibly bellowing in the now cold air. Jasper spotted the beast's teeth through the rotten gaps in slogolyths cheek. The slogolyths head turned to Lee and then to Jasper. Its tongue pulled back and slime spat from the creature's maw and cheeks as it gave an enormous roar so loud and horrifying that Jasper and Lee's bowels almost gave way.

Chapter Twenty: Judgement

Atticus typed relentlessly at the reception desk of the mortuary writing the new slogolyth bounty, trying to disconnect himself from the infected teenager in the other room. He noticed that his foot was tapping involuntarily, and he threw his hand to his leg to steady it. Scoff was sat on the cold ground watching the old man. He tilted his head as he watched Atticus steady his leg and breath. He reached over and wrapped his fingers around a mug.

The old man spotted Scoffs green fur in the corner of his eyes, and he looked over to see the fury monster of myth sitting patiently, watching him. Atticus sighed and took a sip of tea, then pushed his chair back. The chairs wheels rolled along the ground, squealing as they went. Atticus stood, stepping over to Scoff who looked up to him hopeful with his large golden globes. Atticus knelt in front of Scoff and gave him a sympathetic smile.

"You know he's a tough one. First kid I've ever seen to contract Manic, he's even the first being I've ever seen last this long against it". Atticus smiled at Scoff "He's also the first person I know of that's ever got a bogart to care about anything other than eating or destroying things. You lot are like little angry mischievous magpies. If anyone can pull through this its him". Atticus smiled and ruffled the fur on Scoff's head. Scoff instantly grumbled at Atticus, warning him off, Atticus's smile widened. "You're a little softy really, aren't you?" said Atticus falling back into his seat. Scoff not wanting the attention scuttled out of the room and disappeared around the corner. Atticus smiled and returned to typing the new Slogolyths bounty. All the while very aware of the shotgun under the desk and his impending judgment.

Scoff bounced into the utility room, his claws tapping with each step. Jasper lay motionless and sweating on the bed.

Scoff watched the movements of his chest as it rose and fell. Scoff then walked on all fours to the side of the bed and with a little wiggle he kicked off with his back legs, bouncing him up and onto the bed. He walked up the bed and sat on Jasper's chest. His golden globes stared at Jasper, who began to mumble something unintelligible. Scoff's head tilted to one side as a bead of sweat ran down Jasper's brow. Scoff exhaled and plodded down Jasper's body to his feet. He began to pad his paws clawing the blanket like a cat as he walked around in a circle then dropped onto the bed, laying down and resting his head on Jasper's leg. Scoff looked back up to Jasper still unmoving and let out a sigh. His eyes began to get heavy as he blinked each eye individually before they both finally settled to sleep.

Scoff opened his eyes to see a vibrant ancient forest, he was surrounded by beautiful moss and ferns. The sun shone down through the trees illuminating the ground around him and he bounced up sniffing, tasting his new surroundings like a curious spaniel. He could smell a chorus of different scents, from the most sweet-smelling flower to what seemed to smell like a combination of the dankest compost heap and that of fresh tarmac. Instantly Scoff turned his head and his entire body became ridged as he caught a familiar scent.

**

"Lee we can't run from this, we'll never get away. We have to fight, it's our only option". Said Jasper as he grabbed a log from next to him.

Lee gritted his teeth and yelled at the slogolyth. "You want some of this?! I'm gonna show you what happens to guys that mess with Lee Laderman!".

222

Jasper couldn't believe his eyes as Lee placed one hand on the ground and bent his knees like he was about to do a one-hundred-meter sprint. Then like there was a referee in the trees firing a starting gun, he charged head-on into the slogolyth and slammed his fist into the bear's slimy maw, knocking it to the side and splattering slime all up Lee's fist. The bear turned its head back to Lee unfazed. Lee launched a continuous barrage of blows at the slogolyth, slime flying left and right, but as fast as it left the slogolyth it just came rolling back to the slogolyths paws and reformed up to its missing parts. Jasper rushed the creature, each step heavy as he ran through the treacle. The Slogolyth turned to Jasper and he jumped slamming the log with all his weight and strength directly down onto the slogoyths skull. The slogolyth wavered and crashed to the ground. Jasper and Lee stood above it breathing heavily. As they turned to each other, Jasper raised the log to Lee who fist-bumped it triumphantly with bleeding knuckles. Jasper looked up to the Manic Owl watching the fight and he could have sworn the thing smiled. *The damn thing smiled.*

"Lee, step back", Said Jasper and both of them took a step back as the slogolyth slammed each fleshy paw into the slime and pushed itself up. The slime poured into the beast from all over the forest and it grew in size.

The Baba Yaga in its owl-like form looked to the slogolyth then back to Jasper and Lee "I control your dreams, you can never defeat the slogolyth here!" hissed the creature from the tree. Lee let out an almighty battle cry and slammed his fists repeatedly into the slogolyths unmoving snout, his knuckles tearing becoming bloodier with each blow. Jasper lifted the log and slammed it again into the slogolyths unmoving skull. The log shattered sending vibrations like lightning through Jaspers hands and into his wrists. He dropped what was left of the log and looked up to the slogolyth which stared at him bull-like, it's breath visibly pouring out of each nostril. Lee through another right hook to the creature's head, but the creature shifted its weight, lifting its maw out of the line of fire. Lee's fist collided with air, and he lost his footing, the slogolyths massive paw swung up and slammed into Lee's chest throwing him from his feet and sending him flying like a ragdoll into a rotting tree. Falling to the sludge in a heap, he groaned. The slogolyths head then swung to Jasper who took a step back, readying himself. The creature charged at Jasper, slime flinging behind it with each stride. Suddenly like a tiger triggering her ambush, Scoff burst out from some rotting ferns to the right of the creature and dove with a garbling battle cry at the unsuspecting slogolyth.

"Don't think I didn't know you were there", said the Baba Yaga. His enormous wing flung out flinging slime through the trees and Scoff stopped motionless in the air. The Baba Yaga's bird-like appearance shifted again back into its real form, the outstretched wing morphing into the boney claw like fingers of the Baba Yaga's true body. Scoffs eyes shifted left and right to Jasper, the Baba Yaga and the slogolyth. Scoff's entire body was frozen in mid-air. He couldn't move a muscle, he was stuck in unending paralysis. "Let's not have you interfering, shall we?" Hissed the Baba Yaga, "I've had quite enough of you already". The Baba Yaga then dropped his arm down pointing to the ground. Scoffs golden globes looked to Jasper scared and helpless before his entire body imploded and vanished from existence with a splatter of tar and slime.

"No! Scoff!" Jasper cried. But the slogolyth unmoved continued its pursuit of Jasper and charged. Jasper turned his attention back to the slogolyth with a newfound resolve. He jumped aside dodging the massive beast, which turned and skidded to a stop in the slime before charging again. Jasper darted for a tree running as fast as he could through the treacle. The Slogolyth was gaining on him and fast. *I can't beat this thing, it's too powerful*, thought Jasper as he stood just to the side of a tree and waited for the slogolyth, much like a bullfighter waiting for a bull. Just as the creature was about to hit him, Jasper jumped aside, dodging the beast again as the creature tore its claws into a coppice of trees, slicing them to bits. The slogolyth turned almost instantly and slashed its mighty paw at Jasper. Jasper jumped back feeling the claws rip through his top. The beast attacked again and again, never tiring. Jasper ran back dodging again and again before the creature fainted a blow and backhanded him sending him flying across the clearing. Jasper landed on his side and rolled through the slime.

"You're fast boy, but you can't win here Jasper" hissed the Baba Yaga. Pained, winded and with his shoulder throbbing Jasper watched as the Slogolyth began stalking through the slime towards him. Strands of slime clung to its claws with each step. Jasper could only look on in horror as the monster towered over him. Its cold dead eyes looking down at him like he was at the guillotine, ready to die, to be taken by the Manic. "Finish this" Hissed the Baba Yaga.

The slogolyth opened its maw, slime hanging from its canines. It lowered its head to devour Jasper and the last thought that went through Jasper's mind was of Lucy and Billie and the hope that they were safe. Suddenly two arms appeared from around the slogolyths neck, and the beast reared up as Lee squeezed the beast's neck in a choke hold. Lees biceps flexed as he was flung around on the top of the bear holding on for dear life. The slogolyth then reared up on two legs and with its front claws reached up and raked them through Lees back. Lee screamed out in pain as the claws tore through his flesh and he released the bear's neck as he was thrown into the slime. The slogolyth then pounced onto his body sinking its teeth around his torso and shook him like he was a ragdoll. Jasper watched on in horror as Lee was flung across the clearing. Lee landed in a heap, unmoving. The Slogolyth began to slowly make its way over to Lee's limp body, surly to devour him. Jasper pushed himself up out of the pinky puss like slime and ran back to the trees. He searched frantically before finding the coppice of trees that the slogolyth had destroyed. Running over to it he seized the most long, sharp branch he could find. Turning back to the clearing with his new wooden spear he walked back towards Lee and the Slogolyth. The Baba Yaga watched the Slogolyth in delight as it opened its jaws wide to devour its meal. Jasper looked at the slogolyth about to make its final blow as he focused on his target. Jasper lifted the branch like a javelin, leaning back on his right leg as he drew back the Javelin, then taking a few quick steps he launched it at his target so fast he almost lost his balance. The javelin soared through the air past the slogolyth and punctured deep in the Baba Yaga's chest with a thud. The Baba Yaga's milky eyes widened in shock as the branch burst into his bony chest. The Baba Yaga began convulsing as it tried in vain to change form, newly formed feathers fell from its body as it shuddered, the cold dead eyes looked down at the javelin protruding from its chest and it blinked in confusion. Its long teeth shuddered at the realisation of what had just happened.

The Baba Yaga looked up to Jasper and with a twitching tilt of its head it hissed "How, did?-".

The Slogolyth, then collapsed to the ground next to Lee and the world began to dissolve around them. The Baba Yaga fell from the tree as it, like many other trees, dissolved into the ground revealing a deserted wasteland, Mars like and still covered in that same tar-like substance. Jasper ran through the treacle and fell to his knees by Lee's unmoving body.

"Lee, Lee, we did it Lee. It's dead, the Baba Yaga the slogolyth, they're both dead".

Lee coughed up pink oozing slime which bubbled from his lips and he forced himself to spit, "What happened?"

"It was the Baba Yaga, by killing the Baba Yaga we killed the slogolyth. Without him there was nothing to control this world or the Manic. We just needed him to be in his true form before we could attack him, that's why the stones wouldn't go through him before, he wasn't actually there". said Jasper.

"That's great". Lee coughed "But I think that Slogolyth got me again". Lee felt a crawling sensation over his body which caused him to look down. The slime from around them had begun to flow towards him. "What's happening?" said Lee as Jasper looked around to see the slogolyth melting into a puddle of pink sludge which was starting to flow unnaturally towards Lee. Lee's eyes opened wide, and he looked around in horror. "Jasper, Jasper! What's happening?" The slime had crawled up his legs and now held down his arms. He tried to sit up, but the slime reached up from the ground and pulled him down into the ground. "Jasper help!" Jasper tried frantically to hold onto Lee, but his body seemed to be dissolving wherever the slime touched. Jasper's hands passed through the slime as Lee's body dissolved. Lee cried out in pain "Jasppeeerrrr", his yell became drowned out as slime poured into his mouth and covered his face before soaking into the ground all that was left in front of Jasper was a pile of pink oozing slime. Jasper reached into it frantically trying to grab Lee but to no avail.

"Lee! No Lee!" Jasper cried.

The last remnants of slime drained into the ground disappearing all around him. Jasper clawed at it trying to save something of Lee, but it slipped away from him until there was nothing left, and Jasper was left clawing bloody fingers into the dirt. He knelt alone in the barren wasteland triumphant yet defeated, staring into the dirt where Lee once lay. He looked to his right to see the Baba Yaga, it grasped its spidery fingers around the Javelin, and it yanked the Javelin free throwing it to the side. As it struggled in pain to sit up, a foot landed on the wound on the ghastly creature's chest. Jasper pushed it down to the ground and the Baba Yaga laughed in pain as Jasper picked up the spear again.

"That was clever, boy" It hissed. "But not quick enough I'm afraid. She still got him" the creature coughed as it laughed, pink and black ooze streaming from its mouth. "I may have been controlling your dreams but the Manic, that stuff is the real nightmare".

"What do you mean?" said Jasper angrily.

The Baba Yaga coughed and black oozing tar slipped through its teeth, a large phlegm like slime slapped onto Jasper's top and began trickling down. "The world is changing Jasper. Don't worry" the creatures' large pupilless eyes stared into Jaspers "You'll see it all, you'll see her rise again. You survived" The Baba Yaga then placed its hands on the ground and pushed defiantly against Jasper's foot "He won't!" the creature hissed through the toothy Cheshire grin.

Jasper slammed the spear through the long sharp teeth and into the hissing mouth of the Baba Yaga. With a twist of the spear, the whole world suddenly crumbled into darkness.

***

Jasper jolted upright in a cold sweat only to be thrown back down again by an excited Scoff, who licked frantically all over his face. Jasper rolled around on the bed trying to cover his face from Scoffs generous advances.

"Scoff you're okay!" Jasper laughed whilst Scoff continued to try and lick and nibble Jasper's face. Ruffling Scoffs fur Jasper stroked Scoff all over before taking him with both hands and placing Scoff on the ground. Scoff ran around in circles with utter excitement as Jasper, confused and blurry-eyed rubbed at his face. As Jasper sat up he looked around, there was the towels and the cream painted stone walls of the utility room. He sighed in relief at the sight in the room.

"That was quite the dream you were having Jasper", said Atticus as he rounded the corner carrying two steaming cups of green tea with lemon. "It's good to see you back my boy, I thought we were going to lose you for a minute there". Said Atticus stepping into the room and holding out a mug for Jasper. Jasper grasped the steaming mug with both hands.

"Thank you. I thought I was going to lose myself for a minute there too". He sipped the lemon drink tentatively.

"How are you feeling now?" Asked Atticus, sitting on an old wooden chair near the bed.

Jasper looked at the bandages on his arms and shoulders. "I feel, great?" said Jasper, just a little confused.

"That's wonderful news, isn't it?" Said Atticus, his old voice sounding a little laboured.

"It is but I don't understand, I genuinely feel great. No pain, no aching, nothing". Atticus raised an eyebrow as Jasper placed down the tea next and began to tear the bandages off his arm. Atticus's eyes widened in shock as he looked to Jasper's arm then back to Jaspers equally shocked eyes. Jasper's arm was completely healed with not a single scratch or scrape on it, just four lines of perfectly healed scars. Atticus quickly got up from his seat, walked over to Jasper and began to remove the bandages from Jasper's shoulders. Removing the last bandage, Atticus fell to his seat.

"You're completely healed". Said Atticus

Jasper examined his shoulders, eight completely healed puncture scars dotted his shoulders where the monster of the moors had savaged him. Jasper looked up to Atticus and broke into hysterical laughter.

"I feel great!" he laughed. "This is incredible!"
Atticus suddenly broke into laughter too. A wave of relief for Jasper's life washed over him. They both stood and hugged each other happily with Scoff jumping up clawing over them both, trying to join in the excitement.

"This is amazing! Where's Lucy and Billie?" asked Jasper releasing himself from the hug. Atticus's face fell and he suddenly turned serious.

"They went with Jessie, to kill the Hell beast of Bodmin Moor. But it is ok they're with Jessie, He knows what he's doing, they'll be alright". Said Atticus reassuringly.

"What? No! That thing's got manic! They don't know what they're walking into!" Said Jasper as he ran to the other room to get his bag. Atticus followed as fast as he could.

"What do you mean they don't know what they're walking into? They know it's got manic". Said Atticus.

Jasper was rummaging through his bag, putting on his top and changing his blood-soaked trousers as quickly as he could. "If the monster of the moor has the manic and wiped out all the bogarts, what do you think is going to happen next?"

Atticus's old grey eyes widened in horror as the realisation hit him, how could they have been so stupid. "Well, you're not going alone I'm coming with you". Scoff understood the change in mood and stopped running around instead stood bipedal in front of Jasper puffed up his chest. Jasper went to a knee and stroked Scoffs head.

"I'm sorry little buddy, you have got to stay here. It's going to be too dangerous for you out there". Jasper thought back to Lee disappearing into the ground in a pool of tar and slime. Scoff reluctantly dropped back to all fours. "I'm sorry Scoff, I've already lost one friend. I can't lose you too". Jasper smiled a little. Though Lee had been a complete tool, he'd redeemed himself and turned out to be a good friend who faced danger when it came, and even saved his life. Scoff dropped his head sulking as Jasper ruffled his fur. Scoff stood up on two feet, clenched his claws and glared at Jasper. "Hey, don't give me that look".

Atticus watched the moment between Scoff and Jasper. "Ah-ha! Jasper, I've just thought of the perfect thing for you!". Said Atticus as he turned and hurried out of the room.

"What is it?" Jasper shouted, buckling his belt.

"You can't fight those things without a weapon can you!" Atticus shouted from another room.

Excitedly Jasper ran out of the room, closely followed by a determined Scoff.

Chapter Twenty-One: The Hell Beast of Bodmin Moor

The evening was rolling in as the wind continued its unending barrage on the moors. Gorse quivered as the wind thrashed the thorny bushes left and right. The bushes lashed out at every opportunity. Billie, Lucy and Mr J walked in the centre of the path avoiding the tiny daggers around them. Even though their armour would have easily deflected any chance of the daggers stabbing their arms and legs, they still had their hands and ankles to worry about.

"How much further?" Asked Mr J

"Not too far," Shouted Lucy. "There's a tree with no leaves atop a mound of moss and boulders. When you see that tree, then we're there".

Billie looked at the two in front of him being far too serious and thought he'd change the subject for a bit "You know what I can't wait for?" Billie said. Lucy and Mr J looked to him raising their eyebrows. "Just hiding in my workshop. I mean once these A levels are over and you know we have fought the beast yada, yada, yada it will be great to just hunker down and work on a project. Really lose myself you know?" said Billie almost dreamily.

Lucy laughed, "for someone so intelligent you're not very good at focusing, are you?"

"Ha focusing? On our impending doom! Yeah great, I'd rather avoid it as much as possible, thank you very much".

Mr J frowned at Billie, "you know we're hunting it right?"

"Yeah, so?" replied Billie.

"That means we're trying to sneak up on it" said Mr J

"Yeah, alright I see your point, but you know what I mean though"

"Billie just be quiet; we're trying to surprise it. Something we can't do with you yammering on," said Lucy.

"Alright Nanna!" said Billie, taking the piss, but still resorting to keeping quiet.

Mr J looked ahead and just over the hill in front of them, he spotted the tree poking out of the gorse in the distance. Walking closer he spotted the beast atop the mound surveying its surroundings. Mr J Spotted the beast and instantly ducked waving to Billie and Lucy to get down. They both dropped to the ground. Mr J looked to Lucy and at her bow.

"Right, this is the plan", he whispered. "We're going to creep up to it as close as we can without alerting it to our presence. Then, when we're close enough" He turned to address Lucy, "Lucy, you'll shoot it with your bow" Her eyes widened at the thought of this all being put on her. "It's alright I saw your shot earlier, you can definitely do this. This way we'll get a jump on it, and hell even if you don't hit it straight away, at least that will surprise it enough for me to run in and finish it off" said Mr J with absolute confidence.

The three of them then commando crawled down the path through swampy puddles, and under low hanging gorse, until they were only around twenty meters away from the young slogolyth. Mr J was just about to round the corner before he stopped abruptly and lifted his fist, both Lucy and Billie instantly froze. Mr J looked to Lucy dead in the eye and gave her a simple nod. That was all the motivation she needed, she crawled beside Mr J, then as quietly as possible pushed herself to her knees. She then lifted the bow from her back, reaching into the quiver and pulled out a single arrow, nocking it onto the bowstring. With the bow on its side and her thumb cradling the arrow she began to slowly stand, gradually pulling back the string she focused on the wiry tree as it came into sight. Her blood went cold, and she dropped to the ground.

"It's gone!" She whispered.

"What? What do you mean it's gone?" Mr J whispered standing to see what had happened. Billie pushed against the spear on its side and got up to see what was happening.

"Where's it gone?" Billie whispered.

From their hiding spot, Mr J surveyed the area. The wiry tree swayed following the current of the breeze, the gorse rocked back and forth like thorny anemones. He ducked back down to address Lucy and Billie.

"I think it's gone down into the cave again, probably to feed. Let's make our way, over to the cave, then we'll get the jump on it in there". Mr J Unsheathed his sword. "Remember, stay low. We still have a chance of surprising this thing". Mr J crouching, emerged from their hiding spot and began moving towards the cave with his sword low, ready to slash out at any moment. Billie and Lucy looked at each other readying themselves before they too emerged from the gorse, Lucy's bow was held low, ready to shoot at a moment's notice and Billie held his spear ready for anything.

Step by step they moved closer avoiding the bog as much as they could. Mr J reached the entrance to the cave and placed a hand on the cold stone, then looked down the eerie tunnel. Lucy noticed that the boulder that she had covered the entrance with had moved. Now inside the entrance, all Mr J could see was a small dark tunnel surrounded by moss and rocks that was barely even big enough for him to get down. Mr J turned to the teenagers and spoke to them softly.

"Okay, I'm going to head down there, whatever happens, you two look after each other". said Mr J looking at the two armed teenagers.

"We've got this!" Said Lucy. Billie nodded in agreement.

"Cover the entrance, if anything other than me comes out of there, you kill it. Okay?"

"Got it, anything that comes up there, kill it. Unless it's you". Replied Billie. Mr J's face changed, he closed his eyes for a moment, adjusted his glasses and exhaled fortifying his courage, then starting with that first step he descended into the cave. The entrance was too small for him to walk down so he decided to slide down. Holding his sword at a slight angle he slid down the tunnel feet first into the cave. As soon as his feet hit the bottom he took a step forward, dropped to his knee and swept out with the rapier, slashing through low hanging gorse roots and strands of moss. He halted for a moment, sword out to the side steady and unwavering. He observed his surroundings, light shone down illuminating the centre of the cave. The walls were covered in roots from the tree and countless gorse bushes. He took a step forward and felt something soft beneath his foot, He lifted his foot to see a large clump of moss. He took a few more steps and walked carefully into the centre of the cave.

Billie and Lucy stood outside the cave; both of their weapons traced on the entrance. Billie and Lucy's eyes were locked on the entrance, then from the corner of Billie's eye he spotted something large, creeping towards him and his eyes shifted to see the Hell Beast of Bodmin Moor. The beast's eyes shot to Billies, as their eyes locked, it pounced.

"SHIT!!!" Shouted Billie.

The creature kicked itself off the ground and dove at Billie who turned and fell holding out the side of the spear to defend himself. The creature's claws pressed hard against the spear and pushed Billie to the ground, knocking Lucy aside. The Hell beast jaws snapped relentlessly at Billie's face as he pushed back as hard as he could with his arms almost completely outstretched.

"Lucy!" Shouted Billie.

"Guys! There's nothing down here" Mr J shouted. At that moment he noticed a rustle in the roots on the wall.

"Wait!" Mr J walked closer to the wall, peering at the roots. He frowned as all he could see that behind the roots was even more moss. Mr J lowered his sword and adjusted his glasses staring at the moss, it seemed to him that the moss almost had fleshy tones. The moss then opened its eyes, revealing two large milky green globes.

"Oh dear", said Mr J as the moss released its claws from the rock and dived at Mr J, who raised his arm to protect himself. Instantly the manic bogart clamped its angry jaws onto Mr Js arm. Mr J shook his kevlar arm frantically trying to remove the little monster, suddenly bundles of moss with milky green eyes with manic jaws appeared in every direction. He tried to swipe out with his rapier, but his arm was stopped by a barrage of angry garbling jaws, and he fell to the ground in a garbling mess.

Lucy jumped to her feet her heart racing, she turned to the beast trying to savage Billie and threw a kick which connected her boot with the creature's snout. It dove back releasing Billie and shook off the hit to its oversized muzzle. The beast turned to Lucy and snarled a deep leopard-like growl making their hairs stand on end. Lucy nocked an arrow and pulled the bow back, but the sore covered beast darted aside, and the arrow disappeared into the gorse.

Billie scrambled to his feet. With the spear levelled at the creature's chest, he charged. The creature was too fast for him, and it dove to the side and pounced kicking him away with its hind legs, sending him flying into the gorse. Lucy reached into her quiver to grab another arrow, but the beast turned to her and charged. She panicked as the beast drew nearer. She fumbled almost dropping the arrow, and she looked up in a panic as the hell beast pounced soaring through the air. Suddenly, an enormous battle cry came from her side and Jasper slammed a shield into the side of the beast, knocking it to the ground it wheezed from the blow. Jasper wore black and grey padded Kevlar armour like the others. In one hand he held a silver short sword and in the other, he wore a simple round shield. Jasper and the beast circled each other as Atticus, armoured in padded Kevlar and carrying a shotgun, ran over.

"I've got this Atticus you find Mr J" said Jasper, Atticus nodded

"Good! This thing hasn't got any silver!" he replied, pumping the shotgun.

"Mr J's down in the cave! Somethings happening down there!" shouted Lucy.

Atticus nodded, ran to the cave, and slid down the entrance. At the bottom, his eyes widened as at the back of the cave surrounded by roots Mr J, was trying to hold back a swarm of angry bogarts. Mr J had one on each limb trying to gnaw through the Kevlar, he had both hands on another, which was attempting to savage his face. He threw it down to see Atticus in front of him.

"If you say I told you so, I will kill you myself" Shouted Mr J. At that moment, the bogart he threw to the ground turned around and dove for his crotch. Landing the blow with perfect precision Mr J dropped to his knees. The Kevlar helped protect him a bit, but Mr J still squealed as the manic bogart clamped down hard on his genitals.

Atticus cringed at the sight and ran over clubbing one of the bogarts, freeing Mr J's right arm.

Jasper and the beast circled each other until it pounced at him, its pink saliva spraying from its maw as it dove, claws outstretched. Jasper jumped to the side swiping out with the sword, but the blade slashed out cutting nothing but air. The creature took a swipe at Jaspers shield knocking him back, but his footing was sure, and he jumped back with the blow. Shots blasted from within the cave causing Jasper and the beast to jump back. The beast panther-like climbed onto the mound of boulders and turned towards Jasper, who ran back making distance between them, he then turned and planted himself to the ground positioning the sword behind him ready for the killing blow. The beast's claws dug into the boulder, and it roared in defiance as it leapt from the boulder and bounded towards Jasper. Jasper exhaled readying himself. He tightened the grip on his sword and turned the shield to face the beast. It charged, flaps of skin and fur fell from its body as it bounded through gorse and splashed through bogs. The beast pounced claws outstretched. Jasper ducked, shield raised, and threw up his sword slashing the beast's chest. The creature fell in a heap behind Jasper, and he turned shielding himself from another potential attack. His eyes peered over his shield at the unmoving beast, and he spotted an arrow impaled deep in the side of the beast's shoulder. At that moment Lucy walked out from behind a gorse bush.

"Got him, just like I got the rage crawler". Said Lucy strutting past Jasper, whose mouth could not have dropped any lower. Fearlessly she examined the strange head of the beast ensuring it was dead, she pressed her foot against its chest and pulled at the silver arrow. The arrow wrenched free with a sudden gush of pinkish gore. She then turned back and walked past Jasper.

"There is absolutely no way, I slashed its chest". said Jasper.

"Yeah, but I shot it first". She said with a wink.

"But how, you couldn't!" Objected Jasper, lost for words.

Lucy laughed, "You're such a sore loser!"

"Sore loser? How could you even, I came here to save, but then you" He did everything to stifle his rage and she laughed. Suddenly the beast began to convulse on the ground, its muscles twitched. The creature began thrashing around clawing at itself. Both Lucy and Jasper backed away from the panicked creature as it screamed out in pain. Jasper and Lucy watched in horror as the creature rolled back to all fours then began vomiting pinkish slime as its bones began to crack and its muscles bulged. Jasper noticed a large ripple slither underneath the skin of the creature before it burst out the shoulder wound made by the arrow. What emerged from the creature could churn the stomachs of Vikings. An oozing tentacle the size of an adult human's leg had burst from the creature and now was living upon the slogolyths shoulder. The creature's mutations did not end there, bones and muscles had become too large for its skin and fur to contain, giving it no option but to fall from the slogolyth with a sickening squelch. The bones on the creature's joints burst from the muscle protruding out as a bloody boney spike. It's beady grey eyes now dwarfed by the creature's massive bulk glared at Jasper and Lucy with an inexhaustible hatred, fuelled by its pain and suffering. Atticus once said that the beast was a majestic mythical creature that minded its own business. Now it had turned into this flesh and bone monstrosity, even its teeth had grown to grotesque proportions barely even being able to be contained within the creature's jaws.

A chilling sweat of helplessness swept over Jasper as he gazed upon the birth of this new horror. A thought passed through his mind that he really wished he had never left his town, his mother, or his little brother. It occurred to Jasper that the last thing he had said to his baby brother was to yell at him for going in his room. His mind also went to Scoff who he'd made stay in Atticus's car for his own good. At least he'd be safe. Hopefully he would find a way out and the creature won't find him.

Two more shots fired within the cave which drew the attention of the monstrosity in front of the teens. As soon as it turned its head both Lucy and Jasper ran for their lives down the boggy track.

"What the hell is that thing?" Cried Lucy.

"I think that's what Mr J was trying to stop. I think that's what happens to creatures with manic". Shouted Jasper.

"How are you even here?"

"Long story!" Shouted Jasper and the two began running even faster as they heard the crashing of gorse and splashing of puddles as the fully formed slogolyth charged like a raging bull after them.

"We'll never outrun it! What do we do?!" Shouted Lucy.

Jasper's mind raced with different scenarios of how this could go. Not one idea came to him that didn't eventually end with one of them on the wrong end of that slogolyth. Suddenly an idea occurred to him, and he tightened his grip on his sword and shield, he even laughed a little at the idea.

"What? Oh god, what is it?" Said Lucy worried about what they were about to do.

"Just keep running! I've got an idea! I just really hope it works", the latter muttered under his breath. They both continued to run as fast as they could splashing in bogs and tearing past the gorse as they went. The two burst from the gorse to see Atticus's car parked on a dirt track.

Jasper had cracked the windows so Scoff could get some fresh air. Now in the gap of the window Scoff had already squeezed his head through and fell from the car onto the floor to see Jasper and Lucy run up a small ditch to a dirt track.

"Scoff! You were meant to stay in the car! Come on we have to go now!" Shouted Jasper. Scoff watched them run past and tilted his head quizzically. "Scoff! Run! Shouted Jasper. Suddenly the Slogolyth burst from the gorse jumping over the ditch and crashed into Atticus's car. Scoff darted to the side just in time as the tentacle-like appendage lashed out at him. Scoffs ears lowered and his tiny tail pressed tightly between his legs as he cowered in terror as the creature glared down at Scoff, pink slime dripping from its lipless maw. The Slogolyth lurched at Scoff slamming its muscular tentacle into the ground where Scoff cowered, but the furry creature was already gone, bouncing down the track after Jasper and Lucy. The Slogolyth roared and charged down the track after them shouldering the car out of its way. Jasper hearing the Slogolyth's roar looked back to see Scoff scurrying after them and the Slogolyth not too far behind.

Jasper and Lucy emerged from the gorse to the main road and sprinted across it. Jasper turned to look back to the track breathing heavily.

"Okay this is my plan, the creature's going to emerge from that point there" he said pointing to the track. "Now this road has a bend there all we need to do is keep that thing there long enough for a car, bus, or something to come around that corner. It'll crash into the slogolyth then we finish it off".

"That's your great plan!" Shouted Lucy in a rage. "Hope for the best?! Oh, well, I'm so glad you have thought this through! How many cars did you see when we walked down here before? Oh yeah, none because not only were you passed out but there wasn't any!"

Scoff suddenly emerged from the track and ran over the road to Lucy and Jasper just narrowly avoiding being hit by a Land Rover that sped around the corner.

"Well, that would have been just what we needed", Said Jasper. "Wait, where is it? Oh god here it comes" said Jasper as he saw the Slogolyth burst from the track and stopped just on the other side of the road. The grotesque creature paused to let out a throaty roar spewing slime before slowly prowling onto the road. As it moved, each large bony claw hit the ground oozing puss-like sludge.

***

Farmer Barric was driving back home after checking on his sheep. To his pleasure they were all accounted for, not one was missing. He'd had a rather rough couple of days not just because of the loss of many of his flock but because he had an agonising ache in his jaw which he just couldn't shake off. He was from a generation that could shake off anything, so this was a particular thorn in his side especially because he'd been punched by some teenage girl. He swore the next time he saw her, the creature, or either of the boys she was with, they would feel the lead of his pellets. That is not just because of his beating, oh no, they'd also given him no end of trouble because his wife had been in an awful state after seeing her garden destroyed. So, when he turned the corner towards his farm, he couldn't believe his luck when he drove past not only the girl and one of the boys but he almost even hit the little devil spawn they carried with them. Looking in his rear-view mirror he checked to make sure it really was them and to his delight it was. He slammed on his breaks and pulled his land rover to the side of the road. He grabbed his shotgun from the passenger seat and opened the driver's side door already loading the gun.

"Oi! You bloody kids you stay right there!" he shouted at them.

Jasper turned to see the farmer walking towards them shotgun raised and trained on them. Jasper looked at farmer Barrick petrified. The farmer looked at the teens, they were bloody, clothes torn to sunder, and they were covered in sweat. The little creature next to them didn't look much better off. What on earth had these kids been through, that's when stepping a little closer he finally saw it, the mutated fully formed slogolyth of Bodmin Moor. His hairs stood on end at the sight of the terrifying creature and his weakened bladder almost gave way.

"What the bloody hell is that thing" he muttered. Suddenly he gave a joyous shout. "It's bloody real! Ha ha! It's real! I knew it!" He turned the sights over to the creature and fired without hesitation. The shotgun erupted and pellets flew at the creature with devastating speed ripping into its flesh, The second shot even succeeded in decapitating the tip of the tentacle. The creature roared in pain and diverted its gaze to the farmer, who was now frantically trying to reload his shotgun.

"Now!" Shouted Jasper. This wasn't what he planned but this would do. The slogolyth turned and began to charge towards the farmer, Jasper ran after it screaming but it ignored him and was upon the old farmer within a blink of an eye. Lucky for the farmer Scoff was quicker and discarding all terror the creature had previously held over him pounced onto its side and clawed his way up its body to its eyes. Just as Scoff was about to claw into it, the milky white orb shifted to him, and the remainder of the tentacle whipped Scoff from its body. Although Scoff didn't succeed getting to its eyes, he did however manage to throw it off its target and it charged headlong into a ditch full of gorse. The creature roared in anger and frustration rearing back to see Jasper stood in front of it, his tiny shield raised. Lucy nocked an arrow and fired towards the creature. The arrow burst cleanly through the creature's muscular neck and disappeared into the gorse with a spray of blood and slime. The slogolyths anger bubbled over and its jaws opened wide as it dove at Jasper who threw himself at the slogolyth shield being engulfed by the creature's jaws, it clamped down onto the shield and shook Jasper from his feet. Tensing his shield arm, he pulled himself as close to the shield as possible, with the creature shaking him like a toy. He heard the shield creak as it bent under the power of the creature's mutated jaws. It shook him again and he took his chance.

A sudden bloody cry screamed from the creature as Jasper thrust the silver short sword around the shield and pierced through the creature's temple sticking into its brain. It stopped shaking Jasper and he let go of the sword. Holding his body up by the arm still strapped to the shield in the creature's mouth, he swung and slammed his palm against the pummel of the blade, slamming it up to the hilt into the slogolythe's skull, it drove deep and the creature went rigid and collapsed to one side taking Jasper with it. The weight of the creature slammed Jasper into the ground and impaled the sword even further through the creature's head. Loosening the straps on the shield jasper released his arm and pulled it free from the creature's mouth. Both arms were completely covered in the pink slime, and he flicked out his arms in disgust trying to remove it.

"I think that time we got it" said Jasper, wiping his hands on his trousers. Its tentacle twitched, Lucy took a step closer to Jasper and the slogolyth.

"Are you sure it's dead?" asked Lucy. Then suddenly its chest burst open with two blasts as a horrified farmer Barric gave it a double tap to ensure the creature was indeed dead. Jasper and Lucy both knew that a creature like a slogolyth could only really be fully killed by silver but they still both agreed that it was indeed dead, and a couple of shotgun shots would not go amiss. Neither of them could imagine anything surviving a silver sword through its brain.

"Mary's not going to believe this" said the farmer booting the creature. Scoff bounced up onto the creature, startling the farmer who yelped and raised the shotgun again.

"NOOO!" Shouted Jasper. The farmer stopped finger on the trigger, with his sights on the tiny monster. "It's okay, he's okay. He's not hurt anyone" Jasper walked slowly palms up over to Scoff. "He's alright, we were just trying to get him home. Look come with me, we've got a couple of people you should meet, and we will probably need your help". The farmer hesitated for a moment looking back and forth from Jasper and the creature.

"What kinda help you be needing then?" said the farmer raising an eyebrow and lowering his shotgun.
Jasper, Scoff, Lucy and farmer Barric ran at a jog up to the cave all carrying their weapons raised, except Scoff who was bouncing along next to them. All of them flinched as a Kevlar hand appeared from within the cave mouth. It was then followed by an elbow and a coughing Mr J.

"Bloody hell Atticus, I've never seen anyone club something like that. The little guy didn't even know what hit him. Your aim certainly hasn't improved though" said Mr J crawling up from the cave closely followed by Atticus, who laughed.

"I saw what that other one did to you. I may be old but I still need that, I wasn't going to let that thing get anywhere near me" Said Atticus. Mr J laughed and slapped Atticus on the shoulder, before seeing the small army in front of him now lowering their weapons.

"Well, you could have helped" Said Mr J looking at the group. He now noticed that they were all covered in blood, gore, and they'd even managed to gain a new member "What happened to you lot? And who's that?"

"We just killed the Slogolyth. What have you been doing?" Said Lucy. Mr J nodded approvingly "Nicely done guys!"

"I'm just glad this is over". Said Atticus already walking away "I need a cup of tea and I can't wait to get on with the paperwork, I'm not built for field work anymore and we'll have to get all these bodies off the moors".

"All these bodies?" Asked Jasper.

Mr J cringed and pulled at his trousers around his crotch. "The Bogarts had the Manic. Let's just say they took me by surprise" Atticus Laughed at that.

"Took you by surprise alright!"

Suddenly the gorse next to them rustled and they all drew their weapons at the new threat. Billie emerged covered in thorns and scratches, "What happened? Did we win?" He said rubbing at his head.

Chapter Twenty-Two: Reward

The bright afternoon sun shone down on Haywood college. The bell rang, and teenagers ran down the steps pushing each other, laughing and gathering into groups heading back to their homes. Jasper and Billie covered in scratches and bruises ran down the steps towards their bikes.

"How'd you do man?" Said Jasper with a smile.

"Oh, I dunno" Billie's eyes went to his feet. Then he broke into a smile "Totally nailed it!"

"Yes!" Billie and Jasper grasped each other's hands and drew into a bear hug. From over Billie's shoulder, Jasper saw a girl walk through the crowd towards him. Each of her steps were accentuated by her heels and short skirt, though this time uncharacteristically she wore a black hoody. He noticed her usual confident walk was this time marred with crossed arms and her gaze darted around like she was looking for something. Jasper looked up from her hoody to her tired hazel eyes and he released Billie from the hug.

"Hey, Jasp". She muttered

"Hey Mollz, how are you getting on?" said Jasper.

"Yeah, I'm good, how'd the tests go?" She said stroking her hair away from her face with her palm.

"Yeah good, good. How're you doing, like, since the bear?" asked Jasper.

Billie turned and leant back on the rail behind him, trying to make it look like he wasn't listening.

"Yeah, fine, fine. I dunno I just feel a little on edge you know? I know Mr J got the bear but I just feel like it's still around, watching…wating to get us again.". She wiped the hair away from her face again. "I heard Lee had an episode at the hospital. Apparently, he went into a fit or something a couple of weeks ago kind of around the time you lot disappeared. Not much has changed though he's still in the coma. Lillz has taken it pretty badly, hence the whole murderer thing". She looked apologetically to Billie, who awkwardly pierced his lips into a smile, and waved her off.

"I'll live" Said Billie

Jasper looked down to his feet at the thought of Lee being swallowed by the manic, then disappearing into nothingness. He looked up to see Lucy over Mollz shoulder and he broke into an involuntary smile at the sight of her. Mollz saw his smile as his eyes shifted. She turned to see Lucy walking down the steps towards them. She looked back to Jasper, straightened herself and unfolded her arms.

"Okay well, I'll catch you later though yeah Jasp?" Mollz winked at Jasper and looked to Lucy, who eyed her suspiciously. Mollz then whipped her hair to the side and walked with confidence to Lillz and Jordie who were just walking down the steps of the college. Jasper gave her a pained smile; he hated seeing her like that.

He turned to Lucy "Hey, how'd you get on?"

"Yeah, really well actually. What did Mollz want?" Lucy said as she watched the three of them walking away from college.

"She just wanted to know how we did and told us about Lee. Apparently, he had an episode a couple of weeks back, went into shock or something. He's stable now but seems to still be stuck in the coma".

"God that's awful, I hope he wakes up soon. Do you think it has anything to do with your dream? That was a couple of weeks ago, wasn't it?" Said Lucy. Billie jumped off the rail, as carrying a briefcase and cleaning his glasses, he saw Mr J leaving the college and making his way down the steps.

"Mr J!" Billie shouted, running over to him. The teens around them all looked at Billie confused at his excitement, then as if it wasn't confusing enough to see one kid happy to see their teacher, both Jasper and Lucy ran over too.

"Hello you three. How'd your exams go?" he said with a smile. "Oh, wait! before I forget I've got something particularly important for you three. I'm glad I caught you before you all left. It would have been a little difficult to explain me popping to each of your houses". The three teens looked at each other curiously, if Mr J was about to give them all something, it was bound to be something interesting, and monster related. Mr J then placed his tattered briefcase on the wall next to them and shuffled the brass combination lock. "Urgh sorry, these things are always a pain to open" the lock clicked and both latches popped up. Mr J began rummaging through his case. "So, when you three and Scoff headed back on the train Atticus, and I collected up the bodies with the help of Mr Barric and. Ah-ha here they are!" Mr J then stood up holding three large envelopes and handed each to Jasper, Lucy and Billie. Jasper held the envelope, unsealed it and peered inside. His heart skipped as he saw fourteen bound stacks of twenty-pound notes inside. Instantly he closed it and pressed it to his chest. At his reaction, both Lucy and Billie opened theirs.

"Oh my God!" Lucy laughed and she pressed the packet into her chest. Billie opened the packet and his eyes widened at the sight of all the money in front of him then shut it again. Immediately he ran forward and embarrassed Mr J in a massive hug. Jasper and Lucy joined Billie hugging Mr J. Mr J laughed then suddenly became uncomfortable as two teachers walked down the steps out of the college. It was the maths teacher nicknamed handbag and Mr Malak; they eyed the strange interaction curiously.

"They're just really happy with how the exams went". Said Mr J smiling awkwardly. Mr Malak and Handbag face both looked at each other, chuckled and carried on down the steps. Jasper broke away from the hug.

"How come you're giving us this?" said Jasper. They released Mr J from the hug.

"Each stack is one thousand pounds. It's your reward for helping slay the manic creatures, normally there wouldn't be a reward from those mythical creatures because they're quite timid. However, because they had the manic, we did a very important public service for M.I.T.H and they've compensated all five of us for it. So, what you've got there is for both slogolyths, the bear and the beast of Bodmin moor, you've also got some of the bounties from the infected bogarts too. Sorry, Jasper, I tried to tell them about the Baba Yaga but without proof of it being dead there is no way to collect the bounty, we just need to be happy that that thing's gone for good. Shame though that thing with the manic would have added an extra thirty grand to your payday. They are always trying to get out of paying if they can. So, what are you three going to do with all your money?" all three looked at the envelopes then looked back to Mr J.

"I'm upgrading my workshop. It is going to be so amazing kitted out now! My mum also hasn't managed to find a new job yet so this will definitely help us out for a while," said Billie.

"That's really nice Billie, I'm sure she'll appreciate that very much, but be careful telling her where you got the money from. Say it was for a national electronics competition. If she asks anything I can vouch for you" said Mr J.

Lucy thought for a moment "I think I'm going to buy a compound bow and some targets just encase anything like this happens again. I want to be prepared next time. I know it won't cost fourteen thousand, so I'll probably save the rest for now. What about farmer Barric, what happened to him?"

"Oh, he's been compensated too for the help in slaying the slogolyth on the moor. He also complained about some creature destroying his garden. No one had a clue what he was talking about, but M.I.T.H covered those costs too. He seems like a bit of a nut. Atticus was quite excited to be able to tell him about our world though, so I think they're both pretty content now". Said Mr J.

"That's so good I'm glad he's alright and Mary can get her garden back to normal," said Lucy. Mr J raised an eyebrow puzzled. Lucy turned to Jasper. "What about you Jasper? What do you think you'll do with the money?"

"Same as you, I think. I want to make sure I'm prepared for anything; I'm going to get a load of training equipment. Most importantly though, I'm going to do everything I can to make Scoff at home. He's lost everything so it's the least I can do".

"You're a good man Jasper", said Mr J smiling and resting his hand on Jasper's shoulder, giving him an encouraging pat.

Lucy nudged him "Yeah and you're going to need all the training equipment you can get, that's if you actually want to beat me to anything" she laughed.

"Come on! You know I finished that monster!" objected Jasper with a smirk.

"I dunno, I'm pretty sure I shot it first"

"Oh god don't start this again", said Billie dropping his head to his hands.

Later that night Jasper was led upon his bed looking through pages and pages of old drawings of creatures that he'd drawn, when a furry green monster hopped onto the bed with a large red toy in his mouth. The toy made a strange rubbery squeak with each chew, Scoff collapsed next to Jasper's chest chewing loudly. Jasper reached his hand over to Scoff, feeling Scoff's fur in between his fingers as he rubbed his head.

"Good luck destroying that one buddy, it's meant for lions". Jasper's mind wandered and he thought about maybe playing a game, but soon thought better of it. The real thing was more exciting than a game, even if it was one

251

hundred times more dangerous. He laughed to himself, then as he turned a page in his sketchbook something caught his eye. In front of him was something that he drew years ago, it was a strange, floating, dark creature with large milky white dead eyes, floating off the ground with menacing long sharp teeth. Jasper looked up from the page in confusion. Suddenly there was a large cracking noise next to Jasper and he almost jumped out of his bed when he realised the cause. Scoff sat looking up happily at Jasper with his tongue draped out of his mouth. At Scoffs feet was the indestructible toy, broken in two.

To Be Continued...

Epilogue

The room was well lit with a clinical glow typical of any hospital. The walls were a speckled blue and the floors a sickly cream colour. Despite the noise and commotion in the ward outside and the continuous beep of the heart monitor, all was quiet in the patient's room. A blond nurse in blue scrubs opened the door and led in a greying Asian doctor in a white coat passing him a clipboard.

"Dr Sandlebrook left you this, he's made notes on all that's happened to the patient. I hope it helps. He won't be back for another month".

"Honeymoon, wasn't it?" Dr Francis smiled.

"Yes, I think they went to Bali".

"Lovely place, I went there back when I was a student. I'd better get on. Thank you for this, I'll take it from here", said Dr Francis. The nurse nodded and left the room, shutting the door behind her. Dr Francis stood at the foot of the bed of his patient and read through the patient's notes.

Patient - Lee Ladderman,
Sex - Male
Age - 18
Diagnosis – Four severe puncture wounds in chest and back, lacerations across patients back. Severe septicaemia. Due to the patient's severe wounds from a bear attack, the patient was treated and rushed to hospital three weeks ago. Mr Ladderman was placed in an induced coma to allow his body to heal. Two weeks ago, for an unknown reason, his body went into spasm shaking uncontrollably, by the time doctors and nurses arrived to treat the patient he'd stabilized. A greenish tracking still surrounds the lacerations and puncture wounds. The patient was due to wake last week but has shown no signs of consciousness.

"What happened to you, my boy?"

Dr Francis rubbed his greying beard deep in thought. He placed the board down at the foot of the patient's bed. Walking up to the head of the bed he looked down at the curly-haired male in front of him. Tubes extended from the pale patient's nose and mouth. Dr Francis took a small light from the pocket of his white coat and lifted one of Lees eyelids. He frowned seeing cloudy green, white eyes, he looked to the heart monitor which beat with a continuous rhythmic beep, beep, beep. He then flickered the light into the eye and then away repeatedly to see any reaction, but there was none. He stepped back and checked the board, rubbing at his forehead. There was nothing on there about his eyes. He searched the board again and decided to check the healing progress of the wounds. Stepping back towards the head of the bed he started to remove a section of bandage on Lee's shoulder. Just as he was removing it, he began to see the dark green veins tracking up his neck. Suddenly the heart rate monitor flatlined. Dr Francis looked up to the monitor, but just as he was about to shout for the nurse a hand struck out at his throat crushing his windpipe. Dr Francis clawed frantically at the iron grip of the hand, his attacker slowly sitting up and turning towards him. Dr Francis began hitting the arm as hard as he could and tried in vain to scream for help but made no sound except a weak, wheezing, gasping sound. The iron grip on his neck flexed and something popped in the doctor's neck. He felt a sharp pain shoot down his spine and across his entire body, his head flopped to the side, neck broken. The last thing Dr Francis saw was the transformation in his attacker's eyes, as the milky whites disappeared like a sun breaking through a clouded sky, revealing eyes, deep, dark green and surrounded by blackened veins. Before Dr Francis slipped away into the ever sleep of death, he felt as if the stare of the monster in front of him had stirred a manic terror within his soul.

About the Author

Alex Entwisle spent his younger years in rural Somerset, always finding it difficult to fit in at school, he eventually found his calling in nature through Scouting which led him to pursue a career in wildlife. After saving countless animals within local rehabilitation centres, Alex started working with large carnivores in zoos, couple this with a few near-death experiences, it's given Alex a unique outlook on life, one of beauty, humour and if you've got this far in the book you may have noticed a little bit of violence and horror.

Watching lions and wolves sleep for hours on end made Alex's mind wonder and he began to write a series of short stories all with a wild fantasy theme. A wild imagination and copious amounts of coffee eventually led to the birth of The Creatures of Manic, the first book in The Manic Chronicles.

A message from the Author

"I've struggled with dyslexia my whole life. I know how hard it can be. With perseverance you will get there, never let it stop you from fulfilling your dreams. It won't be easy but when you make it, not even the scariest slogolyth will be able to stop you". – Alex

If you'd like to join Alex in his adventures, follow him on Instagram:

@alex_entwisle

Printed in Great Britain
by Amazon

10767731R00150